"It was *bella fortuna* that sent you to me. *Bella fortuna*—luck, fate. Or is your London too dry and serious for such notions?"

"I don't believe in fate," Diana said. "Fate means you've abandoned reason and choice."

"You're listening too much to your head," he said, tapping one finger to his brow. "That is acceptable for London, I suppose, but here in Rome you must rely on your heart. Romans do not think. They *feel*."

"How did you know I'd be here?" she said, her voice sounding oddly breathy. "I certainly didn't tell you."

He smiled. "You didn't have to. I knew you'd come. I knew it here, in my heart."

"That's enough," she said. "My head—my *English* head—makes my decisions for me. I must go now, sir."

"Ahh, you wound me, my lady! Have you remembered so much and forgotten my name?"

She looked up again, unable not to. One minute more with him. That was all she'd allow herself. Maybe two, three, but certainly no more than that. "I haven't forgotten."

"Then say it, my own Diana," he whispered. "Say it to me from your heart, not your head."

"Antonio," she whispered in return, unable to stop herself. There was no one here to help her. But no one to watch and know what she did, either. "Antonio di Randolfo."

Miranda Jarrett's latest Regency trilogy is filled with

Grand Passion on the Grand Tour

The Duke of Aston's beautiful daughters
are in Europe with their governess
on the most exciting trip of their lives…

The daring Lady Mary Farren took France by storm in
THE ADVENTUROUS BRIDE

Her scandalous sister Lady Diana
is thrilled by Italian passion in
SEDUCTION OF AN ENGLISH BEAUTY

Coming soon, their calm English governess,
Miss Wood, has her own romantic encounter…

THE ADVENTUROUS BRIDE
'Jarrett provides readers with a delightful,
charming art mystery set in a colourful palette of the
French countryside, ancient churches and regal Paris.
The interesting backdrop and art history
add that little something different that
many readers are searching for…'
—*Romantic Times BOOKreviews*

SEDUCTION OF AN ENGLISH BEAUTY

Miranda Jarrett

MILLS & BOON®
Pure reading pleasure™

First published in Great Britain 2008
Harlequin Mills & Boon Limited,
Eton House, 18-24 Paradise Road, Richmond, Surrey TW9 1SR

© Miranda Jarrett 2007

ISBN: 978 0 263 86288 1

Set in Times Roman 10½ on 12¾ pt.
04-1108-86863

Printed and bound in Spain
by Litografia Rosés S.A., Barcelona

SEDUCTION OF AN ENGLISH BEAUTY

Miranda Jarrett considers herself sublimely fortunate to have a career that combines history and happy endings—even if it's one that's also made her family far-too-regular patrons of the local pizzeria. Miranda is the author of over thirty historical romances, and her books are enjoyed by readers the world over. She has won numerous awards for her writing, including two Golden Leaf Awards and two *Romantic Times* Reviewers' Choice Awards, and has three times been a Romance Writers of America RITA® Award finalist for best short historical romance.

Miranda is a graduate of Brown University, with a degree in art history. She loves to hear from readers at PO Box 1102, Paoli, PA 19301-1145, USA, or at MJarrett21@aol.com

Recent novels by the same author:

PRINCESS OF FORTUNE
THE SILVER LORD
THE GOLDEN LORD
RAKE'S WAGER*
THE LADY'S HAZARD*
THE DUKE'S GAMBLE*
THE ADVENTUROUS BRIDE†

*A *Penny House* novel
†*Grand Passion on the Grand Tour*

Chapter One

Rome, Italy
October, 1784

Rome was a bore.

Lady Diana Farren stood at the parlor window of their lodgings in the Piazza di Spagna, watching the rain flatten the leaves on the trees in the garden below her. Everyone had promised her that Rome would be enchanting, fascinating, the Eternal City among all other cities on the continent. Yet after a week of steamy rain and tedious company, of endless tours of more old churches, old temples, old statues, old paintings and company old enough to be her grandparents, the only thing eternal she'd discovered here was endless, eternal boredom.

Bore, bored, *boring.*

If her life had gone as she'd hoped and planned, she would have been staying in her family's town house on Grosvenor Square in London by now. She would already be the prize belle of the new season, with a score of young lords vying for her attention and her hand, each willing to duel one another for the sake of a single dance with her. She was eighteen, and she was beautiful: a fact, not a boast, just as it was a fact that she was worth a fortune of at least £20,000 simply by being the younger daughter of the Duke of Aston.

But those facts hadn't saved her from Rome. Nothing had. Instead, one evening in June, she'd been caught in her father's stables with a groom whose face she tried never to recall, and she'd been sent abroad as punishment. She'd been banished, really. There was no other way to look upon Father's decision, and no chance to appeal it, either. She'd finally, regretfully exhausted Father's patience.

But matters had only grown worse in France. Through absolutely no fault of her own, she'd been knocked on the head and kidnapped at the orders of the wickedest old libertine in Paris, the Comte de Archambeault. To her great good fortune, the Comte had been mortally ill and unable to do her any harm. But the scandal had been bad enough, and a whole new set of ill-founded rumors and lies had attached to her name.

Now she was doomed to wander about Italy like some hapless gypsy at least until the spring, with her governess Miss Wood to watch her like a sharp-eyed hawk. By the time she finally returned to England, all the best bachelors would be claimed by other girls, or frightened clear away by her tattered reputation. Only the buck-toothed weaklings and spindle-shanked fools would be left. She'd never discover the kind of love her sister had found with her new husband: joyful, passionate and *forever.* Was it so very much to long for a love of her own? She might not even marry now, but be doomed to empty, loveless spinsterhood, just like Miss Wood.

Diana took a deep breath, trying to keep back her tears. Better to be bored than homesick, but with the gloom of this rain, the homesickness was winning out. She missed her sister and her father and her friends and her cousins. She missed all the young men who'd flirted with her and made her laugh. She missed her corner bedchamber at home in Aston Hall, and the way the sun would stream in the east windows in the morning. She missed England: the words she could understand without a pocket dictionary, the people who laughed at the same things she did, the food and the drink that could comfort her with their familiarity.

She was so lost in her own misery that she didn't hear the other person join her at the window until it was too late to escape.

"*Buongiorno, mia gentildonna bella,*" the gentleman began. "*Mi scusa, non posso a meno di—*"

"*Per favore, signore, no,*" Diana said without turning, giving her refusal the stern conviction that Miss Wood would expect from her. Please, sir, no. What could be more direct than that? She'd already had practice enough on this journey; Italian men could be persistent, and if Diana ever wished to see London again, she had to be as discouraging as possible. "*Grazie, no.*"

"Ahh." The man cleared his throat, perplexed. "*No speranza, mia gentildonna?*"

Suspicious, Diana frowned. She thought he was asking her if she could offer him any hope or encouragement, but she wasn't certain. Her Italian was so limited that she had to be very careful. She'd already suffered through one unfortunate (though amusing) experience when she'd thought a servant had been offering her more tea, and instead he'd been begging to kiss her, and quite shamelessly, too.

"*Sono spiacente, signore, noi non sono stato introdotto.*" I'm sorry, sir, but we've not been introduced. That had become her well-practiced answer to all questions. "*Grazie, no.* No."

But the man didn't budge, and Diana sighed wearily. Until

now, she'd thought that she and Miss Wood were the only guests at Signor Silvani's *palazzo,* and that she'd be left alone here in the common parlor. If this impertinent fellow wouldn't leave her, then she'd have to leave him, and return to the private suite of rooms she shared with Miss Wood and their servants.

She folded the ivory blades of her fan into her palm, and turned away from him to leave. *"Arrivederci, signore."*

"Don't go, please, oh, hang it, that is—*Parla inglese, mia gentildonna?"*

Surprised, she paused, but didn't look back. He didn't *sound* Italian, but he sounded young and charming, and rather handsome, too, if sound alone could be trusted.

"Of course I speak English, sir," she said cautiously. "What else would an Englishwoman speak?"

"Then we've that much in common," he said, "because I'm English, too."

"Are you, sir?" She would have to turn to face him now. What was necessarily discouraging to a forward foreign gentleman would be unforgivably ill-mannered to a gentleman who was English, like herself.

And so she set her face into a polite smile, and turned. The gentleman was not only English, but handsome, with curling blond hair streaked with gold, a smile full of charm and blue eyes that seemed bright enough to light even this gray day. Though not tall, he had the manly sturdiness of an English country gentleman, with a broad chest beneath his well-tailored waistcoat. He was young, too, of an interesting age not much older than her own. Her smile grew and became genuine. How could it not?

"Good day to you, sir." She didn't curtsey, guessing his rank to be below hers, but her smile remained, warm and interested. She let her gaze slide past him, looking for Miss Wood to be their chaperone. The parlor was empty except for the two of them and the dreary sound of the rain echoing up into the room's high coved ceiling. Diana could predict Miss Wood's lecture: to be alone with a gentleman, English or not, was not acceptable, especially not without a proper introduction.

Diana knew the rest, too. Loneliness didn't matter. She shouldn't speak another word to him. She should put aside her smile behind frosty indignation and reserve. She should return at once to her own rooms. If she wanted her banishment from London to end, she mustn't falter now.

And yet how would a few minutes in this gentleman's company hurt? From his accent, his manner, and his bearing, she was certain he was a gentleman, just as he must realize she was a lady. And if he were another guest in this particular palazzo, then he must also have impeccable references and a well-lined pocketbook, for these lodgings were the most exclusive in a neighborhood that already catered to aristocratic British travelers.

Surely, then, he'd understand the value of honor, both hers and his own. Surely he could be trusted, especially with a smile like that.

And surely, too, he must understand the little shiver of excitement she felt at doing something that she'd been so expressly forbidden to do.

"I've frightened you, haven't I?" he asked, misreading her silence. "Coming up behind you like that, taking you by surprise. Ah, forgive me, my lady!"

"I'm not so tender as that," she said. "It takes far more to frighten me. And how did you know I was a lady?"

"I guessed," he confessed, his smile becoming a grin. "I was right, too, wasn't I, my lady?"

"You were." She turned her wrist and tapped him on the

arm with her fan, not hard, not really, but enough to make it clear that she still held the advantage. Oh, this was a hundred times more enjoyable than all the musty old galleries in Rome combined—a *thousand* times! "Just as I will guess, and guess correctly, that you are a gentleman."

He cocked his head to one side. "A gentleman, but no lord?"

"Perhaps," she said, narrowing her eyes to appraise him teasingly. "Your tailor would say so, and so would your tutor at school. And if you're staying here, with Signor Silvani's blessing, then most likely you are what you claim."

"But I'm not," he said. "Staying here, I mean. My rooms are down the street a ways. I'm only visiting my uncle."

"Your *uncle.*" Blade by blade, she opened her fan, holding it just below her chin as she smiled over the painted arc. "And now, you see, you're visiting *me.*"

"Lady Diana?" Miss Wood's voice echoed faintly down the hallway from their rooms. "Where are you, my lady?"

Diana snapped her fan shut. "That's my governess," she said, her eyes round with urgency. "I can't let her find you here with me. Hurry, hurry, you must hide!"

"Hide?" The gentleman smiled indulgently. "There's no need for that, my lady."

"Oh, yes, there is." Swiftly, Diana glanced around the room, searching for a hiding place, and grabbed his arm. "There, behind those curtains. I'll send her on her way as soon as I can."

But he didn't move, only patting her hand as it clung to his sleeve. "I'm not ashamed to be here with you, my lady."

"That is not the point, sir, not when—ah, Miss Wood, you've found me!" Diana smiled brightly, and pulled her hand free of the gentleman's. "I was just coming to answer your call when this gentleman stopped me."

With her hands clasped at the waist of her plain gray gown, Miss Wood didn't answer at first, taking her time to judge the situation for herself. Such silence was hardly new to Diana, and she knew that the longer it continued, the less likely her governess was to decide in Diana's favor. While Miss Wood herself was still a young woman, not yet thirty, in Diana's eyes she would forever be a model spinster-governess: small, drab, inclined to stoutness, severity and suspicion. If Father had sent her away with the head gaoler of Newgate Prison, he couldn't have watched her more closely than Miss Wood.

Even now the governess was studying the gentleman, from the silver buckles on his shoes to the top of his gold-colored head, with the same shrewdness that a farmer's wife used to gauge the worth of vegetables on market day. Finally, she gave a quick little nod, her way of prefacing disagreeable tasks.

"Good day, sir," she said, her voice as chill as ice as she dropped a perfunctory curtsey. "Forgive me for speaking plainly, sir, but I do not believe you have been properly introduced to her ladyship. My lady, come with me."

Diana sighed with frustration. All she'd wanted was a few moments' conversation, a small diversion from this wretched trip's tedium. She'd meant no harm nor scandal, nor had she intended to do anything to put her return to England and London and her season in jeopardy.

But there'd be no use in arguing with Miss Wood, because, as usual, Miss Wood had truth on her side. Diana hadn't been properly introduced to the gentleman; she didn't even know his name. Besides, if he was like all the others, now he'd make as hasty a retreat as he possibly could, the cowards. No man, gentle or otherwise, liked to be reminded of the fearsome prospect of her father's displeasure, even though Father was hundreds of miles away in England.

She swallowed back her unhappiness and raised her chin, prepared to follow Miss Wood back into discretion, gentility and exquisite, undeniable boredom.

But to her surprise, the gentleman spoke first.

"Hold a moment, Miss Wood," he said, his voice strong and sure and not the least cowardly. "If all that's lacking between this lady and myself is an introduction, then introduce us properly, and set everything to rights."

Diana gasped, startled that a gentleman had dared challenge Miss Wood's authority or her father's wrath. None of the other men that she'd known in the past would have. But this one was already proving himself to be a superior gentleman—*quite* superior.

But Miss Wood remained unconvinced. She stopped abruptly, drawing herself up as tall as she could before him. "How could I possibly introduce you to her ladyship, sir, when no one has introduced you to me?"

"Then I shall." He bowed, more towards Diana than her governess. "Miss Wood, I am Lord Edward Warwick, and my father is the Marquess of Calvert, and if you choose not to believe me, you need only ask my uncle, who is also a guest of this house."

"My lord, I am *delighted* to make your acquaintance," Diana said cheerfully, flickering her fingers as she held her hand out to him. True, an heir to a title would have been preferable to a younger son, but after her sister had gone and married a questionable Irishman for love alone, Father would consider the second son of a marquess as a genuine prize. "Not even Miss Wood could object to you!"

But Miss Wood could, and now she stepped between them. "If you please, might I ask your uncle's name?"

Lord Edward smiled past Miss Wood to Diana. "My uncle

is Reverend Lord Henry Patterson, the elderly gentleman residing in the rooms across the hall. He is so occupied with his studies and his writings that he keeps to himself, but there is no more honorable Englishman to be found here in Rome."

"Oh, Miss Wood, not even you could find fault with a recommendation like that," Diana said, her gaze fixed entirely on Lord Edward's charming face. It must have been *months* since an English gentleman had looked at her with such open admiration.

Perhaps she'd been pining after the season for no reason at all. Lord Edward wouldn't have heard of her misadventure with the groom at Aston Hall, or her flirtation with the guard in Chantilly, or even that last dramatic little affair in Paris when she'd been kidnapped for a brief time. All Lord Edward would know of her was what he saw and what she told him. With a little discretion, anything—anything!—could be possible.

"You know exactly what to say to reassure us, my lord," she continued happily. "What better reference for character could there be than the Church of England?"

"None, my lady," Miss Wood said darkly. "But let me please remind you that we must take care, after—"

"Come with me." Lord Edward took Diana's hand—seized it, really, as if he'd every right—and led her from the room and across the hallway. "You can meet the old fellow yourself, and he can set things formally between us."

"This is not proper, my lord," Miss Wood protested, scurrying after them. "This is not *right*. Because her ladyship's rank is higher than yours, you must be introduced to her, not the other way about."

But Lord Edward was already opening the door to the other rooms.

"Uncle, it's Edward again," he called as he entered, not

bothering to wait for the footman that came rushing towards them, still buttoning his livery coat. "I've discovered the English ladies staying beneath your roof, and brought them to you for approval."

In a large room that must serve as parlor, study and dining room sat an elderly gentleman, his armchair drawn close to a large table before the open window. Although rain splattered on the stone sill and curled the papers on the edge of the table, the man himself was oblivious, too absorbed in his work to notice.

Wisps of his white hair poked out from beneath a black velvet beret such as painters wore, and though his black linen waistcoat and breeches were ordinary enough, his bare feet were thrust into outlandish needlepoint slippers embroidered with red roses. Scowling with concentration, he held a large magnifying glass in one hand and a fragment of ancient pottery in the other, while puffing furiously on a long-stemmed white clay pipe.

Lord Edward cleared his throat with noisy emphasis. "Uncle, if you please," he said. "The ladies, Uncle."

"Ehh?" Startled, the Reverend Lord Henry Patterson jerked his head around to face them, his scowl at once dissolving into a beatific smile. He put down his pipe and his fragment, and rose from his chair, sweeping the velvet cap from his head so that the silk tassel swung from the crown. "Why, yes, Edward. The ladies! How do you do, my dears? A damp day in old Rome, isn't it?"

"It is indeed." Diana smiled and stepped forward, determined to put an end to Miss Wood's foolishness about a proper introduction before the governess could start it up again. "I am Lady Diana Farren and this is my governess Miss Wood, and we are delighted to make the acquaintance of two English gentlemen in this foreign place."

The clergyman's expression was so dazzled and doting it was almost foolish. Diana smiled cheerfully, accustomed to the effect her beauty had on men. It wasn't anything she did: it just *happened*.

"There now," Lord Edward said heartily. "I told you I'd discovered true ladies, uncle. Lady Diana, you may be delighted, but I—I am enchanted, and honored, too."

"Her ladyship is the youngest daughter of His Grace the Duke of Aston, my lords," Miss Wood announced sternly, ever vigilant, and Diana could almost feel her reprimand hanging in the damp air. "Her ladyship is not interested in intrigues, my lord. She is traveling through Italy in thoughtful pursuit of knowledge and learning."

"Then you must be her guide in such education, Miss Wood," said Reverend Lord Patterson, slapping his velvet cap back onto his head so he could hold his hand out to Miss Wood. "What a paragon of learning you must be yourself, Miss Wood, if his grace has entrusted his daughter's education and welfare to your hands."

To Diana's amazement, a flush of pink flooded Miss Wood's pale cheeks as the minister shook her hand.

"You are too kind, reverend my lord," her governess said. "But I can think of no more noble calling than to guide his grace's daughter, and to strive to improve her mind and character, as well as my own."

"Of course, of course." Reverend Lord Patterson nodded eagerly. "Might I show you my latest acquisition, Miss Wood? Surely a woman of your scholarly inclinations will appreciate the workmanship of this, from a painted amphora that was already ancient in the times of the Caesars."

"Thank you very kindly, reverend my lord," Miss Wood said, already heading to the table with more eagerness than

Diana could ever recall witnessing. "Nothing would give me greater pleasure."

Diana turned back to Lord Edward, looking up at him wryly from beneath her lashes. "You arranged that quite tidily, didn't you?"

He placed his hand over his heart. "I should rather believe it was fate, my lady, bringing me closer to you."

"I don't believe a word of that," she scoffed, "and neither do you."

His brows rose, his open hand still planted firmly upon his chest. "You don't believe in fate?"

"Not like that, no," she said. She took a single step away from him, taking care to make her white muslin skirts drift gracefully around her legs. "Rather I believe that we control our own lives and destinies, with the free will that God gave us. Otherwise we'd be no better than rudderless skiffs, tossed about on a river's current. That's what *I* believe. As, I suspect, do you."

He sighed, and at last let his hand drop from his chest. "You suspect me already, my lady?"

She smiled, letting him think whatever he pleased. "What I suspect, Lord Edward, isn't you in general, but your actions."

"My actions?" he asked, his blue eyes wide with disbelief. "Why, I've only known you for half an hour!"

"More than enough time, however noble your motives may be." She spread her fan, fluttering it languidly beneath her chin as she walked slowly towards the far window. She hadn't enjoyed herself this much since she'd left England. "I suspect that you are as bored as I here in Rome, with all the best people still away at their villas for the summer."

"Not at all!" he exclaimed. "Why, I've only—"

"Please, my lord, I'm not yet done," she said softly, making him listen even harder. "I suspect that you came to the common room across the hall with full intention of meeting me. And I suspect you somehow contrived for your uncle to entertain Miss Wood and thus leave us together, as we are now. *Those* are my suspicions regarding you, my lord."

"I see." He clasped his hands behind his waist and frowned, thinking, as he followed her. "Yet now you'll fault me because I did not wait for fate to toss you into my path, but bravely bent circumstance to my own will?"

"Oh, I never said I faulted you, my lord," she said, her smile blithe. "I said first that I suspected you did not believe in fate any more than I, and then I offered my other suspicions to prove it."

He raised his chin a fraction, the line of his jaw strong in the muted light. "Then I find favor with you, my lady, and not fault?"

"Not yet," she said, as he came to stand beside her in the window's alcove. "But I must say, it's unusual for a gentleman to be so forthright in his attentions."

"I've no desire to be your rudderless boat, my lady," he said. "Consider me the river's current instead, ready to carry you along with me wherever you please."

She laughed softly, intrigued. Most gentlemen were too awed by the combination of her beauty and her father's power to speak so decisively. She liked that; she liked him. What would he be like as a husband? she wondered, the face she'd wake to see each morning for the rest of her life? "And where exactly do you propose to carry me, Lord Edward?"

He made a gallant half bow. "Wherever you please, my lady."

"But where do *you* please, Lord Edward?" she asked. "Or should I ask you *how?*"

"*How* I please?" He chuckled. "There are some things I'd prefer to demonstrate rather than merely to explain, Lady Diana."

"You forget yourself, my lord." She laughed behind her fan, taking the sting from her reprimand, and pointedly glanced past him to her governess and his uncle, their heads bent close over the broken crockery. "This is neither the place nor the time."

He grinned, not in the least contrite, and leaned back against one side of the alcove with his arms folded over his chest. "We'll speak of Rome instead. That's safe enough, isn't it?"

She shrugged and leaned back against the other side of the window opposite him, leaving him to decide what was safe and what wasn't. The rain had dwindled to a steamy mist, the sun brightening behind the clouds.

"There are so many attractions in Rome, my lady, both ancient and modern," he continued. "It's why we English make this journey, isn't it? Our choices are boundless."

She wrinkled her nose, and turned away from him to gaze out at the red-tiled rooftops and dripping cypress trees. "No tedious museums or dusty old churches, I beg you. I've enough of that with Miss Wood, traipsing across France and Italy with her lecturing me at every step."

"But this is Rome," he said, "and I promise I can make even the dustiest old ruin interesting."

"I'm no bluestocking, Lord Edward," she warned. "Broken-down buildings are never interesting."

"With me, they would be."

She shrugged, feigning indifference. In truth she couldn't imagine anything better than to trade Miss Wood's tours for his. She'd be sure to be ready in the morning, and keep him waiting only a quarter hour or so. "I already have a governess, my lord. I don't need a governor to match."

"Then come with me tomorrow, and I'll show you Rome as you've not yet seen it," he urged. "I'll have a carriage waiting after breakfast. You'll see. I'll change your mind."

"Perhaps," she said, not wanting to seem over-eager. "Look, my lord, there. Can you see the rainbow?"

With colors that were gauzy pale, the rainbow arched over the city, spilling from the low-hanging gray clouds to end in a haze above the Tiber. Diana stepped out onto the narrow balcony, her fingertips trailing lightly along the wet iron railing.

"I can't recall the last time I saw a rainbow," Lord Edward marveled, joining her. "I'd say that's a sign, my lady. I meet you, and the clouds roll away. You smile at me, and a rainbow fills the sky."

But now Diana was leaning over the railing to watch an open carriage passing in the street below. The passengers must have trusted in the promise of that rainbow, too, to carry no more than emerald-colored parasols for cover: three beautiful, laughing women, their glossy black hair dressed high with elaborate leghorn straw hats pinned on top and their gowns cut low and laced tightly to display their lush breasts. The carriage seemed filled with their skirts, yards and yards of gathered bright silks, and as the red-painted wheels rolled past, the tassels on their parasols and the ribbons on their hats waved gaily in the breeze.

"Now that's a sorry display for a lady like you to have to see," Lord Edward said with righteous disapproval. "A covey of painted *filles de l'opera!*"

"That's French." Diana knew perfectly well what he meant—that the women were harlots—but she wanted to hear him say so. "Those women are Italian."

"Well, yes," Lord Edward admitted grudgingly. "Suffice to say that they are low women from the stage."

"But isn't it true that women of any kind are prohibited from appearing on the Roman stage?" she asked, repeating what she'd heard from their landlord. "That all the female parts in plays or operas are taken by men?"

"True, true, true," Lord Edward said, clearing his throat

gruffly at having been caught out. "You force me to be blunt, my lady. Those women are likely the mistresses of rich men, and as such beneath your notice."

But it wasn't the women that had caught Diana's eye, so much as the man sprawled so insolently in the midst of all those petticoats and ribbons. Could he keep all three women as his mistresses, she wondered with interest, like a sultan with his harem?

He sat in the middle of the carriage seat, his arms thrown carelessly around the shoulders of two of the women and his long legs crossed and propped up on the opposite seat. He was handsome and dark like the three women, his smile brilliantly white as he laughed and jested with them, and his long, dark hair tied carelessly back into a queue with a red silk ribbon that could have been filched from one of their hats. But then everything about this man struck Diana as careless and easy, even reckless, and thoroughly, thoroughly not English.

"Will you bring a carriage like that one tomorrow, Lord Edward?" she asked, bending slightly over the rail to watch as the carriage passed beneath them. "One with red wheels and bells, and ribbons and flowers braided into the horses' manes?"

"Only if I hire one from some carnival fair, my lady." Lord Edward shook his head, his expression disapproving. "I respect you far too much for that."

"Do you," she said slowly. "And here I'd thought it looked rather like fun."

"Like scandal, with that lot." He took her by the elbow, ready to guide her from the unsavory sight. "Come away, Lady Diana. Don't sully yourself by paying them any further attention."

He turned away to return to the others, while Diana hung back for a final glimpse of the gaily decorated carriage. As she did, the flutter of her skirts must have caught the eye of the dark-haired man, and he turned to look up at her. For only a second, her gaze met his, his eyes startlingly pale beneath his dark brows and lashes. He pressed his first two fingers to his lips, then swept his hand up towards her on the balcony, a gesture at once elegant and seductive. He didn't smile. He didn't need to. That wind-blown kiss was enough.

"Lady Diana?" Lord Edward's fingers pressed impatiently into her arm. "Shall we join the others?"

"Oh, yes." Her heart racing inexplicably, she smiled at Lord Edward. "The rainbow's gone now anyway."

And when she stole one more glance back over her shoulder, the carriage and the man were gone, too.

Chapter Two

Lord Anthony Randolph tipped the heavy crystal decanter and filled his glass again.

"Summer's done," he said sadly, holding the glass up to the window's light to admire the glow of the deep-red wine. "The English demons are returning to conquer poor Rome again."

Lucia laughed without turning towards him, her back straight as she sat at her dressing table while her maid wrapped another thick strand of hair around the heated curling iron. "How can you speak so, Antonio, when you are one of the English demons yourself?"

"Don't be cruel, Lucia," Anthony said mildly, sipping the wine. "Half my blood's English, true, but my heart is pure Roman."

"Which of course entitles you to say whatever you please." Critically, Lucia touched the still-warm curl as it lay over her shoulder. "Which you would continue to do even if you'd been born on the moon."

"I would, darling," he said, dropping into a chair beside the open window and settling a small velvet pillow comfortably behind his head. Anthony was prepared to wait. Though the days when he and Lucia had been lovers were long past, as friends they were far more tolerant of one another's foibles and flaws. "I cannot help myself. As soon as the days begin to shorten, the whey-faced English descend upon us in heartless droves, complaining because the wine's too strong, the sun's too hot and there's no roasted beef on the menu."

"*I* will not complain about the English gentlemen," she said, holding one eyelid taut as she lined her eye with dark blue. "They are very attentive, and they come to call again and again."

He raised his glass towards her. "How can they not, my lovely Lucia, when you are the golden prize they all wish to possess?"

"Oh, hush, Antonio," she scolded. "You could fill the Tiber's banks with all the idle flattery that spills from your mouth."

"Exactly the way you wish it to be, Lucia," he said, his smile lazy. They would be at least an hour late for the party at the studio of the painter Giovanni, but instead of fuming at the delay, he'd long ago learned to relax instead, and enjoy the intimacy of Lucia's company. "Name another man in this city who knows how to please you better than I."

She made a noncommittal little huff, concentrating on her reflection as she outlined the rosebud of her lips with cerise. Like every successful courtesan, she knew the value of making a grand entrance, even to a party among friends, and she wouldn't leave her looking glass until she was certain every last detail of her appearance was perfect. Besides, tonight she'd been asked to sing as part of the entertainment. Her voice was as beautiful as her face, and she knew the power of both. It was a terrible injustice that Pope Innocent XI had banned female singers from the Roman opera nearly seventy years before. In any other city, her voice would have made her a veritable queen, and free to choose more interesting lovers than the fat, jolly wine merchant who currently kept her.

"You do well enough," she said at last, pouting at herself, "for a whey-faced Englishman."

He groaned dramatically. It was true that his father had been an English nobleman, heir to an earldom so far to the north that his land had bordered on the bleak chill of Scotland. Yet, on his Grand Tour after Oxford, Father had discovered the sun in Rome, and love in the effervescent charm of his mother, wealthy and noble-born in her own right. Anthony's two much-older brothers had dutifully returned to England for their education, and remained there after their father's death, but in his entire twenty-eight years, Anthony had never left Italy, delightfully content to remain in the warmth of that southern sun and his mother's exuberant family.

"I do not have a whey-colored face, Lucia," he said patiently, as if they hadn't had this same discussion countless times before. "Nor am I sanctimonious, or overbearing, or ill-mannered, in the fashion of these traveling English."

"But who's to say you won't end up like that puffed-up fellow we saw on the balcony today, eh?" she teased, hooking long garnet earrings into her ears. "Another year or two, Antonio, and you will look just the same, your waistcoat too tight over your belly and your face pasty and smug."

At once Anthony knew the man she'd meant. How could he not? He'd been leaning from his lodgings to glower with disapproval as he and Lucia and two of her friends had passed through the Piazza di Spagna on their way to an impromptu picnic in the hills.

"That Englishman's younger than I," he said, proudly patting his own flat belly as if that were proof enough. "Lord Edward Warwick. He has been in Rome only a month, yet he believes he knows the city and her secrets better than a mere Roman. I was introduced to him last week in a shop by a friend who should have known better, and I've no further wish to meet him ever again."

"You wouldn't say the same of the lady standing with him." Finally ready, Lucia rose from the bench, and smiled coyly. "You cannot deny it, Antonio. I know you too well. I saw how you looked at her, and she at you."

"I won't deny it for a moment." He savored the last of his wine, remembering the girl on the balcony beside Warwick. She'd been English, too, of course. No one else ever lodged in the Piazza di Spagna. Besides, she'd stood at the iron railing in that peculiarly stiff way that always seemed to mark well-bred English ladies, as if they feared the luxury of their own bodies.

But that could be unlearned with the right tutor. The rest of her was worth the effort. In the soft light as the sun broke through the rain clouds, her hair had seemed as bright as burnished gold, her skin a delicious blend of cream and rose without a hint of paint. Too many of his father's people were pale and wan to his eye, as if they'd been left out-of-doors in their wretched rainy climate to wither and fade away. But this girl managed to be pale without being pallid, delicate without losing that aura of passion, of desire, that he'd seen—no, felt—even at such a distance, and for so short a time before the carriage had turned the corner.

He'd wanted more. He still did.

"Think twice, Antonio, then think again," Lucia warned. She handed him her merino shawl, then turned with a performer's calculated grace. "Will she be worth the trouble she'll bring you?"

He took the shawl, holding it high over her like wings before he settled it over her shoulders. "Who says she'd bring trouble?"

"I do," Lucia said, turning once again so she was facing him. "I am serious, sweet. She is English. She is a lady. She is most likely a virgin. She will have men around her, a father, a brother, a sweetheart, to watch over that maidenhead. That will be your trouble."

He smiled and traced his finger along the elegant bump on the bridge of her nose. "You worry too much, my dear."

She swatted his hand away. "I know you too well."

"And she doesn't know me at all, the poor creature."

"She'll wish she didn't by the time you're through with her," Lucia said darkly. "No woman escapes unmarked by you."

His brows rose with mock surprise. "I don't recall you complaining before this."

"Don't put words into my mouth, Antonio," she said, baring her teeth like a tigress. Lucia might sing like an angel, but she pursued everything else with more inspiration from the devil than the divine. "You know I never complained when I was with you, nor shall I begin now. But for you, love is no more than a game, and that little English virgin may not understand how you play."

He wouldn't disagree. He had always enjoyed women, and he'd been careful to make sure that they found pleasure with him as well. Because of that, and because he was rich, he never lacked for lovers. But although he was nobly born, he preferred the company of the city's more celebrated courtesans and a few married ladies with scandalous reputations, women who understood that love was no more than a passing amusement. Respectable young ladies bored him, and besides, their mothers kept them from his path. He didn't care, either. He'd no need to marry for money, position or an heir. Lucia was right: for him, love *was* a game, and he intended to play it as long as he could.

He smiled at Lucia, hoping to coax her into a better humor. "Since when have you become so kind, darling? That girl is nothing to you."

"And what is she to you, eh? Another of your English demons, ready for your scorn?"

"She's only a pretty little creature I spied on a balcony, Lucia," he said evenly. "Be reasonable, pet. You've no right or reason to be jealous."

"Oh!" she gasped, her eyes wide with righteous fury. "Oh, how dare you say such a thing to me?"

She shoved her hands hard into his chest, and spun away from him. "Why are you so stubborn—so stubborn that you won't give me the truthful answer I deserve? Your oldest friend, your dear Lucia! You are impossible, Antonio! *Impossible!*"

She tossed her head, sending the elaborate construction of ribbons, sugar-stiffened curls, powder and false hair quivering. With her skirts gathered to one side, she swept from the room and down the stairs.

Anthony sighed. Everything with Lucia was a scene, to be performed *grandioso* for the greatest effect. He was fond of her, very fond, but she was also wearying. Surely that lovely English girl would be different. Innocent. Peaceful. Not so eager to bite. A pleasing change, a relief, really, like a still pond in a country meadow after a raging storm at sea.

He slipped on his coat and reached for his hat, letting his mind happily consider the different ways he could steal this delightful blond girl away from the charmless Lord Edward. He paused before Lucia's glass to set his hat at a suitably rakish angle.

He wasn't handsome by English standards. His more fair brothers had always been quick to tease him about his darker skin and black curling hair, his strongly prominent nose and jaw, all inherited from his mother's family. But from his father had come his pale-gray eyes and easy smile, and more than enough wit and confidence to make women forget his craggy, swarthy face. The English girl was sure to be no exception.

He winked at his reflection and headed down the stairs, figuring by now it should be safe enough to join Lucia in the carriage. She should have had plenty of time to calm herself.

Or perhaps not.

"Impossible," she muttered, her face turned away from him as he climbed into the carriage. "You are *impossible*."

He stopped in the carriage's door. "I don't have to go with you tonight, Lucia. If I'm so damned impossible, it might be better for you to go to Giovanni's fete by yourself. Beside you, no one notices me, anyway."

Her head whipped around, her dark eyes wounded even in the half light of the carriage. "Of course they notice you, Antonio. You know as well as I that you are never overlooked or forgotten. That is the kind of man you are."

He dropped onto the leather seat beside her and sighed. "There are so many ways for me to take that, Lucia."

But Lucia didn't answer, turning again to face the open window, and for the next quarter hour they rode in a silence that felt more like an uneasy truce.

"She will be easy for you to find, your little yellow-haired virgin," she said at last. "Your English consul can tell you her name. There are not so many like her in Rome, especially not this early in the autumn."

"I haven't said I was interested in her, have I?"

"You needn't speak the words aloud for it to be understood, Antonio," she said, touching a handkerchief deeply bordered in lace to the corner of her eye. "Not by me."

"Lucia, enough," Anthony said firmly. "Isn't your darling Signor Lorenzo the love of your life? The only man in Rome with devotion enough to tolerate your tantrums, and gold enough to keep you in the luxury you demand?"

"We're not speaking of Lorenzo." Impatiently she flicked

her handkerchief towards Anthony. "We're speaking of you, Antonio, and this English girl that you are plotting to seduce. What if you're the loser in your little game this time? You're already beguiled with her—no, bewitched! What if she steals you from us, and carries you back to England as her prize, eh? What if you abandon all of us for her?"

Amused, Anthony leaned his head back against the leather squabs and chuckled. "It won't happen, Lucia. It can't."

"No?" Her eyes glittered, challenging. "You are very confident."

"I'm confident because I'm right," he said easily. He took her hand and kissed the back of it, right above her ruby ring. "No woman in this world could claim that kind of lasting power over me. You should know, Lucia."

She sniffed, and pulled her hand free, curling it into a loose fist against her breasts. "*I* tired of *you* first, Antonio. Don't let your male pride remember otherwise."

He glanced at her, so obviously skeptical that she hurried on.

"I should just let you marry the underfed little creature," she said. "You could coax her into bearing your weakling children, in the passionless English manner."

"You won't change my mind, darling. I'm not marrying her, or anyone else."

Her fingers opened, fluttering over her décolletage so the half light danced over her ruby ring. "Do you believe yourself safe enough that you'll stake a small wager upon it?"

He smiled. "Small enough that Lorenzo won't question it, but sufficiently large to hold my interest?"

"Exactly." She leaned towards him. "I'll wager that before Advent begins, you will become so obsessed—so lost!— pursuing this English virgin that you will need to be rescued by your friends and saved from marrying her."

"*Marrying* her!" Anthony laughed aloud at the sheer preposterous idiocy of such a notion. Him with a wife, a Lady Anthony to dog him to his grave! This girl might be a delicious change, but hardly enough that he'd give up his cheerfully self-indulgent life here in Rome for the sake of her hand. "I'll take your wager, Lucia, and I'll set your stake for you, too. I'll win. I'll seduce the girl, I'll enjoy her as much as she will me, but she'll never be my wife. I've no doubt of that. And when I win, I'll expect you to sing an entire aria on the Spanish Steps."

She frowned, not understanding, nor wishing to. "Overlooking the Piazza? Before all of Rome?"

"For free, my darling," he said easily. Short of standing on the papal balcony of St. Peter's, he couldn't imagine a more public place. The Spanish Steps had been built earlier in the century, a grand, flamboyant flow of marble cascading down the hillside from the French church of Trinità dei Monti to the Piazza di Spagna centered by one of the city's more celebrated fountains, the Fontana della Barcaccia. The piazza was not only a favorite idling place for Romans, but a prime attraction for foreign visitors, too. Lucia would be guaranteed an enormous audience on the natural stage formed by the steps, and the fact that her performance would be within view of the English girl's lodgings would serve as an extra fillip of amusement to their wager.

Anthony smiled, savoring the possibility. "A small gift of your voice to all of Rome. Nothing that will be missed from Randolfo's pockets, yes?"

"For *free!*" Lucia sputtered, outraged. "I never sing for—for *nothing!*"

He crossed his arms over his chest. "That's my stake. If you choose not to accept it, why, then the wager is—"

"Then if you lose, *you* must sing instead!" she said quickly. "You, Antonio, who bray like a donkey! If this girl ruins you, as is sure to happen, then you must sing to her yourself on the same steps!"

"Agreed." He did sing like a donkey, and even then only after a sufficient amount of very strong drink, but he was confident that the wager would never come to proving it. How could it, really?

"And—and a hundred Venetian gold pieces!"

"Venetian it is," he said, amused. Only Lucia would be so specifically greedy. "Prepare your favorite aria, darling. You'll want to sing your best for the people of Rome."

"I promise I'll rehearse and rehearse, Antonio." Her smile indulgent, she reached out and patted his cheek. "For your wedding, eh? For your *wedding*."

"That, ladies is the great Coliseum." Reverend Lord Patterson paused for solemn effect, pointing his walking stick out the carriage window. "Where pagan warriors battled for the amusement of the Caesars, and where countless victims were slaughtered at the whim of a ruthless dictator's down-turned thumb. Within those very walls, ladies!"

"Gracious," murmured Miss Wood, mightily impressed. "To think that all that happened inside those very walls! Lady Diana, you recall reading of the gladiators in the Coliseum, don't you?"

Diana glanced dolefully out the window at the huge stone ruin looming beside them. She'd been trying hard these last three days to be enthusiastic for Edward's sake, and interested in what interested him. That was what her sister Mary had done with Lord John Fitzgerald. It had worked, too, because he'd fallen so deeply in love with Mary that he'd eloped with her in the most romantic fashion imaginable.

But it wasn't easy for Diana, not when Edward found ancient Rome the most interesting topic imaginable. She leaned forward on the seat, trying to see if there was more to see that she was missing, but still the great Coliseum looked suspiciously like yet another tedious pile of ancient stone.

And Edward, bless him, realized it, too.

"Come now, Uncle, be reasonable," he said, taking advantage of the darkened carriage to slip his fingers into Diana's. "You can hardly expect a lady as gently bred as Lady Diana to share your bloodthirsty fascination with pagan warriors slaughtering one another a thousand years ago."

"But his grace the duke expects his daughters to have a certain degree of education about the past, my lord," Miss Wood said firmly. "Not so much as if they were boys, of course, but sufficient for them to separate themselves from common women, and to make their conversation pleasing to his grace, and other gentlemen."

"Then I'll speak as a gentleman, Miss Wood," Edward said, raising Diana's hand to kiss the air above in tribute. "I'd prefer Lady Diana kept her innocence about the barbaric, debauched practices of the Caesars, even at the expense of her so-called education. Better she appreciate the beauty of the place, than dwell on the villainy it once harbored."

Diana smiled, touched by his defense of her innocence. True, what he was defending seemed to her more ignorance than innocence, but she'd let that detail pass for the sake of sentiment. She'd never had a champion like this, and she liked it.

But Miss Wood wasn't ready to give in just yet. "I'll agree that his grace desires his daughter's innocence preserved, my lord. But he also wishes her to acquire some sense and appreciation for the greater world of the continent, including the Coliseum."

"I've a notion, Miss Wood." Reverend Lord Patterson leaned forward, eager to make peace. "Have my nephew escort Lady Diana inside for a moment or two so that she might see the Coliseum for herself. Surely the moonlight will banish the harsher realities of the place from her ladyship's memory, yet help her retain a suitable awe for its history."

"What a perfect idea!" Diana exclaimed, ready to jump from the carriage at once. They had been so thoroughly watched together these last days that the chance to be alone with Edward was irresistible. "That is, if Lord Edward is willing to—"

"I'll be honored, my lady." Edward reached for the latch to open the door, his eagerness a match for Diana's. "What better way to view the Coliseum than by moonlight?"

"What better, indeed?" Miss Wood said, rising from her seat. "I should like very much to see that myself."

Edward's face fell. "That's not necessary, Miss Wood. That is, I don't believe that—"

"You don't have to come with us, Miss Wood," Diana begged. "Please, please! You can trust us this little bit."

But Miss Wood shook her head, her mouth inflexibly set. She still faulted herself for Mary's elopement in Paris, and since then she'd been determined not to let Diana have the same opportunity as her sister. "It's not a question of trust, my lady, but of respectability. I needn't remind you of—"

"I *am* respectable, Miss Wood," Diana said quickly. She'd been able to make a fresh start here in Rome with Edward. With the city still so empty of foreign visitors, there was no whispered gossip to trail along after her, and sully her attempt to rebuild her reputation. The last thing she needed now was for her governess to dredge up old tales and scandals before him and his uncle. "And there couldn't be a more respectable gentleman than Lord Edward."

"Oh, let them go, Miss Wood," Reverend Lord Patterson said indulgently. "I'll vouch for my nephew's honor, and besides, they'll scarcely be alone. There will be more visitors inside now than there are by day, along with the constant crowd of priests and biscuit-vendors and trinket-sellers that clog the Coliseum day and night."

Edward pressed his hand over his heart. "You have my word, Miss Wood. I shall guard her ladyship's honor with my life."

Miss Wood hesitated, then sighed with resignation. "Very well, my lady. I will trust you, and his lordship as well. You may go view the ruin together. But mind you, you must return here within half an hour's time, or I shall come hunting for you."

"Then let us go, Lord Edward," Diana said, seizing his hand. "We haven't a moment to squander."

"I'd never squander a moment with you." He was always doing that, taking her words and turning them around into a romantic echo. He slipped his hand free, and tucked hers into the crook of his arm. "The entrance is down this way."

"We could just walk around and around outside for all I care, my lord," she said, feeling almost giddy to be finally alone in his company. "All I truly wanted was to be with you."

He chuckled, patting her hand as he led her towards the small canvas awning that marked the ruin's entrance. "Your governess is wise to guard you. A lady's reputation is an irreplaceable treasure."

"It can be an intolerable burden as well," she said wryly. "Sometimes I wish that I were only ordinary, without all the fuss of being the daughter of the almighty Duke of Aston."

"You couldn't ever be called ordinary, my lady," he said gallantly, misinterpreting her complaint. "Nor could his grace your father."

"Father's ordinary enough, especially for a peer," she said.

"That rubbish from Miss Wood about how he wanted to discuss history and art with me—all he's really expected from me or my sister is that we're able to exclaim and marvel at the proper moments during his hunting stories."

"I should rather like to meet his grace one day," he said, so clearly taken with the idea that he gave an extra little nod to reinforce it. "I've heard he is a man of great vision. I hope I have the honor of his acquaintance."

"I can't fathom why," Diana said, amused. The only vision she'd grant her father was his ability to stare up at the clouds and predict if they were carrying sufficient rain within to cancel the day's hunt. "Unless you wish to be bored to tears by how high a gate he can jump on his favorite hunter."

"We'd find other matters to discuss," he said, and nodded again. "You, my lady, for one."

She glanced up at him again, startled into speechlessness. There was only one reason a gentleman wished to address a lady's father to discuss her, and that was to ask for her hand. Of all the men she'd met in her short life, none had dared venture such a desire. It was early days with Edward, true, and much could go amiss between them before the banns were cried. But for him to hint at such a possibility so soon—ah, that delighted her and stunned her at the same time. He was *courting* her.

Was he falling in love with her, she wondered, to make such a suggestion?

"Is that notion so appalling to you, my lady?" he asked lightly, making her realize how long she'd been silent. "That I sing your praises to your father? Is that what you were thinking?"

"Magic, my lord." She smiled up at him, hugging his arm. "*That's* what I was thinking. How everything you say and do feels that way to me."

But instead of agreeing with her, or sharing a similar confession, he only smiled pleasantly, as if he didn't understand at all.

"I enjoy your company, too, my lady," he said, stopping to search through his pockets for the entrance fee. He gave the coins to the bored-looking man sitting on a tall stool beneath the awning, and handed Diana through the gate. "Always a garnish, eh? These infernal Romans would bleed a gentleman dry, then try to figure a way to make a profit from his blood."

"It must cost a great deal to keep a place like this," Diana said. Despite the lanterns hung sporadically along the walls, the arched passageway ahead was dark and forbidding, and she hung close to Edward's side. "It's larger than any building in London. Imagine how many charwomen must be employed in sweeping it out!"

"Imagine, yes, because it never happens," Edward declared, not bothering to hide his disapproval. "You can see for yourself how shabby the Romans have let things become. They haven't a care for their heritage. Once this city had a system for water and sewers that would shame London today, and look at it now, so foul a fellow can hardly bear to breathe. It's almost impossible to believe that these scruffy latter-day Romans actually descended from Caesar's mighty pagan breed."

But Diana didn't care any more about Caesar tonight than she had the previous two days. What she cared most about was Edward. More specifically, what she cared most about was hearing more about how Edward cared for her.

"I hope we'll see the moon again soon," she said, trying to steer the conversation back to more interesting topics. She liked moonlight better than these murky passages lit with foul-smelling tallow candles. Moonlight was bright and romantic and flattering to the complexion. Besides, moonlight generally made men want to kiss her, and for all that it was a delightful change to be respected, she thought it was high time for Edward to try to kiss at least her cheek. After what he'd said earlier, he deserved a kiss, but he'd have to be the one to claim it. "It's nearly full tonight, you know. Didn't you see? It's like an enormous silver coin in the sky."

"Isn't that like you, my lady, to notice the moon!" She could see the curve of his white teeth as he smiled indulgently at her, as if she'd said something remarkable for its foolishness rather than making perfect sense. "I have to admit my thoughts were elsewhere than dangling up in the sky."

"The moon doesn't 'dangle' in the sky, my lord." She gave a little toss to her head and lifted her chin, *willing* him to kiss her. For a gentleman who was so learned about ancient history, Edward could be remarkably thick about what was happening in the present. "The moon rises and sets quite purposefully each night, just like the sun does by day."

"Well, yes, I suppose it does." With a small flourish—but no kiss—he led her around another corner and into the open. "There now! *That's* what you've come to Rome to see!"

Dutifully Diana looked. The Coliseum seemed far larger from inside than she'd imagined outside from the carriage, an enormous stone ring made ragged and tattered over time. Half of the wall with its rows of arches had been broken away like a shattered teacup, and the flat rows that once had been benches or seats now sprouted tufts of grass and wildflowers. Other tourists and their guides wandered about the different levels with lanterns bobbing in their hands, their figures like aimless ghosts in the gray half light. Diana was disappointed. If the Coliseum by moonlight was the most romantic place in Rome, the way all the guidebooks claimed, then the guidebook writers had far different notions of romance from hers.

"Where did they stage the fights and shows?" she asked,

peering downward. The ground floor in the center was criss-crossed with a labyrinth of open corridors that bore no resemblance to the engravings in her old history book. "That looks more like a marketplace with farmers' stalls than an arena for warriors."

"That's because what we see now were once tunnels for bringing in the gladiators and the wild beasts." Edward's voice rose with relish. "Once there was a plank decking laid across the top as a kind of stage, covered with sand to soak up the spilled blood of the dying. Oh, imagine the spectacle of it all, my lady! Sixty thousand strong, cheering for the mortal combat from these very stands!"

"I'd rather not." Diana sighed. This masculine blood-lust of Edward's seemed awfully similar to her father's boundless enthusiasm for slaughtering stags, pheasants and foxes at Aston Hall, and on an even grander scale. "What's that curious little house down there, my lord? Do they offer refreshments? I'm rather thirsty."

"That's a papist chapel, my lady," he said, making his disregard for the chapel plain. "You know how the Romans are, throwing up a church anywhere they can."

"But in the middle of such a pagan place?" Her earlier travels through France and the great Catholic cathedrals built there had given her a much healthier appreciation for the powers of that faith. "They must have had a reason, a saint they wished to commemorate or some such."

He frowned, perplexed. "My knowledge is limited to the glorious ancients, my lady, not their ignoble descendants."

"Perhaps it's in honor of the fallen gladiators," she suggested. "Miss Wood said that early Christians were martyred here, and so—"

"My lady, I wouldn't know," he said, clearly weary of the

topic. He smiled, and swept his hat from his head. "But I'd guess that the keepers might still be persuaded to prepare a glass of orange-water for you. Would it please you, my lady, if I asked them?"

"Oh, thank you, yes, Lord Edward!" She opened her fan and smiled over the top. She wasn't really that thirsty, but she'd drink a barrel of orange-water if it made Edward forget his glorious ancients and think more of her. "You're too kind."

He crooked his arm and offered it to her. "Then come join me, my lady."

"Down there?" Dubious, she looked from him to the delicate pointed toe of her slipper, raising her hem a fraction to better demonstrate her reason, and to keep his interest as well. "I'm sorry, my lord, but I'm not shod like a mountain goat. I didn't know we'd leave the carriage tonight. I'll wait here while you go inquire."

"Leave you here?" he asked with surprise. "I can hardly abandon you like that, my lady!"

"Of course you can." She smiled happily. Sending him off on an errand at her bidding wasn't quite as satisfying as a kiss, but it was close. "What could befall me with so many others around? I'll be waiting here where you can see me the entire time."

He shook his head. "I'm not sure that's proper, my lady."

"It is, my lord," she said, sweetening her smile, "because I'm growing more thirsty by the moment."

"I can't permit that, my lady, can I?" He jammed his hat back on his head. "I'll return as soon as I can."

She watched him as he made his way down among the broken seats, picking a path towards the lowest level. The Coliseum was a good deal larger than Diana had first thought, and now she realized Edward would be gone longer than she'd first guessed. He stopped once to turn and wave, and she almost—almost—considered calling him back before she waved in return. Better to have him wandering about this old ruin than to let him call her indecisive, and besides, all that talk of orange-water had only served to make her thirst genuine.

But now she must wait here for however long it took Edward to return. She'd looked up at the row of broken arches along the Coliseum's skyline, then down to where the stage had been, and finally once again across to the little chapel, snugged into the side of the ruin. What was left, really?

She fidgeted with the cuffs of her gloves, and glanced back into the murky corridor that they'd come through, half expecting to see Miss Wood charging up after her. How much time had passed since they'd left the carriage?

"Buona sera, bella mia." The words came in a deep, rumbling whisper from the shadows behind her. "The moon is like molten silver tonight, is it not?"

Diana whipped about, peering into the shadows. "Who's there?" she called sharply. "Who speaks? Show yourself, sir!"

"Ah, but you show yourself too much," the man said. "Come beneath these arches with me, and see what a pleasurable difference a bit of shadow can make."

"I'll do nothing of the sort," she declared, folding her arms over her chest. "If you've come here seeking the use of a—a harlot, then you have made a most grievous mistake."

"I think not," the man said with an easy confidence. "I came here seeking you, lovely lady of the moon, and I've succeeded, haven't I?"

Diana gasped indignantly. She didn't like how he seemed to have all the advantages, hiding there in the dark where she couldn't see him. It was worse than not fair; it was *cowardly.* "How dare you say you sought me, when you don't even know who I am?"

"But I do know you, *cara.*" His laugh was as rich and dark as the shadows that hid him, a masculine laugh that, under other circumstances, would have struck her as infinitely appealing: no wonder he was so irritating to her now. "One glimpse was enough to know our souls were meant for one another."

"That's rubbish," she said tartly. "You mean nothing to me. This city is overrun with conceited Italian men like you."

"How barbarously wrong you are, sweet," he said easily, as if he'd expected no less from her. "I assure you, I'm quite unique."

"And I'm just as sure you're not," she insisted. "You're only another preening cockerel who believes he can seduce any woman he spies."

Determined that that would be her final word, she turned away, giving her skirts an extra disdainful flick. The man in the shadows didn't deserve more. Clambering after Edward would be preferable to listening further to this nonsense.

But the man wasn't done. "Not any woman, my Lady Diana Farren. I prefer only the rare birds, like you."

She stopped abruptly, stunned that he'd called her by name, and he laughed softly.

"You see, I do know you," he continued. "I spoke to you in your own language, didn't I? I know that pasty-faced mooncalf's unworthy to spread your...*fan* for you. And I know how much you delight in the silver glow of the moon's own fair goddess. Oh, yes, I know you, *cara.*"

How had she not noticed that he'd addressed her in English? How had he known her name, her title? How could he make every word he spoke sound so wicked?

"You were eavesdropping on me with Lord Edward, weren't you?" she demanded, turning back to confront him. "You were *spying!* He's ten times the gentleman you'll ever be—no, a hundred times! *You* followed us, and listened to our conversation, and—"

He laughed again, infuriating her all the more. "Do you truly believe that I care what another man says to you?"

"I know that *I* do not care what *you* say!"

"How cruel," he said mildly, and took a step towards her. One step, but exactly enough to carry him from the shadows and into the moonlight.

He was dressed in plain black, his broad shoulders relaxed, his weight on one leg, his elbow bent where he'd hooked his thumb into the pocket of his waistcoat. The muted light sharpened the strong planes of his face and accentuated his jaw and a nose that, from the bumps and bends across the bridge, must have been broken at least once. His long black hair was shoved back with careless nonchalance, a single loose lock falling across his broad brow.

But what Diana noticed first were his eyes, pewter pale against so much somber black. She'd always recollect eyes like those, but the unabashed male interest in her that now lit his gaze was so blatant that she felt her cheeks grow hot.

"You were in the carriage with your mistresses," she said slowly. "I saw you from the balcony."

"I knew you wouldn't forget, *cara*." His smile came slow and warm and seductive, and she recalled that from the balcony, too. "Not you, not me. Not ever."

Chapter Three

So she *was* brave, Anthony decided with satisfaction. He'd guessed as much from that first glimpse of her on the balcony in the Piazza di Spagna, and how she'd held his gaze without flinching.

Now he had the proof. When he'd stepped from the shadows like the villain in a bad opera, she hadn't shrieked, or run away, or worst of all, fainted in a white-linen heap at his feet. Instead Lady Diana Farren had stood her ground, and spoken up for herself in a way that was both unladylike and un-English. Bravery like that was a rare quality in a woman, and one that would be altogether necessary for the little game they were about to play together.

No, the game they'd already begun. She just didn't know it yet.

"How ridiculously arrogant you are!" she exclaimed, her blue eyes round with her outrage. "To think that I would ever remember you longer than—than this!"

She raised her hand and snapped her fingers, and though the effect was muted by her gloves, the look of indignant triumph on her lovely face more than made up for it.

"Longer, indeed," he said easily. "As long as it took you to remember seeing me from your balcony. And you were mistaken about my companions in the carriage. They were my friends, not my mistresses."

"They're of no importance to me either way. I remembered because you reminded me," she said, so promptly that he nearly laughed. Brave *and* quick, and unperturbed by possible rivals: a most unusual combination. His life was so filled with beautiful women that a new one needed to be extraordinary to catch his interest. And wager or no, this one was extraordinary.

"The only reminder I gave you, *cara,* was to stand before you," he reasoned. "If that was enough, why, then I must already have been in your thoughts, and in your—"

"I don't even *know* you," she said imperiously, every inch the peer's daughter with her aristocratic nose in the air. "Who are you? What is your name? Answer me, sir, answer me at once."

He smiled, and took his time with his reply, knowing that nothing would vex her more. "Orders, orders, like a petticoat general," he scolded mildly. "It's hardly becoming to you, *mia signora di bella luna.*"

She glared at him, her uncertainty so transparent that he spared her and translated.

"'My beautiful lady of the moon.' Diana was the Roman goddess of that luminous orb over our heads, you see."

"I know that," she protested sharply. "I'm hardly so ignorant that I wouldn't recognize my own namesake."

"Ignorant, no," he said. "Ill-mannered, perhaps."

"You are the one who's ill-mannered, sir. What kind of gentleman withholds his name from a lady?"

He brushed an invisible speck from his sleeve. "Who said I was a gentleman?"

"You did," she insisted, seemingly unaware of how she was inching closer to him, her hands clenched into tight fists at her sides. "That is, you pretend to be, by addressing me with such—such familiarity, as if we were equals."

He made a mock bow, waving his hand through the air. "I'm honored, my lady, to have my nobility confirmed simply because I dared to speak to you."

"That's not what I meant at all." She was almost quivering with indignation now, such furious spark and fire that he half expected her to burst into flame when he finally touched her. "I meant that by your speech and manner—"

"You meant that?" He leaned back against the arch, folding his arms over his chest with a nonchalance that he was certain she found maddening. "My ill manners, instead of yours?"

"No, no, no!" she cried, stopping just short of stamping her well-bred foot at not being obeyed. "I meant that your English speech is that of a gentleman, but that no true gentleman would behave towards me in this barbarous fashion. Refusing to tell me your name! It's not fair, sir, not fair in the least."

"What's not fair, *cara,* is seeing you squander yourself on a man like Warwick." Anthony made sure to keep his judgment no more than a stingingly idle observation. "My lady of the moon deserves far better than that pompous yellow-haired *sciocco.*"

"*Sciocco?*"

"A fool," he explained, happy to do so. "A dolt. A popinjay. A fellow not worth your notice."

"A *popinjay!*" she exclaimed. "How can you call Lord Edward a popinjay? He's worth ten of you—no, a hundred! He treats me with respect and regard as does no other man. Why, do you know where he is this very moment? He has

gone to fetch me orange-water, just because he was thoughtful enough to anticipate my thirst!"

"Admirable qualities in a lackey or footman, true,"
Anthony said with a shrug of indifference, "but not in a lover,
not for such a passionate woman who—"

"How *dare* you!" she cried furiously, and jerked up her
hand to slap him.

But Anthony was larger, stronger and all too accustomed
to such female outbursts. He easily caught her wrist before
she could strike him, holding her hand away from his face.

"A passionate woman, yes," he said, his voice low as she
struggled to break free. "You prove it yourself. Not a lady, but
a woman first, eh, *cara?*"

"And you're—you're no gentleman, but a vile, low, ill-
behaved beast!" she cried, practically spitting the words. "Let
me free at once!"

"If that is what you truly wish," he said easily, "then I will."

"What I wish!" she sputtered. "What I *wish!*"

"What you wish as a woman." He liked how her temper
had shattered that aristocratic shell of propriety. In his experience, temper and passion were the closest of cousins, and it
never took much to introduce one after the other. "If you wish
me to release you so you can flee to Warwick, then all you
must do is ask."

Instantly she stopped struggling, her wrist still in his fingers.

"Why wouldn't I wish to go back to Lord Edward?" she
asked suspiciously. She was watching him closely, the moonlight casting long curving shadows from her lashes over her
cheeks. "He is a gentleman, and you are not. What other
reason could I possibly have for fleeing from you back to his
safekeeping?"

"You know that better than I," Anthony said. It was clear

that she already had her own doubts about Warwick; it wouldn't take much to tip her to his own side. "If you're the lady you claim to be, and he is the gentleman, that is."

"I *am* a lady," she said quickly, and he noted how this time she didn't defend Warwick. Poor bastard, his days basking in her favor must be numbered.

"I never said you weren't." He lowered his face nearer to hers. He liked her scent, lilacs with a hint of spice. "But while you're here in Rome, you should let yourself be a woman first."

"I'll ignore that." She raised her chin, just a fraction, but enough to challenge him. Lady or not, she must have felt the tension swirling between them. "And you're still a beast."

"I never said I wasn't." He retained his hold on her wrist, but the fight had gone from her hand and her fisted fingers had begun to unfurl. Yet he could also feel how her pulse raced, her heartbeat quick there beneath his fingers. "Perhaps I feel an affinity for all the poor beasts killed within these walls."

From the look in her eyes, he knew he'd caught her interest now. That was good. He knew he couldn't have much more time before Warwick would come bumbling back with whatever it was she'd sent him to fetch.

"The ones killed by the gladiators?" she asked. "The wild beasts from the jungles and forests?"

"The same," he said quietly. Slowly he lowered her captured wrist, his grip on it so light now that they might be dancing partners instead of adversaries. "But I like to think the wild beasts killed a few of those butchering gladiators in return, too."

For the first time she smiled. "You sound as if you sympathize with the lions and tigers."

"I do." He drew her a fraction closer, and she leaned into him another fraction more. He liked how her body was fuller, more rounded, than he'd realized from the balcony, and he liked how near that body was to touching his. "How could I not? Their spirit, their savagery, their magnificence. Most of all, their refusal to be tamed into submission."

"Indeed." She tipped her head to one side, her glance slanting up at him from under her lashes: hardly the sort of glance most young English ladies had in their arsenal, and he liked that, too. "Then you consider yourself untamed as well?"

"Oh, completely." He rested his free hand on the back of her waist, lightly, as if by accident. "I'm as wild as any lion."

She eased herself away from his hand. She didn't fuss or squawk in a maidenly scene. She simply moved, silently establishing her boundaries, and his estimation of her rose another notch.

"Not so vastly wild," she said, still smiling. "I'd wager that would change if only you'd meet the proper lion-tamer."

"I wouldn't offer that wager, *cara,*" he said, spreading his fingers along her back with just enough pressure to feel the bones of her stays and her body beneath. "I *devour* lion-tamers for breakfast."

She chuckled, a throaty sound that delighted him. "Do you eat them with jam and butter?"

"This is Rome, not barbarous London," he said. "I prefer a splash of olive oil and sweet basil to taste."

She chuckled again. "Pity the poor lion-tamers, to meet such an end!"

"Pity me, for having to make such a dish of the wretched beings." He sighed dramatically, even as he reached out to touch her cheek. "I suspect the real problem is that I've yet to meet the right golden lioness."

"Ahh." She went still, but didn't pull away from him. "You must recall that I'm here with Lord Edward."

"I remember," he said, lowering his face to hers, "though I'm determined to make you forget he was ever born."

He kissed her then, exactly as he'd planned from the moment he'd followed her here. He swept her from her feet before she could stop him, leaned her back into the crook of his arm, and kissed her as she deserved to be kissed, with skill and passion, admiration and desire, and as the first, inevitable step to seduction.

He kissed her, and Diana stiffened with surprise. It wasn't that she was surprised that he'd kissed her. She knew when men were contemplating her with that in mind, and she'd been expecting this man to kiss her ever since he'd grabbed her by the wrist.

But she'd never anticipated *how* he'd kiss her. It wasn't like any other kiss she'd ever experienced. He didn't slobber, or grunt, or press too hard, or bump his teeth against hers. He didn't taste like his pipe, or the onions he'd eaten earlier. What she'd always liked best about kissing came afterwards, when the man was so grateful and devoted because he wished to do it again. That was the only reason she ever permitted it.

But the way that this man kissed stunned her with its intimacy. She couldn't begin to fathom it. He kissed her, and made her lips tingle and grow warm, her head spin and her heart quicken. He coaxed her, teased her and yet there was never any doubt that he was the untamed lion he claimed to be. His mouth tasted inexplicably male, just as kissing him made her feel not like a schoolgirl burdened with her governess, but a woman. It didn't matter that he was a stranger to her. She sensed that he could teach her mysterious things she didn't yet know existed, things her body ached to know, and eagerly she parted her lips to let him deepen the kiss.

To her dismay, he didn't answer, but drew back, into the darkest shadows.

"I must go, *bellissima*," he whispered, brushing his finger-tips lightly across her cheek. *"Buona sera."*

"No!" she cried in a breathless whisper as he turned away from her. "I don't even know your name!"

"You don't need to," he said, backing away. "You have Warwick."

Lord Edward. Oh, how had she forgotten him so easily? She took a single step towards the stranger, wishing she could follow.

"Don't go," she said softly. "I beg you, please!"

He didn't stop. Yet as he walked away, he turned back to smile one last time at her over his shoulder. He touched his fingers to his lips and swept his hand towards her, the same salute he'd made to her when she'd stood on the balcony. Then he turned through an arch and vanished into the night.

Diana pressed her fingers to her mouth, wishing she could magically keep the sensual memory of the kiss alive though its giver was gone. Her lips felt ripe, sensitized in a way that was new to her, almost as if they were no longer her own.

How could the stranger have done this to her and disappeared without even telling her his name? How could he have changed everything she thought a kiss could be and then be gone from her life? She'd wanted adventure to break this tedious journey, she'd longed for a romantic intrigue, but now that she'd been tantalized with both this night, all she could do was wish for more.

"Lady Diana!"

She turned away from the shadows and into the moonlight. Edward was coming towards her with a small glass clutched in his hand, puffing from his climb up the steps.

"I couldn't see you, my lady," he said as he reached her. "When I looked up from the floor of the Coliseum, you were quite lost in the shadows. I worried, you know."

"There was no need, my lord," she said, praying that the shadows would hide her a bit longer, and mask the guilty confusion she felt sure must show on her face. "I was well enough where you'd left me. It must have been some oddity of the moonlight that hid me from your sight."

He nodded, and held the little tumbler out to her. "Your orange-water, my lady," he said, striving to be gallant even as he wiped the rivulets of sweat from his forehead with his handkerchief. "It was chilled when I bought it, but that was a devilish hard jaunt back up here, and I fear it may have grown warm."

She smiled automatically, though the curve of her mouth felt as stiff as if it had been carved from wood.

If she'd truly been the honorable lady she'd been trying so hard to be these last days, she would have rebuffed the dark-clad man. She would not have let him kiss her, nor kissed him in return, nor begged him to stay….

"Thank you, my lord." She took the glass tumbler from him, and sipped at the orange-water. It was sickly sweet, almost a syrup, so thick with sugar that she could scarcely make herself swallow it.

Yet how easy it had been to let that other man's lips caress hers, to open her mouth to take his—

"Are you ill, my lady?" Edward was peering at her face with a frown of concern, his handkerchief clutched in a knot in his hand. "Has the closeness of this place affected you? Forgive me for speaking plain, my lady, but you don't appear well."

She let her gaze sweep around the great curving ruin. Likely she'd never see the black-clad man again. He was really no better than the crude rascals who tried to pinch women's bottoms in the market, and the sooner she forgot how he'd taken advantage of her to kiss her, the better.

At least that was what her poor beleaguered conscience told her.

Her wicked body whispered otherwise.

"It's not so much the closeness of the place, my lord," she said with careful truth, "but the—the mystery of it that has left me rather—rather breathless."

"It often has that effect on those who visit for the first time, my lady," Edward said, tucking his handkerchief back into his waistcoat pocket. "It's not surprising, really. Consider how many wicked, heathen souls must haunt this place!"

Wicked, heathen...and untamed.

She set the tumbler with the barely touched orange-water onto a nearby ledge, the heavy glass clicking against the stone. "Forgive me, Lord Edward, but I should like to return to the others now."

"Of course." He held his arm out to her, and when she took the crook of it, he laid his hand protectively over hers. "Whatever you wish, my lady."

But what she wished for most was not in Lord Edward's power to give.

"Wake up, Edward." Reverend Lord Henry Patterson yanked the bed curtains open, the brass rings jangling mercilessly across the rod as the late-morning sun burst across Edward's face. "We must talk."

But Edward didn't want to talk. He didn't even want to open his eyes. He wanted to slip back into blissful unconsciousness, where he could forget the queasiness in his belly and the thickness of his tongue and the way that blasted sunlight seemed to pierce right into his blasted aching skull to find whatever poison remained of that blasted Roman wine.

"Edward, enough." Impatiently his uncle smacked

Edward's leg with his newspaper. "The day is half gone, and you've yet to drag your drunken carcass from this bed."

"I'm not drunk, Uncle," Edward protested weakly, burrowing against his pillow to defend himself from the sunlight. "I'd be much happier if I were."

"Now that's a proper attitude for a Warwick man, isn't it?" Uncle Henry's disgust was as sharp as that sunlight. "No wonder my sister despairs so, cursed with a worthless son like you."

Edward groaned against the pillow. He could make an excellent argument for his being cursed with a shrill, meddlesome mother, too, but not right at this moment.

"Get up, Edward!"

The water that splashed over Edward's face seemed enough to drown him, and he jerked upright, sputtering and gasping for air to save himself.

"Oh, quit your complaining, Nephew," his uncle ordered, the empty pitcher from the washstand still in his hands. "What do you think Lady Diana would say if she could see you now?"

"She'd say you were a damned wicked old bastard to treat me so." Edward squinted at his uncle as he blotted the water from his face with the sheet. "She'd be right, too."

"What she'd say is that you're a lazy sluggard with no respect for your elders." Uncle Henry pulled a chair close to the bed, flipped the tails of his coat to one side, and perched on the edge of the seat. "While you've been snoring away your wine, I've been to the consulate this morning. I've made a few inquiries, and on your behalf, too. Lady Diana Farren is indeed Aston's daughter, exactly as she and the governess have claimed. They'd letters of introduction so grand that there was no doubt of it. But of greater interest to you, however, is that she'll bring £20,000 a year to whichever lucky gentleman claims her hand."

"Twenty thousand?" That was enough to clear anyone's head. Edward swung his legs over the side of the bed, ready to hear more. "A pretty penny by any reckoning."

His uncle nodded, patting his pockets until he found his pipe, and the tinderbox with it. "You'll never have a sweeter plum drop into your undeserving lap, Edward. And you'll have none of the competition here in Rome that you would back in London."

"That's precious hard." Edward scowled, his pride wounded by the unfortunate truth. "You've seen how Lady Diana looks at me. I'd venture she's rather fond of me already."

"Perhaps." His skepticism obvious, Uncle Henry thrust the stem of his pipe into his mouth. "Though you haven't had much luck with ladies before this, have you?"

"I haven't been trying, that's all," Edward said defensively, running his fingers back through his bed-flattened hair. This was a difficult enough conversation without having to conduct it in his nightshirt, rank with last night's excesses. "Those smug overbred London bitches—they're not easy on a man, you know. They'll cut you off at the knees as soon as look at you."

"Don't try to bluff me, Edward," Uncle Henry said sternly as he concentrated on lighting his pipe, puffing furiously until the tobacco finally sparked. "I know your situation, and why your poor widowed mother put you into my safekeeping here in Italy, away from the bailiff's reach. You've squandered what little inheritance you had on kickshaw schemes."

"They were legitimate investments in inventions with great promise." There'd been a sure-fire method for converting wood into coal, a proposal for a wagon-tunnel from Dover to Calais, a way to turn brass into true gold: all that had been wanting had been a cagey investor, capable of the vision to see the potential. How he loved to listen to the scientific gen-

tlemen explain their genius, and how, after a suitable investment, they'd all become rich as Croesus without a day of un-
gentlemanly toil on his part!

"Such ventures offer enormous opportunity for those clever
enough to see it, Uncle," he continued. "It's hardly my fault
that my funds weren't sufficient to see the projects through
to fruition and profit."

"Tossing good money after bad into the ocean is more the
case," his uncle said with contempt. "You've scarce a farthing
left to your name, Edward. You might as well have lost it all
at cards or dice for the good it's done you. There's only one
venture left open for you now. You must marry soon, and
marry well. Otherwise you'll be doomed to keeping yourself
by the gaming tables in Calais, or saddling yourself with
some thick-ankled coal heiress from the north."

"I know, Uncle, I know," Edward said with frustration. Blast,
but he was still a young man, and as such he'd hoped to sow a
few more wild oats here in Italy before he had to play the docile
husband. This was his mother's idea, of course. She might be
three countries away, but he could feel her tentacles reaching
out to control him through his uncle, just as she had in London.

But twenty thousand a year would change everything.
Twenty thousand, and marrying into the exalted family of the
Duke of Aston. Of course he'd have to bow to the traces in
the beginning, but once he could pack Diana off to the country
to breed like every other noble wife, then he could begin
living his life the way a gentleman should. He'd finally have
the funds to back his favorite ventures, and see them made
real. Let the others invest in old-fashioned plans like fur-
trading in Canada, or tea from the Indies. He'd make more
than the rest combined, and be lauded as a visionary, too.

And Diana Farren wasn't some coarsely bred heiress,

either. She would make a first-rate wife, the kind of filly that other men would envy. Delighted by such a glorious prospect, he reached for the wine bottle—ah, Virgil's own inspiration!—that he'd left beside his bed last night.

"No more of that," his uncle snapped, reaching out to rap Edward across the wrist. "Tell me instead how far you've proceeded with the lady."

"I've treated her as her rank deserved," Edward declared. He'd planned to kiss Lady Diana last night at the Coliseum, but by the time he'd brought her that blasted orange-water, she'd turned odd towards him, and he'd lost his nerve. Beautiful women did that to him, and Lady Diana was very, very beautiful. "You can't fault me there. I've done nothing but blow her the usual puffery about admiration and respect."

"Then perhaps it's time you did a bit more," his uncle advised. "She's a lady, yes, but she's also a woman. Women like having a man behave as the master, so long as it is decently done."

"Uncle, I've known her less than a week!"

"Twenty thousand pounds are at stake, nephew, twenty thousand that you could sorely use," Uncle Henry said through the wreaths of pipe smoke drifting about his face. "You can't expect to live out your life on my generosity, you know. My regard for your poor mother will go only so far."

Now that was true enough, thought Edward, his resentment bubbling beneath the conversation. Uncle Henry had more money than Croesus to squander on bits of broken ancient crockery, yet still he made Edward grovel and beg for every favor. But with twenty thousand a year, Edward would never have to ask for anything again, either from his uncle or his mother. He'd be his own man. Why, Mother would even have to bow down to his wife because she'd be a higher rank. Hah, how he'd like to see that!

He rubbed his hand across his mouth, imagining every detail. His wife, Lady Diana Warwick. His children, with a duke for a grandfather. His pockets, filled with guineas. How could he ask for more?

"God helps those who help themselves, Edward," Uncle Henry was droning on, as pompously as if he were standing in his pulpit. "Remember that, and how you must always take whatever—"

"Consider it done, Uncle," Edward said with more determination than he'd ever felt in his life. "By the time we leave Rome, I assure you, Lady Diana Farren will be my wife."

"Is that how you wish the curl to fall, my lady?" Diana's maid Deborah stepped back, comb in hand, to let Diana study her reflection in the looking glass at her dressing table. "Because you must wear your hat with the widest brim against the sun, my lady, very little of your hair shall show beyond that single curl."

Diana sighed unhappily, touching the silvery-blond lovelock that hung across her shoulder. Deborah was right. Traipsing through yet another pile of ruins offered little inspiration for dressing with elegance. It was more important to dress sensibly, to hide one's skin from the burning Roman sun while still keeping as cool as was possible in the wicked heat.

But in Diana's eyes, the sensible dress was ugly and uncomfortable. And how was she supposed to beguile Lord Edward while bundled up in scarves, hat and gloves from her head to the tip of her dreadful, sturdy walking shoe? Swaddled away like this, how could she possibly inspire him to be more romantic, more passionate, more able to make her forget the stranger she'd kissed last night?

"It's well enough, Deborah," she finally said, reaching for

her wide-brimmed leghorn hat from the dressing table. "I don't even know if his lordship will notice."

"Oh, my lady, what a thing to say!" Deborah clucked her tongue, taking the hat from Diana's hand and pinning it into place on her piled hair. "'Course his lordship notices you. Any gentleman worth his salt notices as soon as he sets his eyes upon you, my lady, and that's the good Lord's honest truth."

Any gentleman worth his salt. The stranger had noticed her from a distance, and for only a handful of moments, yet that had been enough that he'd followed her for the chance of seeing her again and then—

No. She closed her eyes, her conscience at war with her memory. She must not think of that man; not with interest, regret, longing or even curiosity. She must purge him from her thoughts forever, and forget how his kiss, his touch, his—

"Ah, my lady, look what just arrived for you!"

Diana opened her eyes just as Miss Wood handed her a bouquet of flowers. Late red roses, some kind of wild daisies, mixed with curling grasses and other local flowers she didn't recognize, framed with lace and tied up with an extravagant bow of black and white ribbons. There was an effortless art to how the bouquet had been gathered, the costly roses combined with weedy wildflowers into a beautiful design that was unlike any bouquet she'd ever received before.

"Oh, Miss Wood, how lovely!" she cried, cradling the flowers in her hands. "Who sent them?"

Miss Wood was smiling so broadly that her eyes were nearly hidden by her round cheeks. "I should venture after last night that it was Lord Edward, my lady."

"But there's no card or note," Diana said, searching through the leaves. "Did the servant tell you nothing?"

"They were brought not by a proper servant, but by a

scruffy small beggar-boy, doubtless in the employ of the flower-seller," Miss Wood said. "But they must be from Lord Edward. Who else could it be here in Rome?"

Diana didn't answer, holding the flowers close to her face to hide her confusion. Who else, indeed? But how could a man who'd spoken so disparagingly of the "dangling moon" be inventive—and romantic—enough to combine these flowers in this way?

What if the stranger had sent them to her? She wouldn't even have recognized his name. But as she breathed deeply of the bouquet's scent, fresh and wild and still redolent of the fields outside the city, she knew—she *knew*—that the flowers had come from him.

"There now, my lady, didn't I tell you?" Deborah asked, thrusting one final pin into the crown of her straw hat. "And you thought his lordship hadn't noticed you!"

"Of course he noticed, Deborah," Miss Wood said. "Now that you're done here, would you fetch a pitcher or vase to put the flowers in?"

The maid dipped her curtsey, and, as she left, Miss Wood settled herself in the chair across from Diana. She was already dressed for going out, in the same practical gray linsey-woolsey gown and jacket and flat-brimmed hat that she would have worn whether striding about the grounds of Aston Hall or the Forum here in Rome. If anyone exemplified Sensible, it was Miss Wood.

She folded her gloved hands in her lap and beamed at Diana. "It would seem you've made a genuine conquest, my lady. Ah, the look in Lord Edward's eyes when you returned to the carriage last night! He is besotted, Lady Diana, completely besotted."

"Yes, Miss Wood." Diana tried to smile in return. She and

Edward had barely spoken on the walk back to the carriage, each of them lost in their own thoughts. She'd no experience beyond this with a gentleman who might wish to ask for her hand, but if in fact Edward were besotted with her, then he'd a mighty peculiar way of showing it. "He is a fine gentleman."

"He is more than merely fine, Lady Diana," Miss Wood said. "Last night while you and Lord Edward were inside the Coliseum, Reverend Lord Patterson told me a great deal about his nephew. Lord Edward is a younger son, which is unfortunate, his brother having already inherited the family's title. But he does have a small income through his mother, the Dowager Marchioness of Calvert, and Reverend Patterson says Lord Edward is very devoted to her—a model son. It was her notion that Lord Edward come with his uncle here to Rome to continue his education. He'd never dreamed he would meet a lady such as yourself."

"No, I don't believe he did." Diana looked down at the flowers, tracing the petals of one daisy with her finger and remembering how vastly more interesting the stranger's conversation had been than Lord Edward's. One had spoken with too much relish of the violence that had once filled the Coliseum, while the other had expressed a rare empathy for the same wild beasts who'd lost their lives entertaining the Caesars. "In fact I rather doubt Lord Edward has the imagination to dream at all."

"Oh, that cannot be true, my lady!" Miss Brown exclaimed. "Whatever gave you such an idea?"

"He did himself," Diana said promptly. "He perceives everything in Rome to be inferior to what he judges it should be. He seems incapable of accepting that there might be another way of doing or seeing things besides his own."

"And you in turn should not be so quick to judge him, my lady," scolded Miss Wood gently. "Come, come, Lady Diana!

He is an educated gentleman, and his opinions are informed by deeper studies than you, my lady, shall ever be inclined to make."

Diana sighed, and glanced up at her over the flowers in her lap. "You rather sound as if you're taking Lord Edward's side over mine."

"Not at all, my lady, not at all." The governess leaned forward and smiled, resting her hand fondly on Diana's arm. "It's only that I wish you to be as happy in love as your sister Lady Mary is. Of all the men who have attended you, Lord Edward strikes me as the first one who has shown you the respect and admiration that you deserve, the kind that can grow into lasting love."

"Love," repeated Diana with more sadness than she'd intended. "I cannot even tell if Lord Edward so much as *likes* me!"

"I believe he does, my lady," Miss Wood said gently. "To be sure, I cannot see all the secrets of Lord Edward's heart, and I would never suggest that you entertain the overtures of any gentleman you found odious. But I believe that the quiet regard his lordship can offer would be worth far more to you than the idle, empty flirtations that have been your indulgence in the past."

Once again Diana looked down at the flowers cradled in the crook of her arm. Miss Wood was right: she had had more than her share of "idle, empty flirtations" that had led to nothing. It was past time she changed her life. What kind of lasting love could she ever hope to find with a man who wouldn't so much as tell her his name?

Deliberately she set the flowers down on her dressing table. "Deborah can see to those," she said, rising. "The gentlemen must be with the carriage below, Miss Wood. We shouldn't keep them waiting."

She followed Miss Wood down the stairs and into the bright afternoon sunlight. Edward had suggested that because of the late-summer heat, they restrict their sightseeing to the end of the day, though Diana secretly suspected this was also because Edward and his uncle had fallen into the Italian habit of rising late, then drowsily napping through the midday.

Waiting at the door was their hired carriage—not decked with ribbons and bows like the one Diana had seen that night from the balcony, but still the same high-wheeled open carriage that was the standard here in this city, with the broad seats cushioned with loose pillows and a canvas awning rigged for shade. The driver sat nodding beneath the awning, his cocked straw hat pulled low to hide his doubtless closed eyes, while the young groom stood beside the horses, shouting oaths at the cluster of laughing beggar-children if they came too near.

Reverend Lord Patterson greeted them in the hall, dressed in a plain, unlined linen suit that made Diana wish that ladies were permitted the same kind of cooler undress. Already her gloves felt glued to her hands, and beneath her shift and stays she could feel the rivulets of perspiration trickling down the hollow of her back and between her breasts.

"Good day, ladies," he said, touching his hat to them. "My nephew should be down directly."

"Oh, we'll forgive his lordship," Miss Wood said cheerfully, squinting as they stepped out into the sunny plaza. "Gentlemen can't be rushed."

But Reverend Lord Patterson was too busy glowering at the beggars to worry about Edward. "Away with you, you vile creatures! *Andare via, andare via!* Shiftless, dirty creatures! Why, they're like a flock of magpies waiting to steal anything their grasping claws can reach! Don't encourage them, my lady, else they'll never leave us alone."

"They're children, reverend my lord," Diana protested as she and Miss Wood each tossed a handful of coins into the little crowd. "They can't help it if their parents don't feed them. That's all we have, children. *Quello e tutto, bambini!* No more!"

She held up her open palms as proof, and the children shuffled away.

"Magpies, my lady. Small thieving papists." The minister sniffed with a disgust that seemed to her misplaced for a Christian gentleman, but unfortunately close to his nephew's opinions. "Before they summon their fellows, I suggest we situate ourselves in the carriage."

"We do take situating, reverend my lord, don't we?" Miss Wood said as she climbed up first over the high wheel and into the carriage. For all her practical nature, Miss Wood loved the fuss of embarkations, the same fussing that drove Diana to distraction. She sighed, and followed her governess. With Miss Wood, it always seemed to take double the time necessary to settle their petticoats around their legs, open their parasols, and arrange the basket with the refreshments, and even then her governess was never quite done.

Now she began patting her pockets, a look of chagrined surprise on her face. "Forgive me, my lady, but I appear to have forgotten my little traveling journal."

"Then you can write in it when we return, Miss Wood," Diana said. "It's likely sitting on the desk where you left it."

"But my observations will have lost their freshness, my lady," Miss Wood said, rising swiftly enough to set the carriage to rocking. "I'll run upstairs for it, and be back before you know I've gone."

"I shall join you, Miss Wood," Reverend Lord Patterson declared, clambering after her. "I must see what's detaining my nephew. You will excuse me, Lady Diana?"

"I wouldn't dream of keeping either of you." Diana sighed again, stuffing a pillow behind her. They hadn't even ventured near a single ruin, yet the day seemed to stretch endlessly before her, and already she had a headache. With a grumble of discontent, she leaned back against the pillow and closed her eyes, willing the headache to go away.

"Ah, *carissima*," the man said softly behind her. "And here I thought my flowers would bring you pleasure!"

Chapter Four

"You!" Diana twisted around in the seat. The man was standing behind the carriage, his face level with hers. He looked different in the daylight—less mysterious, less the wild beast with his jaw cleanly shaven and his black hair combed more neatly, dressed in light blue-gray instead of black—yet still she'd know him anywhere. "What are you doing here?"

"Here?" He spread his arms wide, encompassing the entire crowded piazza. "'Here' is my home, my lady. I was born in Rome, and I've never lived anywhere else, nor wished to."

"No, I meant *here*," she said, jabbing her finger at the paving stones at his feet. "You must stop following me!"

He smiled, that lazy smile that revealed its charm slowly, a smile she'd come to recognize all too well.

"No, I mean what I say," she said indignantly. The last thing she wished was to have Edward come out and see this man lurking behind her as if there were some sort of—of *acquaintance* between them. "You must leave at once, or I'll have the driver send you away!"

His smile widened, and he made a nonchalant little sweep of his hand, a dare if ever there was one.

She jerked around in her seat and leaned towards the driver. "Driver, this man is bothering me."

The man didn't move, wheezing—or snoring—gently beneath his lowered hat.

With the ivory handle of her parasol, Diana tapped him on the shoulder. "Driver, please make this man leave me alone. *Driveri, drivero*—oh, how must I say it in Italian to make him understand?"

"*Questo uomo mi da fastidio. Farlo andare via,*" the man behind the carriage helpfully supplied. "That should do it."

Diana whipped around to face him once again, the parasol clutched tightly in her hands. "What did you just tell him?"

"'This man is bothering me. Make him go away.' That's what you wished me to say, isn't it?" He leaned his arm on the back of the carriage seat, as comfortable as if it were a chair in his own parlor. "But I doubt the fellow is going to pay you any heed."

"And why not?" Diana asked imperiously, though she'd wondered, too, why the driver was ignoring her. She was a duke's daughter; she was accustomed to being obeyed. "He must do as I say. He's in my employ."

"Yes, my lady, but you see the last coin he took was mine, so I expect he'll do as I ask instead," the man said. "Which is to turn both a blind eye and a deaf ear to whatever protests you make about me."

Diana frowned, restlessly tapping the handle of her parasol against her knee. She'd been in Italy long enough to understand the truth in what he said: there was almost no loyalty to be found in this country except to whomever waved the brightest coin last.

But that didn't mean she was going to let him stand there like a grinning, handsome signboard. "This piazza is full of people, including English people. If you don't leave directly, I shall shout and scream and make a general racket until others come to see that you do."

"Will you now?" He lowered his voice a fraction, forcing her to lean closer to him so she could make out his words. "But then, dear, dear Lord Edward will understand if you turn into a shrieking banshee in the middle of the Piazza di Spagna. Even the daintiest of English ladies is permitted to draw a crowd on occasion."

But Edward wouldn't understand. He believed her to be refined and demure, a model English lady. Edward would be mortified if she created a scene, and blast this man for knowing it as well as she did herself.

She glanced over her shoulder, back to the doorway of their lodgings. "You must go now," she said, her voice taut with urgency. "I don't want you here, and I don't want to see you."

"But you do, *cara*," he said softly, and it was the warmth in his gray-blue eyes that could convince her even if his words didn't. "When you took my flowers into your arms and held them close, you thought of me, and how much you'd like to see me again. And I obliged."

Her cheeks flushed with confusion. "You—you don't know what I did. You *can't* know."

"But I do, my lady," he said, and the way he smiled proved it. "You cannot deny it, can you? I chose every flower, every ribbon, knowing how they'd make you long to see me."

Her back straight, she turned away from him, away from his eyes and his smile and his certainty. "You know nothing of me."

"I know you wanted to see me, and now that you have, you'll want to see me again, and again after that," he said, his whispered voice so low and seductive behind her that it would almost have been better to have remained facing him. "I know that you don't belong in this stuffy little carriage, with its stuffy little passengers, *bella mia*."

"You don't know anything about—"

"Hush, hush and listen," he interrupted. "I know you belong with me, riding along the Palatine Hill and among the ruined palaces of the Augustans at sunset. With the kestrel's cry overhead, we would laugh as the stars first showed themselves over the river and the dome of St. Peter's. And I would kiss you, my wild lady, because that is what you want most of all from me. I would kiss you, and you me, there beneath the stars."

She squeezed her eyes shut as if that were enough to close her ears as well. God forgive her, but she could imagine it *all*. Yet how had he known she'd prefer to see Rome on horseback instead of in this clumsy carriage? How had he understood that she was at heart a country girl who missed riding?

How had he known she would want him to kiss her again?

"You're guessing," she said defensively. "That's all your prattle is. You can't possibly know me as well as you pretend."

"But I do, *cara*," he reasoned, "because I know myself, and thus I—"

"Then why won't you tell me your name?" she demanded. "You continue to insist upon this—this false connection between us, yet you can't even bring yourself to tell me so much as that."

"Antonio di Randolfo," he said softly, surprising her. "My name is Antonio."

"You mean Anthony," she repeated with triumph, as if getting him to surrender his name was a great victory. "Like the Mark Anthony who murdered his Caesar? You were named for a traitor?"

He didn't answer, and her triumph grew. At last she'd said

something he couldn't answer, and she turned around again to confront him, eager to see the confusion that must surely be marking his face.

But to her chagrin, he'd vanished. She looked across the piazza, to the left and the right, yet there was no sign of him. How could so large a man disappear so suddenly, and so completely?

"Anthony?" she called crossly, holding the back of the seat to peer down beneath the carriage. It would be entirely like him to hide underneath so he could suddenly pop up like a jack-in-the-box. "Anthony, where have you gone?"

"Lady Diana, what are you doing?" asked Miss Wood, her disapproval clear. "Hanging upside down like that! Come, sit properly, so Lord Edward and Reverend Lord Patterson might see your face instead of your—your other side."

At once Diana spun around and dropped into her seat. "Good day, Lord Edward," she said, concentrating on opening her parasol so she didn't have to meet his gaze just yet. What if they'd actually seen her *speaking* to Anthony, with him leering over the seat? "I hope you slept well?"

"It was the wretched beggars again, wasn't it?" Reverend Lord Patterson glared over the back of the carriage. "I've never seen such packs of the audacious rascals as here in Rome. I'm sorry, my lady, for leaving you to their depredation."

"No better than thieves," Edward agreed, dropping heavily into the seat across from Diana. "You should have come inside with Miss Wood, my lady, instead of having put yourself at risk alone. These Italian drivers and servants wouldn't lift a pinkie in your defense. I say, it is warm today, isn't it?"

"Thank you, my lords, but there was no harm done." Diana smiled at Edward, whose own smile seemed somewhat sickly. His face was pale, too, with greenish undertones that made Diana suspect overindulgence in the local red wine after he'd left her last night. But she wouldn't tempt fate. She'd say nothing. If they hadn't noticed her talking to Anthony, then she wouldn't notice Edward's bleariness.

But Edward had other ideas. "You shouldn't have insisted on sitting out here alone, my lady," he said. "It's not proper. You've no notion of the liberties these Roman men will take if you let them."

"I told you, my lord, that I was quite well enough on my own," Diana said, her displeasure simmering. She wished to make a favorable impression on Edward, true, but they certainly hadn't reached the point where he was entitled to lecture her. "Do you see any Roman men within twenty feet of me at present? I may have no notion of their liberties, but I doubt they can take them at such a distance."

He raised his chin like a bulldog, showing the softness beneath his jaw. "You shouldn't underestimate them, Lady Diana. They are rough and daring, and all too willing to take advantage of an innocent lady."

"Indeed, my lord." She should have been comforted by his insistence on her innocence, and that she protect herself. But instead of his concern, she found herself hearing only the overbearing authority in his words, and thinking of how vastly more agreeable she'd found the stranger's velvety, bemused tone instead. Nothing the stranger had said came close to being as vexing as Edward insisting she was a helpless imbecile.

No, he wasn't a stranger any longer. His name was Anthony. Antonio di Randolfo. The name of a handsome, charming rascal, for whom pursuing her had become some sort of ridiculous game.

Antonio….

The driver turned the carriage about, the scraping of the

metal-bound wheels against the paving stones a match for the discord in Diana's mood.

"That was a beautiful bouquet you sent to her ladyship, my lord," Miss Wood began, obviously trying to ease the strain within their little party. "A very unusual collection of blossoms."

"Flowers, Edward?" His uncle beamed, turning towards him. "I didn't know you'd sent her ladyship flowers!"

"Yes, my lord. I cannot thank you enough." Diana smiled at Edward, waiting. He could confess the flowers weren't his, or he could accept Anthony's gift as his own. The difficult truth, or a comfortable, self-serving lie.

He smiled in return, and to her disappointment, she understood at once which path he'd take.

"I'm glad you liked the bouquet, my lady," he said, touching his forehead. "Though the beauty of the flowers falls far short of your own, nor can they begin to express the admiration you inspire."

She nodded in acknowledgement of his compliment, then looked away to the shops and houses they were passing. How could he so easily claim what wasn't his? To take credit for flowers he hadn't the imagination to gather, let alone the thoughtfulness to send to her—it made her both sad and resentful that he'd do such a base thing. Edward had seemed so honorable, so respectable. She'd wanted to trust him, even to love him, but after this she was inclined to do neither.

Not that she could ever challenge him about this, or the bouquet. To do so would be to admit that there was another gentleman sufficiently fond of her to send her flowers, another man who'd taken special care to please her.

And as she glimpsed her own sad-faced reflection in a passing window, she realized the only face in her thoughts belonged to the indubitably unsuitable Antonio di Randolfo.

* * *

A glass of red wine in his hand, Anthony stood on the palazzo's balcony, only half listening to the singer's aria as it drifted to him on the warm evening from Lucia's sitting room. He'd lost track of which of the boys were performing now; there'd been so many eager to perform tonight.

With the summer heat finally fading, more and more of the city's aristocrats were returning to their town palazzos from their villas in the hills, and soon the theaters would reopen for the season. The companies were already rehearsing, and while the leading roles had long ago been filled, there was always the chance for a newcomer to earn a small part in a production by proving himself at one of these private musicales. While Lucia herself could never sing at the Capranica, she adored being the patroness of these aspiring young men, fawning over her favorites and plotting against the rest.

But Anthony was in no mood for Lucia's intrigues tonight. He was, in fact, in no mood for company in general, which was why he'd retreated to this balcony, where the only company he was likely to have would be the omnipresent shadow of St. Peter's dome, looming there against the star-filled sky.

Had there been so many stars two nights ago, when he'd kissed Diana Farren? Had the moon been full, or only a bright sliver in the sky above them? What he remembered was how the light seemed to come from her: the gleam of her golden hair, the brilliance of her eyes, but most of all the fire of her temper, her passion, and how it had burned so hot and bright through her kiss that he'd been unable to put her from his thoughts since then.

Seeing her today outside her lodgings had only made matters worse. He'd sent her flowers from his mother's old garden, a mix of cultivated and wild, just like her. She'd been amazed to see him there in the piazza, though it was no real mystery. In Rome, every servant's knowledge was for sale for a few coins, and her party was so slow and predictable that it hadn't taken much for him to be waiting when she appeared. All women were beautiful by moonlight, but she'd proven to be one of the rare ones who was just as extraordinary in the unforgiving light of the afternoon sun. She'd been as fascinated with him in return. He'd seen it in her eyes, felt it in the air between them and in the plaintive, disappointed way she'd called his name when he'd ducked away.

Now experience told him that tomorrow he needed to avoid her entirely, to let her fancy he'd left her, to keep her off balance and uncertain. By keeping away, he meant to increase her interest in him, letting her curiosity and desire grow and ripen until she'd be the one begging for him.

But it wasn't working entirely the way he'd expected. He'd meant to leave his mark on her, the first step in any decent seduction, yet somehow this little English virgin had turned the tables, and left her imprint on him. He'd have to take back command, of course, and steer this whole affair back the way he wished. But how in blazes had such a thing happened at all to him—to *him?*

"You were wise to retreat, my lord," said the heavy-set man as he joined Anthony on the balcony. "The air in there is insufferable."

Anthony nodded, and shifted along the railing to give the newcomer room to join him. He'd rather have been left alone, but if he had to be interrupted, it might as well be by Alessandro Dandolo. Dandolo was not only the most popular and gifted singer in the Roman opera and the Vatican's favorite soloist on holy days, but also the most amusing. He had risen far from his birth as an orphaned bastard in the Roman streets, though the price he'd paid as a boy—his manhood in exchange for a heavenly voice—for his success now as a *castrato* was too grim for Anthony even to consider.

"It's a warm night for so late in the summer," Anthony said. "If we'd any sense, we'd all have stayed in the hills for another fortnight."

"I didn't mean the heat of the air, my lord." Dandolo paused for effect, gently stroking the cascade of lace ruffles he always wore beneath his chin to mask his lack of a manly Adam's apple. "Though I'll grant that any room with our dear Lucia in it will be...*fervid*."

Anthony chuckled. "How can she not be, surrounded by so many pretty, fawning boys?"

"How, indeed?" Dandolo's sigh was purposefully melancholy as he glanced back through the open door to where one more hopeful youth was attempting an aria. "But they're so sad, the little pigeons. So much yearning, so much striving, and for what?"

"They look at you, sir," Anthony said dryly, for this was exactly the answer that the other man sought, "and wish the same prizes. The best roles, the acclaim of the crowds and wealth beyond reason."

"Yes, yes, there is that." Dimples showed in his plump, smooth cheeks, making Dandolo look like a crafty, oversized cherub. "Fame is a most heady potion."

Anthony raised his own glass towards the woman now addressing the audience inside. "It's certainly one our dear friend Lucia would love to sip."

"Oh, Lucia, Lucia." Dandolo waved his hand through the air, the moonlight glancing off the large ruby on his middle finger. "Poor dear, forced to heed the words of St. Paul—'Let the women be silent in church.' Forbidden to sing in the cathedral or a theater! They say her best performances are the private ones, singing in the bedchamber. But then why need I tell you, my lord, when you've occupied her most private box yourself?"

"Enough, Dandolo," Anthony warned mildly. "I'll not hear you slander her."

Dandolo arched one carefully painted brow. "What will your new mistress say to that, eh, my lord? What will she make of such loyalty to her predecessor?"

"My new mistress?" Anthony smiled, and sipped his wine slowly before answering. Dandolo was a notorious gossip, never letting the truth interfere with a good story. "You make no sense to me, sir."

"No, my lord?" Dandolo tipped his hand towards the sky, idly admiring the ring on his finger. "Lucia told me you're much taken with a certain fair English lady. She swore on her mother's rosary that it was true, and that because of a wager she'd made with you, we'd have an English wedding before Christmas."

"Lucia is confused, my friend," Anthony said easily. "It's true that she and I have made a small wager between us regarding that fair English lady, but it's a wager I've every intention of winning. Lucia's stake is that she will perform on the steps above the Piazza di Spagna, a generous gift to all of those Romans unfortunate enough never to have heard her sing. As for my stake—ah, it's of no importance, sir, for I will win. Have no doubt of that. I'll win, and Lucia shall sing."

"Then with such confidence, you'll have no need for my little news, my lord," Dandolo countered with a sniff of wounded disdain. "It's from an impeccable source within the British consulate, mind you, but of no consequence to a great lord of such indubitably seductive prowess, such magnificence in the bedchamber, such—"

"Oh, hell, Dandolo, tell me your news." Anthony was disgusted with the other man's game, but more disgusted with himself for wanting so badly to know the scandal being blatantly dangled before him. "What have you heard?"

Dandolo's wide red mouth curved into a smile of happy complicity. "You have a rival for the lady. The English Lord Edward Warwick has shown a determined attachment to Lady Diana, and she to him."

"Oh, Warwick," Anthony said, more relieved than he wished to admit. "He's nothing to her."

"Nothing, my lord? Then why are both parties making discreet inquiries regarding the, ah, situations of the other?"

"What? Warwick's asking about the lady's past?"

"No, no, it's far more serious than that, my lord," purred Dandolo. "He's asking after the size of her dowry, and how she stands in her father's favor."

Anthony frowned. "If her people ask after Warwick, then they'll learn what a wretched rascal he is."

"What they'll learn is that his family is wealthy and noble and respectable," Dandolo said. "The consul is well-acquainted with them, and so willing to vouch for this Warwick that he is promoting the match to her people himself. All expect an announcement any day."

"That's ridiculous, Dandolo," Anthony snapped, remembering how weakly she'd defended Warwick. "The lady is clearly not inclined towards him."

Dandolo's smile widened slyly. "But what if the lady must heed reason, instead of her heart? What if she must view his offer as a great gift?—or perhaps the only gift she deserves?"

"She's a peer's daughter, doubtless with a dowry to match,

and she's a beauty. She'll have more men wriggling after that bait than she could count."

"But I've heard the English expect their lady-brides to be without a smudge of scandal," Dandolo said with relish. "I've heard tales of certain, ah, adventures in Paris involving quite the wickedest old *debauché* that might lessen her virginal value."

"So that Warwick might be her best offer?" Anthony didn't care one way or the other if the girl was a virgin—he thought virginity in general was overrated, and something of a bother that too often fostered hysterics—but he'd guess his more tedious English cousins would insist on being first with their wives. "What a pity for her."

"But a great benefit to you with your wager, my lord," Dandolo said with a droll chuckle. "If the lady is already inclined towards *inclination,* then I'd venture Rome will soon be hearing the fair Lucia's song."

Anthony laughed with him, but his thoughts had returned to Lady Diana herself, remembering how her cheeks had flushed and her blue eyes had sparked when he'd teased her over the back of the carriage. She was so quick and full of spirit that it saddened him to imagine her with Warwick. If she were going to be forced to settle for such a dour match, then she deserved a few rich memories to sustain her for the rest of her life. Anthony would gladly give her that, wager or not. But he'd have to proceed more quickly than he'd first intended. Once Warwick claimed her, then likely his opportunity to win the wager would be over.

He swirled the half-forgotten wine in his glass. "Have you told any of this to Lucia?"

"By all the saints, no," scoffed Dandolo. "We men must support one another, my lord, eh? Why should I wish you to wed against your will? I'll send you passes to one of our rehearsals tomorrow. So far our company's in shambles, the musicians are sour and clumsy, and the settings are little more than ruins. Yet still the English ladies do crave admission to our follies, as if they've been given a great bowl of clotted cream and honey for supper."

"She's English to her bones." Anthony chuckled, imagining the girl's delight at such an invitation. Not that he'd send the passes to her directly; he'd another plan in mind, a more entertaining way to bring them together again. "Likely she and her governess will think it's cream and honey and some of that hideous English treacle, too. I thank you, Dandolo."

"Not that you need my paltry bait," Dandolo said, pretending to disparage his offering even as he preened at Anthony's thanks. "Not you. You're such a clever one, you've not even told the chit your name yet."

"I let her believe I'm Italian," Anthony said with a shrug. "Antonio di Randolfo. It seemed less…complicated at the time."

"Surely less inconvenient if she never learns the name of her ruin." Dandolo smirked and cocked his pinkie in an affected gesture of over-refinement. "Lord Anthony Randolph, the youngest son of the oh-so-English Earl of Markham."

Anthony glanced over the rail, towards the house in the distance where he knew Diana Farren must now be asleep. No, she'd never learn his name, or his title, or the fact that half of him was as impeccably English as she herself. She'd never hear of the wager he'd made with Lucia. All the golden Lady Diana would know was that he'd given her greater pleasure than she'd ever find with her doltish husband. He'd become no more than a bittersweet memory that would fade with time, like a brittle, crumbling rosebud pressed between love letters.

That was all he'd ever intended to mean to her, and all he'd ever wanted to be. Yet when he remembered how she'd smiled at him, the realization that he'd fade away like that brittle rosebud made him feel unexpectedly melancholy.

With a frown, he gave himself a small shake. What had come over him, anyway? He'd never been sentimental about a woman before. He wasn't about to start now.

He raised his glass towards the open door, and Lucia beyond. "To the triumph of men, eh, Dandolo?" he said with his best rakish grin. "And to the wager that will settle it between us."

Slowly Diana followed Miss Wood down the staircase to the first floor, and the carriage waiting with Edward and his uncle. She took longer and longer between steps, making sure that Miss Wood was well ahead of her, almost to the door.

Two weeks ago—even two days ago!—she wouldn't have dared so much as to imagine what she was going to do next. But after yesterday, she could think of nothing else. She swallowed back her excitement, relishing the old familiar sense of rebellion from before she'd tried to reform herself, and finally stopped on a middle stair.

"Oh, Miss Wood, I've forgotten something in the room!" she called, turning on the step. "You go ahead without me and make my excuses to the gentlemen, and I'll join you directly."

"Lady Diana." Miss Wood looked up at her, her hands at her waist. "My lady, I vow you'd forget your own head if it weren't on your pillow each morning. Go on, go on, but pray don't keep the rest of us waiting any longer than you must."

"Yes, Miss Wood." Diana was glad her governess couldn't see her grin, nor see how quickly she began undressing as soon as she reached her bedchamber, kicking off her slippers and yanking her hat off without pausing to draw the pins.

"Hurry, Deborah, be quick!" she ordered her maidservant as she wriggled free of her gown. "My riding habit!"

"Your habit, my lady?" asked Deborah, even as she hurried to present the habit's navy superfine bodice. Her fingers flew over the double rows of pewter buttons, fastening one side over the other. "I didn't know you was riding, my lady, else I would have laid out the proper clothes."

"No one else did either, Deborah," Diana said breathlessly, hopping as she pulled on her boots without pausing to let Deborah help her. "Quickly, my hat!"

"Yes, my lady." Deborah stepped back, letting Diana settle the hat onto her head herself.

This particular riding hat was Diana's favorite: light-blue dyed beaver, with a cunning plume that curled over one eye like a quotation mark. She angled it to one side, then shifted it lower still, so the plume nearly brushed her cheek. If that didn't inspire a gentleman to kiss her, then nothing would, and she blew a kiss to her reflection in the glass to make sure. Then she grabbed her crop instead of her parasol, and ran down the stairs, through the door held by the gaping footman, and into the street to the carriage with the others.

One look at the three faces before her, and she knew she'd done the right thing—irresponsible and impulsive, yes, but also the right thing for *her*.

Miss Wood spoke first. "My lady, might I ask why you are dressed in such a fashion?"

"Because I am weary of being hauled about in the back of an open cart like a farmer's goodwife," Diana said cheerfully. "Lord Edward, I have decided that today we shall go riding together instead. I wish to view the ruined palaces on the Palatine Hill. I've heard they are quite fascinating."

He stared at her with blank incomprehension, as if she'd

just proposed he flap his arms like Icarus's wings and rise to the sun. "Ride, my lady? On horseback?"

"Yes, on horseback," she said, her gaze locked with his "Unless there is some other beast preferred for the saddle by Romans."

"My dear Lady Diana," his uncle said, clasping his hands before him in a conciliatory manner. "I know how confined you must feel by the carriage, but I must assure you that this is the most comfortable and approved manner of travel for ladies in Rome."

"Perhaps it is for Roman ladies, reverend my lord," Diana said, "but I believe today I should prefer to ride. Lord Edward, will you accompany me?"

Miss Wood stepped forward, her hands likewise clasped before her and the flat brim of her hat quivering.

"My lady, please, this is tempting, yes, but quite rash of you," she said, her voice low and earnest. "You must reconsider. This *is* Rome, a foreign place, and for you to ride unaccompanied with a gentleman, even so honorable a gentleman as his lordship, would not be proper."

"But I am not a Roman lady, Miss Wood. I'm an English one." Already Diana's wool riding habit was too warm for the afternoon sun, and she could feel the prickle of heat growing beneath her shift. But to back down now would be to admit that she'd been wrong, that she'd been impulsive, that she hadn't been able to put Antonio di Randolfo's vision from her head as she should have. "You and Reverend Lord Patterson can follow behind in the carriage. Besides, how can one possibly be indiscreet whilst riding?"

"My lady," Miss Wood said in an ominous whisper. "If there is a way, you will be sure to find it. Now for once in your life, show some sense, and—"

"We'll ride, my lady," Edward interrupted evenly. "To the Palatine Hill. If that is what you wish, then that's what we shall do, as soon as I can send for the proper mounts."

Diana tipped her head to one side. She was daring him, and they both knew it. "You will oblige me, my lord?"

"I'll do whatever it takes to please you, my lady." He bowed slightly, his golden hair slipping over his forehead and his pale eyes never leaving hers. He was smiling, but there was no humor or good will in the set of his mouth. He'd accepted her challenge. It was surprising, yet pleasing, too, that he hadn't backed down as she'd suspected he would. He'd do as she'd asked, yes, but he clearly wasn't happy about it.

Yet instead of feeling wary, Diana found his displeasure oddly exhilarating, as if by being herself for the first time, she'd managed to uncover a more genuine Edward as well. Perhaps he was stronger, more manly, than she'd first judged him to be. Perhaps he truly could make her forget she'd ever kissed Antonio di Randolfo.

The plume on her hat tickled her cheek as she held her gloved hand out to him. "If you wish so much to please me, my lord, why, then surely I shall do my best to please you in turn."

"I should hope you will, my lady." He took her offered hand, his fingers closing tightly over hers. "I should hope you will."

Chapter Five

The Palatine Hill that Diana had imagined had been colored through Antonio's description. She'd seen a wild, romantic place, with a gentle evening breeze tossing the stars over the sky. She'd ridden hard among ghostly white ruins, her horse's mane whipping back against her hands, her own hair inexplicably loose and the man had ridden laughing beside her.

But the reality of the Palatine Hill was far more dusty and uncomfortable. She hadn't realized it was so distant from their lodgings, across the city and near the Coliseum. Any of the stars she'd been promised were bleached out by the unrelenting afternoon sun. The wildness was confined to the great numbers of mangy, underfed cats that hid and darted among the broken walls, and as for romance—there was next to none of that.

"Please slow your pace, my lady." Edward scowled as her mare—a neat little bay named Zucchero—gave an emphatic toss of her head. "We're getting too far ahead of the carriage again."

"Oh, don't make jests, my lord, I beg you." Diana wanted to be agreeable to him since he'd taken her side to please her about the horses, but she also wished he wouldn't be so quick to give orders to her, as if he were her master. "The streets have been so narrow and crowded today that I couldn't begin to outrace the carriage if my very life depended upon it."

"You're an experienced horsewoman," he said, clumsily guiding his own gelding around a man with a cart full of bottles who refused to move from his path. It was obvious he was an uneasy rider at best, which, in a way, made his concession to her all the more generous. "Even in this twisting old city, my lady, you can adjust your haste as it suits you."

This was true. The little mare that had been hired for her was spirited and quick, and in better circumstances would have proven a delight to ride. But experienced or not, Diana hadn't been on a horse since she'd left England nearly four months ago, and riding on the lady's saddle with one knee hooked over the pommel was reminding her of muscles she'd forgotten she possessed. Her back ached from the careful balancing, and the woolen habit that was so appropriate for an English spring had made her sticky, over-warm, and cross beyond measure.

She looked longingly up the hill to the leafy shade of the cypress trees that poked through the jagged pattern of broken columns and roofless walls. "Why don't we ride up there where it's cooler?"

"Because the carriage couldn't follow us," he answered with infuriating patience. "I know you've no concern for what becomes of Miss Wood, but I won't abandon my uncle, nor put your reputation at risk."

Her reputation was her responsibility, not his, but still she bit back her retort, determined to keep peace at least a while longer.

"What if I should wish to learn more of that ruin, my lord?" she asked, appealing to his scholarly pride as a way of making the conversation more agreeable. "What if I wished you to explain it to me in detail?"

"You mean the Domus Flavia?" He smiled, and his face

relaxed and warmed. Perhaps she'd misjudged him. Perhaps he didn't want to be her overbearing master. "It's a remarkable building, isn't it? Though the palace is a shambles now, when one considers how long ago it was built, it's a wonder there's any of it surviving at all."

Diana nodded. She didn't particularly care if the wretched palace had been built a thousand years ago, or last week. What mattered most to her was that the tension seemed to have lessened between them, and Edward was once again the agreeable golden-haired gentleman she'd first met.

She smiled, encouraging. "Was it as grand as our royal palaces?"

"Oh, far grander," he said, warming to his subject as he gazed back at the rows of broken arches. "The Domus Flavia was the official residence of the emperors. It represented not only their majesty, but the majesty of the entire empire. Not that it looks like much now."

"No," Diana agreed, comparing it to Kensington Palace, Whitehall and the other great palaces where the English kings and queens lived in London, and where, if she were honest, she rather wished she were right now, on a cool autumn day. "It doesn't at all."

"That's the fault of these lazy latter-day Romans again, my lady," he said firmly. "They've let these palaces all tumble down, just as they have the Coliseum and their temples and everything else left in their keeping. Do you know that all the work to discover and restore this palace has been done by Englishmen in this very century, with English money to fund the labor? Why, the emperor's throne room itself wasn't discovered until two years ago!"

Diana shook her head, and wished he could speak as passionately to her as he did to moss-covered columns.

"You certainly couldn't leave it to the Romans themselves, my lady," he said with a self-important sniff. He'd tied his neckcloth too tightly for the warm day, and a glossy ripple of pink neck bulged over the damp white linen. "Their entire moral ethic changed the minute they let popery take its greedy hold over their souls, and gave them all the excuse they needed to become idle and uncaring of the magnificent ancient heritage in their city's possession."

"So you would discount everything built since the fall of Rome, my lord?" Diana asked, curious. She and her sister Mary had discussed this very topic after seeing the breathtaking medieval cathedrals on their journey through France. Because she and Miss Wood had fallen in with Lord Edward and his uncle, their sightseeing here had been limited to the remnants of ancient imperial Rome, but she'd glimpsed enough of the rest of the city to decide that there was much that was splendid built in the last thousand years.

"The Roman faith was the only Christian faith for many centuries," she continued. "Would you fault all that was created in the time since?"

"Oh, I'll grant there are a handful of exceptions, my lady, to be sure." He waved one hand impatiently in the air as if brushing away an impudent fly. "But considered as a whole, there is an unpleasant sensuality to the newer architecture and painting of this city, a surfeit of base, overwrought passions that are encouraged by the Roman church. Everything is for pleasure, without a breath of useful or gainful purpose."

At once Diana thought of Antonio. She wasn't in the habit of describing men as sensual, but as soon as Edward used the word, her head applied it to Antonio. He *was* sensual: from the easy confidence of his smile, the way he moved with a dancer's unconscious grace, his deep, melodious chuckle, even the rumbling, rolling pattern of his accented English, seasoned with Italian words, all tossed her conceptions of a gentleman's behavior to the unruly winds.

And when she considered how he'd kissed her—oh, heaven deliver her, was there anything more blatantly sensual than how he'd teased her with his lips, his teeth, his tongue?

"You can see the sensual excess in everything these people do, my lady," Edward was saying, continuing his lecture, "from that gaudy, vainglorious dome of St. Peter's Cathedral, down to the merest urchin whose hair is coaxed by his mother into outrageous curls."

Immediately Diana thought again of Antonio di Randolfo, of the glossy black curls of his careless queue and how a few more fell over his brow.

"To imagine that an entire city—no, a small country!—has done nothing of any worth or value for a thousand years seems a harsh judgment, my lord," she said slowly. "I cannot believe that the ancient Romans were as perfect as you claim, nor that their descendents today are so very wicked."

"But that's just it, my lady," he said, his voice rising for emphasis. "These modern laggards are poor descendents of the noble ancients."

"Oh, my lord, that is *preposterous!*" scoffed Diana as she drew her horse to a stop. "Of all the narrow-minded declarations I've heard in my life, that is surely the most foolish. If you have so little use for this city and its people, I cannot fathom how you can bear to stay in their midst."

He reined his horse up sharply before hers. "I'm sorry I offended you so, my lady, but I refuse to retract what I know to be the truth. The modern Romans are a slothful breed, a disgrace to—"

"What of the people who've been so agreeable to you?"

Diana demanded. "At our lodgings, everyone from Signor Silvani to the cook to the youngest scullery maid has been the very soul of good humor and hospitality!"

"Do not mistake familiarity with hospitality, my lady," he warned. "They'll take any excuse to stop their tasks and make forward conversation. It's a problem I've observed in all the houses in Rome. Servants forget their stations, and their masters neglect to correct them."

"Where is the sin in being agreeable?"

"The sin comes from forgetting one's station and the order of society with it," he said. "It's a lesson you might do well to recall yourself, my lady."

"*I* should recall, my lord?" repeated Diana, stunned. "You would dare tell me I've forgotten my station?"

"You have, my lady," he said doggedly. "You are the daughter of a peer, one of the highest-born gentlemen in England. Yet once you've been infected with the Roman fever, you wish to traipse about unaccompanied like—like some gypsy-strumpet, with no regard for your dignity or honor."

"Like a gypsy-*strumpet!*" Diana cried, so loudly that her mare danced nervously beneath her. She had done her very best always to be the lady around Edward, working harder at it than she'd ever done before, and yet that effort wasn't enough? "My lord, you go too far!"

"I did not say you *were* a gypsy, nor a strumpet," he said hastily. "I said only that you were beginning to act more like a woman of this place, instead of the fine English lady that you are."

"'Fine English lady,' hah," Diana said, wheeling her horse sharply away from his. "If you're so quick to make pronouncements, then I'll show you exactly how a fine English lady can traipse away!"

Before he could answer, she smacked Zucchero on the flank, dug in the heels of her boots, and guided the horse up the side of the hill. Delighted to be free, the little mare surged forward, nimbly picking a path through the tall grass and stones up the hill to the ancient palace.

"My lady!" called Edward behind her. "My lady, don't be so rash! I beg you, come back!"

"A pox on his infernal rashness," Diana muttered, leaning lower over the horse's neck. "And a pox on his traipsing gypsy-wench, too. On, on, Zucchero!"

The mare scrambled up to a flat plateau on the hillside, perhaps once a walkway, now overgrown with grass and weeds. Ahead lay a long, narrow alley lined with stone arches, some broken to their bases and others nearly whole, that must once have been a kind of covered cloister or balcony. At once Diana turned the mare's head towards the passage, and sent her clattering down the length of it.

The feather on her hat wasn't tickling her cheek any longer, and the brim was folded back by her speed, but she didn't care, nor did she look back to see if Edward was following. She was sure he wouldn't, or more rightly, that he couldn't, and it served him right for insulting her the way he had.

Yet as she raced along the passageway, her main feeling was one of glorious, untrammeled freedom. With her skirts flying around her legs and her hair coming unpinned around her hat, the warm wind in her face and her heart thumping in rhythm with the mare's hooves, she felt finally free of everything that had held her down here in Rome: Miss Wood's rules and Lord Edward's expectations, and even her fear that she'd somehow lost herself by trying to please everyone else.

It was a false freedom, and wouldn't last—she wasn't so foolish as to believe otherwise—but for these precious moments, here where emperors might have walked, she'd take any freedom she could. If that made her more Roman than English, then so be it. She'd have to return to the others soon enough, before they came hunting after her. But for now, with the city laid out before her, orange-tiled roofs and gilded domes, she felt as glorious as any ancient empress ever could.

The little mare snorted and slowed as they reached the end of the passage. The horse was winded, and likely thirsty, too, on this warm afternoon. In a courtyard through one of the arches, Diana could make out the glittering reflection of water, a small impromptu pond filled by the sliver of a spring or stream. She slid from the saddle to the ground, and with the reins looped in her hand, led the horse around the low stone walls to where she'd seen the water. She hoped Edward's excavating scholars weren't at work here today; she would rather not have to explain either who she was, or how she'd come to be there.

She ducked beneath the low branch of a cypress tree that long ago had sprouted and grown through the emperor's marble floor. She pushed aside another branch, turning back to make sure the horse could pass through with her.

"Here you are, Zucchero," she said, giving the horse a fond pat as she bent over the pond. "Drink your fill, sweet, and then we must go back before Miss Wood calls out the army."

"Not just yet, *cara,*" the man said. "I've been waiting so long for you, that they can wait a little longer."

Diana looked up sharply. Antonio was standing before her. He wore no coat, and the collar of his white linen shirt was open, with the full sleeves rolled up to his elbows to leave his forearms bare. He wore dark breeches and boots, and when she glanced past him she could see a large black gelding grazing in the distance.

"What do you mean by that, sir?" she said. Yes, he'd been much in her thoughts since she'd seen him by the carriage in the piazza, but to have him appear so suddenly again made her uneasy, and too aware of how solitary—and vulnerable—she was. "How can you have been waiting here so long?"

"An easy answer, my lady." He sighed, and placed his hand over his heart before he bowed. Somehow he managed to make the gesture at once deferential and courtly, heart-felt and self-mocking, and altogether devastatingly charming. "How can it not be, when I've been waiting all my mortal days for you?"

A little frisson of pleasure at the compliment rippled through her, pleasure she'd no business feeling from him.

She straightened her hat with both hands, an efficient, practical gesture to counter his.

"Now that's empty foolishness," she said. "How can you have been waiting all your life when you didn't know I existed before this week?"

"Because it was *bella fortuna* that sent you to me." Slowly he walked towards her, his arms outstretched in supplication, or perhaps to demonstrate he meant no harm. "*Bella fortuna,* luck, fate. Or is your London too dry and serious for such notions?"

"I don't believe in fate," she said. "Fate means you've abandoned reason and choice."

"You're listening too much to your head," he said, tapping one finger to his brow. "That is acceptable for London, I suppose, but here in Rome, you must rely on your heart. Romans do not think. They *feel.*"

He covered his heart again, more meaningful this time because he stood so much closer. Without realizing it, she'd inched backwards away from him, bumping into the rounded side of the mare, the stirrup of her saddle pressing into her spine.

"How did you know I'd be here?" she said, her voice sounding oddly breathy. "I certainly didn't tell you."

He smiled. "You didn't have to. I knew you'd come. I knew it here, in my heart."

"You couldn't have," she insisted, clutching at reason to protect her. Oh, why couldn't Edward talk like this to her? "I didn't plan to come here. I—I ran away. So there's no way I could have told you."

"Yes, there was," he said, reaching out to touch his fingertips lightly to her forehead. "Your head didn't know it, but your heart—"

"That's enough," she said, swiftly swatting away his hand before he reached for her heart. "My head—my *English* head—makes my decisions for me."

He shrugged. "Perhaps. But yesterday, when I came upon you in your carriage, I told you how much I should like to show you the view from the Palatine Hill. I put that much into your heart, *carissima*."

"You did not!"

"Didn't I? Then why did you choose to come here today if you hadn't hoped to see me? If I hadn't haunted your dreams last night as you did mine?"

"I—I came because Lord Edward likes to show me the ancient places," she said, so blatant a half truth it wouldn't have fooled even Miss Wood. "And I did not dream of you."

"As you say, my lady, as you say." There was that lazy smile again, his eyes half closed beneath the dark sweep of his lashes. He had the most extravagant lashes she'd ever seen on a man, long and silky, the equal to his pale-blue eyes.

What was it Edward had called it: the "sensual excess" of the Romans? Could such a term apply to a man's eyelashes as well as a cathedral's dome?

She swallowed, wishing she'd the power to look away. "I did say it, because it's true."

"Then it's just as true that you remembered how I wished to see you on horseback," he said. "You remembered, and here you are."

"Lord Edward chose for us to ride!"

"He agreed, *cara.* You suggested it, didn't you?"

"I—I must go." At last she broke her gaze from his to stare at the white linen-covered wall of his chest. The finest Holland linen, she observed, striving to distract herself, the linen expertly pressed by a skilled laundress, a gentleman's shirt without a doubt, even if it weren't being worn by a gentleman, but a rascal. "I must rejoin Lord Edward before he comes and finds me here. I must go now, sir."

"Ah, you wound me, my lady! Have you remembered so much, and forgotten my name?"

She looked up again, unable not to. One minute more with him, that's all she'd allow herself, maybe two, three, but certainly no more than that. "I haven't forgotten."

"Then say it, my own Diana," he whispered. "Say it to me, from your heart, not your head."

"Antonio," she whispered in return, unable to stop herself. There was no one here to help her, but no one to watch and know what she did, either. "Antonio di Randolfo."

"Say it properly," he asked softly, leaning into her. "Say the name of the one who worships and desires you the most. Ann-TON-nee-yo. Like a caress in the night, languid and sweet. Antonio."

"Antonio," she repeated, drawing the syllables out as he'd asked, as if she were the one giving the caress, not receiving it. "Antonio di Randolfo."

And then she kissed him. There was no way she could shift

the blame to him, or cry that he'd taken advantage of her solitude. In truth she'd taken advantage of *him*. She arched up on the toes of her boots, lifted her mouth to his, closed her eyes, and kissed him, her palms resting lightly on his chest.

She kissed him, because she wanted to, and in return he let her do all the work, the rascal, standing there as she moved her lips gently over his, trying to coax him to respond. All his babble about *feeling*, yet here he was pretending he was as dispassionate as the shattered marble columns and walls around them.

"Your heart, Antonio," she whispered, feathering her breath over his ear. "What has become of your blasted heart now?"

She felt his laughter before she heard it, a low rumble building deep in his chest as his arms circled around her waist and drew her close.

"You think you must remind me, eh?" he asked, brushing tiny kisses over her nose, her cheeks, the underside of her chin as she turned towards him, teasing, tickling kisses. "You think that is your role, *carissima?*"

"If you are a man, you need reminding," she said, chuckling with delight.

"Oh, I'm that," he said, his mouth finally reaching hers. "And I don't need reminding of anything."

He proved it to her by kissing her the way she remembered from the Coliseum, and yet different enough to surprise her all over again. She felt as if she were melting into a pool of sensation, a warm, delicious pool where she wanted to linger forever.

And where, most sadly and regrettably, she'd no right to remain even another second longer.

She pulled away, and turned her face. "I must go."

"I know you must," he said softly. "Just as I know you don't wish to."

She sighed and closed her eyes, for he was right about that as well. "I have no choice."

"And I know that, too." Gently he turned her face back towards his. "Do what you must, *cara*. Go back to them now. But I will find you again, and kiss you again."

She pulled her face free, and shook her head. "Please don't," she said sadly. "It's not right. If you know as much about me as you claim, then you must understand that."

To prove she meant it, she slipped free of his embrace, and was both thankful and disappointed that he didn't try to draw her back.

"You cannot meddle with fate, my lady," he said, his smile resolute. "Fate doesn't care if you're a princess or a serving girl. If you're meant to be mine, then be mine you will. That's Roman fate, my lady, not English."

She tried to smile in return, to make light of this whole foolish affair, but somehow couldn't. "How should I say it? *Arrivederci, signore.*"

"Not goodbye, *cara*." He kissed his fingertips in parting, the farewell she'd come to expect, and one that nearly melted her resistance all over gain. "Only a brief parting, until I find you—"

"My lady!" Miss Wood shouted from the far side of the wall. "My Lady Diana, where are you?"

"Oh, heavens, it's my governess!" Swiftly Diana scanned the ruined walls for Miss Wood's inevitable approach. "Hurry, Antonio, hurry, you must go! I can't let her find you with me!"

But when she looked back, Antonio was gone. She caught the blur of black that was his horse, and no more. If he appeared with breathtaking suddenness, he also seemed able to disappear just as thoroughly.

Beside her Zucchero's ears pricked up, and the mare whinnied softly at the fading click of the gelding's hooves over broken marble, as if she, too, lamented the hasty departure.

"My *lady!*"

Diana turned in time to see Miss Wood laboring up the hillside towards her. She held her skirts bunched in her fists at her sides, her round face flushed and sweating, and her mouth puckered with mixed emotions. It was an expression she'd come to recognize all too well over the last few years: relief that Diana was safe, mingled with irritation for the anxiety she'd caused, and a resolution that it would not happen again.

Which, of course, Diana knew it likely would.

"There you are, Miss Wood." She'd try to bluff her way clear with pleasantries; sometimes that did work. She patted the mare's side. "My horse was growing weary from the heat, and I was fortunate to find this little pond."

"If your horse was weary, my lady, it was from you driving her up the hill like a vengeful fury." Miss Wood glanced at the horse and the water, then back to Diana. "What *possessed* you to abandon your senses like that?"

"I told you, Miss Wood, my horse—"

"I'm not a complete fool, my lady! What must Lord Edward think after that display?"

"Lord Edward was addressing me in an offensive manner," Diana said. "He was saying the most barbarously rude things, and I couldn't—"

"*You* are the rude one, my lady," Miss Wood declared. "The poor gentleman was devastated to see you ride off as you did, convinced that he had in some fashion upset you."

"How perceptive of him, considering how he'd—"

"Hush, my lady, and listen to me," ordered the governess

sternly. "If you've any hope of maintaining any acquaintance with him, you must apologize to him at once—at *once!*"

Diana began to answer, then stopped short. If she was honest with herself, what she'd done to Edward was equal, perhaps even worse, than what he'd said to her. She'd even guessed that he wouldn't be skilled enough with the hired horse to follow her, which, considering how he'd agreed to riding instead of the carriage to please her in the first place, likely did tip the scales against her. He deserved an apology from her.

So why, then, was she so reluctant to give one? Was she so besotted with the notion—and it had to be only a notion, for she'd no true acquaintance with the actual man—of Antonio di Randolfo that she'd toss away a perfectly good suitor like Lord Edward for the sake of—of nothing? All too easily she could imagine her father's response to Antonio, how he'd sputter and fume over her even speaking to such a man. A damned dark dago: that's what Father would call him, lumping anyone who wasn't English into the same pot. She'd rather not imagine Father's reaction to her having kissed Antonio, and so eagerly at that.

Perhaps that was why she'd tried to send Antonio away forever today. Perhaps she was finally beginning to show some common sense. Perhaps she'd finally realized that he could have no lasting place in her life, and worse, could cause great havoc with her future.

And yet here she was back where she'd started, wondering why she was still thinking of Antonio, and reluctant to apologize to Edward.

"My lady!" Edward was waving his hat as he rode towards her. "My lady, thank God you're safe!"

"Of course I'm safe, my lord," she said. "I didn't go far."

"But when your horse bolted, and you vanished from my

sight—what was I to think?" He practically flung himself from the horse, his haste to reach her making his dismount so clumsy that Diana reached for his horse's bridle to steady it. "My lady, if any harm had come to you on account of me—"

"But it wouldn't, my lord," she said, gently stroking his horse's nose to take attention away from her own confused emotions. What was happening here, anyway? Edward was angry at himself, not her; he was even making excuses for her, blaming her abrupt departure on her horse instead. "It couldn't."

"Oh, yes, it could." He took a deep breath, working his fingers around the brim of the hat in his hands. "In this city, there's no real safety for an unaccompanied lady. If anything I said or did had caused you distress or unhappiness, if it had been my fault, then I'd never have forgiven myself."

Heaven help her, he was going to apologize to *her*. She'd been at least equally at fault, but he hadn't seen it that way. He'd worried for her safety, and blamed himself, and now he stood before her, his full face flushed and his voice so earnest that she knew she'd no choice but one to make.

Slowly she lifted her gaze to meet Lord Edward's, and offered him her hand.

"My lord," she said softly. "What can I ever do to thank you?"

"That aria has turned out far better than I'd thought it ever would," Lucia declared, clapping her gloved hands together up over her head as the singer bowed in appreciation. "The suggestions I made were well taken. That composer shows promise."

Beside her, Anthony stifled a yawn. The two of them were the only audience for the rehearsal, invited by Dandolo to watch from the royal box while they ate cold chicken and melon brought in a basket. "You like that composer because he is young and beautiful, and fawns over you."

"He *should* fawn over me," she said proudly. "I'm his most important backer."

"You?" asked Anthony, incredulous yet amused. Despite all the money Lucia had coerced from rich lovers over time, she always claimed to be perilously close to the edge of bankruptcy, and the thought of her gathering up enough funds to invest in an opera seemed far-fetched at best. "A backer, Lucia?"

"Very well, then, it's Lorenzo," she admitted, daintily nibbling the skin from a chicken leg, "or more properly, it's Lorenzo's money. But he's done it because I wished it. He has no ear for music himself, and thus has asked me to oversee his investment for him."

Anthony laughed. "You must have been very persuasive."

"You know me as well as any man." Lucia's small white teeth sank into the leg's meat. "Which in turn reminds me to ask you, Antonio, how matters are progressing with your little English dove."

Anthony settled into the high-backed armchair that mimicked a throne, running his fingertips over the bristling red plush upholstery. How were matters progressing with Diana Farren, anyway? He wasn't sure how to answer that, because he wasn't quite sure himself.

Oh, he'd gotten the details of the pursuit down effortlessly. He'd followed her, teased her, showered her with rare flowers and rarer kisses. He'd made certain to be so fascinating, so engaging, so *different* from the other poor wretches she'd known that she thought of him at least every quarter-hour of the day. He'd seen that much in her eyes when she'd tried to banish him earlier today on the Palatine.

Quarter-hour, hah. He'd wager a pile of gold that she was thinking of him every minute of the day, and dreaming of him during the night.

But what made no sense was that he was thinking of her just as frequently. It could be anything: the way her voice could turn husky without warning, or how the seaming on her riding habit curved in to define her waist with exhilarating precision, or the unusual rosiness that colored her cheeks when she blushed, a delectable color that put him to mind of the ripest of summer peaches, or the velvety perfection of her mouth when she'd just parted her lips to his tongue.

He could not recall another woman who'd so thoroughly overwhelmed him like this, and it made him feel unbalanced, as if his world had tipped a fraction off its axis with no hope of being righted.

Lucia prodded his arm with the chicken leg. "Are you searching for the words to admit your loss, Antonio? Are you hearing the bells that will peal for your wedding? Or is your defeat so complete that love for your virgin has struck you dumb?"

"Not at all," he said, unwilling to be taunted by her. He seized her wrist and twisted it so he could bite the chicken himself. "I'm only imagining my victory, and the great joy that you'll give to this city when you sing in the piazza."

She snorted, and jerked her wrist free of his grasp. She ran her tongue along the now-ravaged chicken leg, and smiled wickedly, an invitation if ever there was one, an invitation he no longer had any wish to accept.

Maybe this was the problem with Diana. He'd been so busy wooing her, that he'd forgotten the wickedness. Surely she must be simmering by now, the same as he was. Better to bring them both to a boil, and this wager with it.

Suddenly he noticed one of the boys who helped with the staging standing at the open door to the box, shifting from one foot to the other.

"What the devil do you want?" he growled, more irritated

at being caught thinking than alone with Lucia. "Spit it out, boy, spit it out."

The boy stepped forward, and made a grandiose bow at odds with his ragged dress. "A thousand pardons for interrupting, my lord. But Signor Dandolo sends you his most humble regards, and these four passes to tomorrow's performance, specially signed by our manager."

He held out a fat, sealed packet for Anthony's approval, and Lucia frowned.

"Passes, Antonio?" she asked suspiciously. "What need do you have for manager's passes to the opera, when your family has held a private box to this theater since before you were born?"

"These are for other acquaintances, Lucia," he said, purposefully vague as he waved away the boy's offering. "You know where to deliver them?"

"At the lodging house with the red shutters on the Piazza di Spagna, my lord," he answered promptly. "For the two English gentlemen in the front rooms."

"Two English *lords,*" Anthony said. "Mind you recall the difference, because God knows they will. Patterson and Warwick."

"Warwick?" Lucia narrowed her eyes. "That's the Englishman who's in the hunt for your Lady Diana. What are you plotting, Antonio? What mischief is this?"

"All's fair, Lucia." He flipped a coin to the boy. "There you are, you rascal. That should triple whatever Dandolo gave you. Now go, away with you."

The boy caught the coin, bowed and darted off down the hall. Lucia made a low, ominous growl of displeasure, and drummed her fingers on the arm of her chair.

"I don't like this, Antonio," she said slowly. "You're plotting some advantage against me, and I don't like it."

He thought of how he meant to make Diana Farren's lovely blush spread over her whole body, how he'd make her writhe against him and cry out with pleasure.

"I am plotting some advantage, darling," he said. "Only it's not against you."

"I told you, Antonio," Lucia said. "I mean to win."

He smiled. "All's fair, Lucia. All's fair."

Chapter Six

⁓⁓⁓⁓⁓⁓

"I cannot fathom how you came by tickets to this opera, my lord," said Miss Wood as their carriage drew away from their lodgings. "From what I have heard, such tickets are nearly impossible for foreign visitors like us to find for love or money."

Reverend Lord Patterson chuckled, and patted the pocket of his coat where the precious tickets lay.

"I have my ways, Miss Wood," he said. "But yes, we are fortunate indeed to have such a treat. I'm told these first performances are often the best, before the true season begins and the singers are still filled with fresh inspiration. While the audience may be a bit less refined than later in the fall, after the subscription owners have all returned to the city, I think we'll find the glorious music will be worth it."

In the gray light of the closed carriage, Diana glowed with excitement, her anticipation so great she could hardly sit still. After days of poking around grubby old ruins, she was finally having an evening that suited *her*.

She was going to a beautiful modern building to hear music among attractive, appreciative company. She was wearing one of her favorite gowns for evening, a pale-green lutestring *polonaise* dressed with pink ribbons, and lavender silk slippers instead of ugly, sensible shoes for trudging. Her hair was dressed high and lightly powdered, and crowned with more ribbons and a black ostrich plume, bought specially earlier in the day. Miss Wood had even permitted her to paint her eyelids and her cheeks in a manner that made her feel elegantly alluring, and in keeping with the sophisticated spirit of Rome. She'd not dressed so well since they'd left Paris weeks ago.

Most of all, she hoped tonight would celebrate the improvement of matters between her and Edward. He'd been courtly when he'd called to ask her and Miss Wood to join him and his uncle, so courtly as to be almost humble. Of course she'd accepted; of course she'd been charmed. Now she smiled almost shyly at him, sitting across from her, and thought how handsome he looked in his glossy evening suit and embroidered waistcoat that echoed her own garments for magnificence.

She suspected he'd once again had a glass or two of wine before he'd joined them—his cheeks and nose were a bit too rosy for good cheer alone—but this time all the wine had done was to take the sharpness from his personality and make him more agreeable. If Edward could only stay like this, a model English lord with his golden hair and a pleasing smile on his face, then she was certain he could make her forget Antonio. He might even make her happy as well.

After waiting their turn in a winding queue of other carriages along the Via Alibert, they finally reached the entrance to the Teatro delle Dame, overlooking the Piazza del Popolo. Eagerly Diana looked from the carriage window at the crowds gathered before the open doors.

The evening was cool with a first hint of autumn, and many of the gentlemen and ladies wore black evening cloaks that flicked open as they moved to show the bright satin linings within. Vendors shouted their wares, offering oranges and small bouquets for the ladies, while singers with no place on the stage inside sang extravagant ballads on either side of the door, their hats lying hopefully on the pavement at their feet. Footmen jostled one another to reach the next carriage first, not so much to be helpful, but to throw open the door with an outstretched hand to claim their garnish.

Diana nodded her thanks to Edward as he handed her from the carriage, striving to maneuver her skirts and make as graceful an entrance as possible. She heard appreciative whistles and a small chorus of appeals as the footmen fought to keep the usual beggars from pushing towards her. With relief she claimed Edward's arm, and let him guide her inside.

"I'm sorry you had to contend with that rabble," he said. "A lady like you shouldn't have to suffer like that. You wouldn't in London, but this is Rome."

"Yes, it is," she said, gazing around the candlelit lobby at the painted murals on the walls and the many-branched chandeliers overhead that were unlike anything she'd seen in England. "And how wonderful Rome is, isn't it?"

"It is because you're here with me, my lady." He smiled, clearly pleased by his own gallantry. "This theater was commissioned for a carnival earlier this century, by the Conte Antonio d'Alibert."

"Antonio?" she repeated foolishly, without realizing what she said.

"The Italian version of Anthony, my lady," Edward said indulgently, suspecting nothing. "The theater's plans were drawn up by one Ferdinando Fuga, and built in record time."

She smiled, more from nervousness than humor. Oh,

how had she been so careless? "You surprise me once again, my lord. And here I thought your knowledge was limited to the ancients!"

"I asked specially about this theater so I could impress you." He winked broadly. "You are looking most handsome tonight, my lady. Very *bella*."

Her smile relaxed, and became genuine at the compliment. "*Bellissima,* you mean. That's how they say very beautiful."

"How'd you learn that, eh?" he asked curiously. "Listening to what these greasy Italian rakes say when you pass them by?"

"How wickedly rude of you, my lord!" she exclaimed, giving his arm a little swat for good measure, and deftly avoiding answering him as well. Twice now she'd slipped like that, and guiltily she remembered how Antonio had predicted he'd always be in her thoughts, no matter how hard she fought it. A pox on the man, for being right like that, and on her, too, for being so susceptible!

She pointed her closed fan across the crowded lobby. "There go your uncle and Miss Wood. Hurry now, I don't want to lose them in this crush."

They followed the others up the narrow staircase. They hadn't far to climb: their box was in the first tier, close to the stage. However Reverend Lord Patterson had come by such seats, he'd done very well for them.

Diana leaned over the railing, eager to see as much of the theater as she could. There were four tiers of boxes, lavished with great quantities of red plush and gilding that shone with muted magnificence in the candlelight. The front panels of each box were painted with different mythological scenes, and though at a distance Diana couldn't tell exactly which myth was represented, the artists had embraced the opportunity to show a quantity of naked nymphs and goddesses.

Few of these lower, more expensive boxes were occupied yet, for it seemed that fashionable Romans shared the habit of Londoners to arrive late for performances. Farther up, however, the boxes were alive with chattering, eager patrons, busily waving, fluttering fans, shouting back and forth, and drinking toasts to one another, as if the boxes were balconies over a narrow street.

The lowest level—what in London was called the pit—seemed to be much the same here in Rome as well. Instead of chairs, long, rough benches served as seats, and already the places were mostly taken by a churning mix of apprentices, lower tradesmen, sailors and a well-seasoned smattering of obvious prostitutes, their breasts brazenly displayed above their tightly laced bodices. This crowd seemed cheerfully contentious, and while some pushed and shoved at one another, most seemed to be preparing for the performance, lining up rows of rotting tomatoes brought specifically to hurl at any hapless singers who displeased them.

"Come away from there, my lady," scolded Miss Wood, taking Diana's cloak from her shoulders. "It's not proper to display yourself like that."

"But I want to see *everything!*" Diana protested. The Teatro delle Dame might not be the elegant retreat she'd imagined, but it was so gloriously alive that she didn't want to overlook a single ill-behaved apprentice. "This is why we traveled here to Rome, Miss Wood, to see sights we'd never see at home!"

"Yes, my lady, and a good thing we don't, too," her governess said with a disapproving sniff. She took Diana's arm and forcibly sat her in a high-backed armchair. "You can see your fill from here, my lady, and still be a credit to your rank and breeding."

"Here now, what's this?" exclaimed Edward as two servants carried a table into the box, and swiftly began to set it with napkins, cutlery and glasses. "What are we to have here?"

A waiter with a thick ribbon-wrapped braid to his waist and fat curls over each ear bowed deeply over his leg before Edward.

"*Mon signore*, supper it is," he said, clearly expecting his wide smile to make up for his deficiencies in English. "Supper and wine plenty, *per favore, sì? Rosso vino, sì?*"

"*Rosso vino*—that's red wine," Edward said happily. "What a splendid idea, having supper and drink while watching an opera! Why don't the theaters in London offer the same? *Rosso vino, cameriere, sì, sì,* yes, yes, and plenty of it!"

The waiter and the other servants bowed their way from the box, hurrying to bring Edward's order while he dropped into the chair beside Diana's.

"Do you believe that's wise, Edward?" Reverend Lord Patterson said grimly. "Ordering more wine like that? I trust you do recall our conversation earlier, and the promises you made to me."

"Of course I recall it, Uncle," Edward said with a breezy wave of his hand. "But I do not see that either our conversation or my promises have any relation upon this happy little party here tonight."

He inched his chair closer to Diana, leaning forward to give her his full attention, and also to more fully ignore his uncle. "So tell me, my lady. Are you a connoisseur of the opera?"

"I've only seen two others before this, my lord," Diana confessed. "I know that must make me sound like the backward country sister, but my father believes the opera, like the theater, is not a suitable amusement for young ladies."

"His grace must be a wise lord, my lady," Edward answered as one of the servants handed him a full glass of wine. "And I'd venture he's likewise an excellent father. There is much about the opera that can be unsavory for ladies."

"Indeed." Diana's glance slid away from him, down towards the stage. "Oh, look, Edward, it's about to begin!"

"Not really," Edward said, drinking deeply of his wine. "You may watch if you wish, but there'll be nothing worth seeing."

The small orchestra had finished tuning their instruments, and with a half-hearted trumpet fanfare, had launched into an overture. A half-dozen dancers, costumed in vaguely historical tunics, winged caps and buskins skipped out onto the stage and began a dance in a rhythm that seemed to have little relation to the music being played.

But the ballet served its unenviable purpose. At once the crowd in the pit began to jeer and boo with lusty enthusiasm, and before long the dancers fled beneath a splattering shower of overripe tomatoes. While the orchestra continued to play, sweepers cleared the stage of tomato wreckage.

"That wasn't very nice of them," Diana noted, taking a small slice of melon from the tray the servant was offering. "How dreadful for those poor dancers!"

"But you see, my lady, they've served their purpose," Edward said, holding out his wineglass to be refilled. "By drawing the fire of the pit, they deplete the arsenal, and lessen the attacks that can be directed towards the singers."

"They would assault the singers?" asked Diana, shocked.

"Oh, yes," Edward said, pausing to drink more. "Every Roman man considers himself a critic. A pleasing singer is rewarded with applause and wreaths of flowers, while a bad one receives what you just saw. But considering tonight's leading role will be sung by the great Signor Dandolo, I doubt we'll see any more assaults on the stage."

Diana twisted around in her chair to face him. "Even I've

heard of Dandolo," she said excitedly. "Have you ever listened to him sing before?"

"Only once," Edward admitted. "Last season, when he gave a week of performances in Florence. He leaves Farinelli and Marchesi clean in the dust. I vow he made the very hair on my head rise, his voice is that fine. One would almost forget what an unfortunate, wretched creature he is."

"Unfortunate, my lord?" Diana asked with surprise. "I've heard that only the Pope himself lives in more luxury than Signor Dandolo."

"Don't you know?" Edward came closer, lowering his voice to a whisper as if offering the deepest secret. The flush across his cheeks had deepened as he'd continued to drink, and the scent of wine was heavy on his breath. "He's half a man, for sake of his voice. A gelding. What they call a *castrato*."

Diana frowned. Being from the country, she knew perfectly well how a stallion became a gelding, but part of her balked at considering the same done to a man.

"I don't understand, my lord," she said slowly. "If he is—"

"Oh, it's not hard to understand at all," Edward said carelessly. "It's common enough here in Rome. A poor boy sings like an angel, and before he knows it, he's hauled off to one of those foul little surgeries near the Vatican, trussed up for sacrifice and dosed with liquor so he won't realize when he's given the knife to his—"

"That's quite enough, Edward," his uncle interrupted sharply. "I believe you owe this lady an apology for such ill-chosen words."

Edward's eyes widened with unfocussed surprise. "She asked, Uncle, and all I was doing was—"

"You're forgiven, my lord," said Diana quickly, her cheeks pink with horrified embarrassment. "It's true, reverend my lord. I did ask him for an—an explanation. All Lord Edward did was answer me."

"He could have used more genteel language, appropriate for a lady," the other man insisted sternly. "The Roman *castrati* are indeed unfortunates, mutilated as innocent children in order to preserve the fullest range of their voices."

"How—how barbaric, reverend my lord!" exclaimed Miss Wood, her face showing the same shock that Diana felt must surely be on hers as well. "How unspeakably cruel!"

"It is indeed, Miss Wood," he agreed. "I cannot fathom how the same holy men who deem it sinful for women to appear on the stage can offer such an abomination in their place. True, those *castrati* who find success on the stage, like Signor Dandolo, or with places in the Vatican choirs, are richly rewarded by the world for their sacrifice. But that cannot lessen the hideous nature of the practice, nor how it is encouraged by the Roman church. It is truly a bargain with the devil."

"I—I thank you, reverend my lord," Diana said, stunned and sickened by what she'd just heard. "I appreciate your—your illumination as well as your discretion."

Reverend Lord Patterson nodded his head in solemn acknowledgement just as the music swelled, and cheering applause burst from the crowd around them.

"But judge for yourself, my lady," he said, speaking over the roaring crowd. "There's the famous Dandolo himself."

Diana looked, and to her shock saw not the man she expected, but a tall, beautiful woman, her bosom full and white, her face radiant with emotion as her gaze traveled slowly across the tiers of boxes. Every poignant gesture seemed drawn from a woman's heart, every step in the wide panniers and trailing skirts seemed to embody feminine grace.

"You saved me there with my uncle," Edward whispered

hoarsely into her ear. "You did that for me, lamb, and I can't thank you enough."

She didn't answer, for no answer would be right. She hadn't spoken for him; she'd spoken for herself, to try to keep herself from one more lie, one more twisted half truth. Dandolo lifted his arm as if beckoning to her, the deep lace ruffles on his sleeve falling back over his elbow, and opened his mouth to sing.

The voice was like nothing Diana had ever heard, angelic sweetness combined with a strength that stunned her with its power, not of this world, nor yet the next. She didn't need to comprehend the foreign words to understand this aria. This voice understood her confusion and torment, and how she could be so torn between two men, two choices, between a good and a bad that seemed to shift and change by the minute. Around her she felt the sigh of the audience come as a single rush of emotion, a willingness to surrender to such a rare gift, and she felt herself slip into the tide of sensation with them.

"I won't forget this, Diana," Edward was saying, distracting her with his wrongful words. "What you just did for me— why, I couldn't have asked for more from you."

She ached to experience the love that filled this song, the love that this voice brought to life. *That* was what she wanted, what she desired, and not Edward's empty protestations.

Yet still Edward placed his hand on her knee and pushed through her heavy skirts and between her legs, daring such a caress when all others were turned away and bound by Dandolo's magic. Startled, Diana looked down at Edward's hand, then began to look back to his face to question him.

But in the middle of that slight shift of her gaze, she realized Antonio had found her again.

As clearly as if he'd called to her, she knew to look across the theater to the darkened box opposite theirs. Dressed in his usual black, he sat deep in the shadows, barely visible beyond the pale outlines of his white shirt. She'd sensed his presence even before she'd seen him, and her heart quickened within her breast.

How long had he been there, she wondered. How long had he been watching her?

Now the unbearable yearning that she heard in Dandolo's voice spoke to her with fresh intensity, echoing all the feelings she'd been struggling to deny. Antonio knew it; he knew everything. He leaned forward just far enough to clear his face from the shadows, and touched his fingertips to his lips—a kiss for her, for *her.*

She rose so abruptly her chair rocked backwards.

"Here now, my lady! Ah, no need for that!" Edward exclaimed as he reached for her hand, and was greeted by a chorus of hisses for him to be quiet.

"I—I must go outside," Diana stammered, pushing away from him. "I'm sorry, but I must."

Miss Wood's whisper was full of concern. "Are you ill, my lady? Are you unwell?"

"I'll be only a moment," Diana insisted, fearing they'd try to stop her. "The box is close and I need to—to be by myself, that is all."

She stumbled towards the back of the box, grabbed her skirts to keep from tripping, and ran into the empty hallway. She was risking everything, she knew, but she had no choice. She *had* to find Antonio, and tell him—

But Anthony found her first.

He'd never doubted she'd come, or that she'd be able to keep away from him. How could she, when he couldn't keep from her? He was waiting for her in the curtained doorway to an empty box, and as she passed, he reached out and caught her, drawing her back behind the curtain and into his arms. There were no lit candles in the box, with only the distant light from the stage to filter through the shadows. No one would see them, nor would they see one another. She said nothing, and neither did he, leaving it instead to Dandolo's voice, filling the theater behind them. Even an English virgin must be lured by the unearthly power of that voice, and hear the overt sensuality of it.

She came to him eagerly, no, more than that; he could taste the heat of her desperation as soon as their lips met, desperation and desire. She turned her face upwards to meet him, her mouth open and giving, yet taking as well. He pressed her close against the wall, letting her feel the force of his body against hers. To his surprise, she pressed back, molding herself against him as much as her whalebone-stiffened clothing would permit. He deepened their kiss, roughened it, to make her know that he was possessing her, and she answered back, her fingers clutching into his back.

He realized that, if he wished it, he could take her here, against this wall, and win his wager now.

And in some last sputtering scrap of her conscience, she realized it, too. She twisted her mouth away from his, and put her palms flat against his chest.

"I—I must go," she whispered hoarsely, her breathing ragged. "I only came to tell you that I—we—must never meet again."

"Liar." He kept her trapped by his body against the wall, noting how she made no real effort to escape. "You couldn't keep away from me if your very life depended upon it."

"That's not true," she protested, her eyes full of fire that he knew had little to do with her argument. She pushed against him, trying to sidle free. "Let me go. Let me go now, or they'll come looking for me."

"Not yet, *cara,*" he said, his own breathing harsh now. "Not yet."

"But if Lord Edward—"

"The devil take Lord Edward, for you've no use for him." Before she could protest again, he turned swiftly and took her with him, pulling her back to his chest and pinning her there with his arm.

"Does Lord Edward make your blood race faster in your veins, Diana?" he asked, his whisper close to her ear, so close that he knew she'd feel each word warm upon her skin.

"Lord Edward is a gentleman!"

"Is that what you want, then? A gentleman?"

"Then I wouldn't want you!" She lifted her chin, twisting around to taunt him, her excitement palpable in the air between them.

"No, you wouldn't," he agreed, and bent to kiss the vein pulsing faintly on the side of her slender throat. "But then could a *gentleman* like Lord Edward kiss you like this?"

"You don't know," she said, arousal giving an edge to her voice as she tested the barrier of his arm around her waist. "You don't *know.*"

"But I do, *cara,* and so do you," he said, bending to kiss her and prove it. "You do, or you wouldn't have come back to me."

She arched back against him as they kissed, reaching for what she claimed she didn't want. He slipped one hand inside the low neckline of her bodice, tugging it down to free the warm, soft flesh of her breasts. Each filled his palm, the size and weight exquisitely perfect for him, with small, neat nipples that rose tight and taut beneath his touch. She gasped, and he could feel how her knees weakened with pleasure as her weight sagged against his arm. He pulled her hips back against his, so she could feel the urgency of his own desire, how hard she'd made him.

"I could love you now, Diana," he whispered roughly. "*Dannazione,* I could give you exactly what you wanted, what we were both made to share, what you'll always come back to me to find again."

"Please, Antonio," she whimpered, her eyes squeezed shut. "Oh, please, please!"

He could take her against this wall, or on that table, or bent over the chair, or a score of other ways his raging body was urging. No one could fault him if he did, not the way she was pleading with him now. But the uncomfortable truth was that he liked her too much for that, and far too much, really, for this ridiculous wager with Lucia. When he finally claimed Diana, he wanted to take his time, to savor her, to give her such delight she'd never forget it, or him. When he took her body, he wanted part of her soul with it.

Struggling to keep his own body in check, he grabbed a fistful of her skirt and pulled it up high over her bare thigh. He pushed his bent knee between her legs to keep her from closing them, and then touched her.

Merciful heaven, but she was wet, already full and ripe and ready for him, sweet honey in his hand, and once again he was forced to stop himself. Instead he caressed her, finding the one sure place that would give her release. She was panting and writhing against him, her cries lost in the drums and crashing cymbals of the orchestra below, until suddenly she arched back one final time, then melted against him.

"Ah, *carissima.*" He let her skirts drop and turned her around to face him once again, folding her into his arms. She was limp now, her pleasure spent. He suspected he'd been the first to give her such a gift; certainly that oafish Warwick wouldn't begin to know how. "I told you that you were meant for me."

She disentangled herself from him to stand apart, swaying unsteadily as she pulled her gown back into place. She took a deep breath to compose herself, then another with her eyes closed. She'd turned just enough in the dimness for him to see how her face would betray her, no matter what she said. She looked sated yet still wanton, her mouth swollen from kissing and her eyes heavy-lidded with pleasure and shadowed with the smudged remnants of her paint—the kind of beautiful face every man would give his eyeteeth to find in bed with him when he woke in the morning.

"For what you just did to me," she said, "my father would have you claimed by the press gang."

"I'd do it again, Diana, and more." The tension that still coiled through his body kept him from laughing the way he otherwise would. "Much, much more. And I'm not afraid of your father."

"He's had other men I've known carried off for less, you know," she said. "He's had them sold for indenture in the colonies, too."

"This is Rome, not England," he said. "And I'm still not afraid of your father."

"Neither am I," she confessed, surprising him. She raised her chin higher. "And what happened before… I kissed you, and begged you for—for the joy, didn't I?"

The joy. He was hard again in an instant. "There's never a sin in asking for what pleases you."

She sucked in her lower lip, considering. "Not when you and I—oh, heaven help me, that's the end of the first act, isn't it?"

The music had ended with a fanfare of trumpets, and the singers were bowing to great applause, Dandolo to the most.

"I can't let them find me here with you," she said with fresh urgency. "I must go."

She turned to leave him, and he caught her arm to hold her back. "When will I see you again, *cara?*"

She shook her head, and tried to pull free, but he held her fast.

"Next time come to my villa in the hills," he said. "Stay the night with me there, and I'll give you more pleasure than you've ever dreamed possible."

She flushed and looked down. Now she understood what he offered, and how much she'd risk to have it. "No, Antonio, I cannot."

"You will," he said softly. "Not tonight, no, but you will soon enough."

He raised her hand to his lips and kissed it, and when she pulled free again, he let her go.

He could do that now, knowing he'd soon see her again. It was only a matter of time, and then—then she would be his.

"I know an excellent physician here in Rome," Reverend Lord Patterson said. "A Scotsman, trained in Edinburgh. I'll send for him directly as soon as we return to our lodgings."

"I pray it's not Roman fever," Miss Wood said, rubbing Diana's hand. "I thought by coming here so late in the year we'd miss it."

"I'm fine, Miss Wood," Diana murmured wearily. "Truly. You needn't worry."

They'd wrapped her up in her cloak with as much care as if she'd been made of the most delicate porcelain, and tucked her into the carriage with an extra coverlet over her. It had been like this ever since she'd come back to the box, and Miss Wood had pounced on her with tears of relief in her eyes.

Yet what would her governess have done if she'd known

the truth? What would Edward or his uncle have said if they'd seen her ten minutes before in that other box with Antonio, shamelessly behaving like the lowest of slatterns? What would they think of her if they'd heard her crying out, begging for her own ruin to a man she scarcely knew?

"She seemed much affected by the music, Uncle," Edward said. "Perhaps it was too loud for her constitution."

"I doubt it was the volume of the music so much as its passion," his uncle said. "Dandolo's voice possesses a kind of sorcery to it, a rare quality that makes him so special as a singer. But like a strong liquor, it can overpower those too tender for its effect."

"I understand now why his grace her father has limited her experience with such music," Miss Wood said. "My poor lady! The opera was too much for an innocent like you to bear!"

Diana closed her eyes, using that as an excuse not to answer. Let them think what they would. She'd felt the magic of Dandolo's song, true, but that was nothing compared to what Antonio had done to her. All he'd had to do was smile, and toss her a kiss across a crowded theater, and she'd melted. The way he whispered her name was worth an entire book of poems from any other man. Why was it that she could sit for hours beside Edward and feel nothing more than a pleasant regard, yet the very sight of Antonio consumed her with passion and made her ready to toss away all honor and caution—and an eminently acceptable suitor—for his sake?

With her eyes closed like this, it was all too easy to remember how he'd kissed her, how he'd touched her, how he'd made her feel a wonderful, wanton joy she'd never experienced before. She'd let other men kiss her and sometimes permitted a few other liberties because they'd wished her to so badly, but Antonio was the first one to show such concern for pleasing *her*.

Was this how her sister had felt when she'd first met the man who'd become her husband? How she wished Mary were here now, so she could ask her! Was this love—lasting, true love—or only desire? He'd made her forget all about London and the young gentlemen she'd hoped to meet there. In fact, Antonio had managed to make her forget nearly everything and everyone but him. He kept telling her how they were meant to be together. What if he were speaking truthfully, and not simply making idle romantic prattle?

What if Antonio was right?

She knew next to nothing of him. She did not know where he lived, or anything of his family, or if he worked at some profession, or lived on an elegant patrimony. He had lived his entire life in Rome; he was thoroughly, completely un-English. He spoke of a villa and a palazzo. But for all she could tell, he might already be married, a man with a wife and a brood of beautiful children, who amused himself by following after foolish, foreign women like herself.

If she'd any sense, she'd stick to her vow never to see him again. But what if she were falling in love—really, truly in love—with the most unsuitable man she'd ever met?

"I'm sure you'll feel better in the morning, my lady," Edward was saying. "I know a good night's sleep always puts me to rights."

She opened her eyes and saw his blandly handsome face and his slightly desperate smile. Suddenly she realized he was terrified that his single fumbling caress of her knee through her petticoats had been so shocking to her tender, innocent constitution that she'd fled, and worse, that she'd tell his uncle and Miss Wood what he'd done. Poor Edward! His misplaced anxiety over nothing would amuse her if it had happened to anyone else. Yet still she smiled, not wanting him to worry for no reason.

"Here we are at last," said Edward's uncle as the carriage stopped in the Piazza di Spagna. "I'll go send for Dr. Shaw at once."

"I'll have the servants send up hot water for a bath, my lady," Miss Wood said. "Nothing else will take away a dangerous chill."

The two of them hurried inside, leaving Edward to help Diana from the carriage.

"Oh, Edward, I've forgotten my fan in the carriage," she said, pausing before the door. "Would you please fetch it for me so it's not lost?"

Edward bowed and obediently returned to the carriage. As she waited alone by the door, a small boy darted from the shadows towards her. Yet another beggar, she thought sadly, and began to reach into her pocket for a coin. But before she could, the child reached up to her and pressed a folded, sealed letter into her hand. Then he ran away, gone before she could reward him.

She looked at the note for only a second: there was no address, nor sender, written on the face, and the sheet had been sealed without a stamp's impression. But it had to be from Antonio, already pining to see her again: who else would send her such a hasty note, by such a manner? Swiftly she tucked it into her pocket before Edward returned, to read later when she was alone.

"Here you are," Edward said, handing her the forgotten fan. "I know how you ladies guard what you value most, eh?"

But for Diana, it felt as if it were already too late.

Chapter Seven

"And I'm telling you what I know, Uncle," Edward said glumly the next morning over breakfast. "The lady doesn't care for me, leastwise not in the way to make her accept an offer."

"Nonsense, Edward," Reverend Lord Patterson said, briskly stirring precisely half a spoonful of sugar into his tea. "You're exaggerating in a pessimistic fashion. Lady Diana has given you no inclination of disfavor that I can see."

"Well, I can see it clear as day." Slowly Edward dragged his knife back and forth across the ruby-colored jam on his slice of toasted bread, making small, sticky waves in the shimmering surface. "She scarcely says a word to me unless I speak first."

His uncle chuckled and folded the newspaper in his hand to a fresh sheet. "There's plenty of husbands who'd regard that as a divine quality in a wife."

"She smiles at me just to be polite," continued Edward. "Not as though she's truly happy to see me."

"A maidenly demeanor is a fine thing, Edward," his uncle said. "The daughter of a duke is bound to be reserved in her manner."

"More like cold than reserved," Edward said, remembering how she'd recoiled when he'd finally dared touch her knee. "Cold as the first day of the year."

His uncle lowered the paper, and stared sternly over the rims of his spectacles. "You can invent objections and obstacles all the day long, Edward, and they won't serve you at all. The lady *is* a lady. She expects to be wooed properly, and won. She's not going to tumble into your lap like some sort of tavern girl. You must invest a bit of gallantry in your pursuit."

"In pursuit of her fortune, you mean."

"In pursuit of both the girl *and* her fortune," his uncle said. "Edward, Lady Diana is a beautiful, charming young woman, and yes, her fortune is sizable, certainly to a man in your situation. But I urge you to recall that the state of matrimony is a holy sacrament, and I will not give you my blessings in this match until I see some sentiment, some genuine care for the lady, on your part."

"You want me to love her?"

"Love would be most desired, yes," his uncle said. "But I'll grant that sometimes in a marriage, love must be nurtured and grown from the seeds of mutual affection and regard. *That* is what I should like to see you apply to Lady Diana."

Edward sighed mightily, and carved a small circle in the center of the jam. "Maybe you should be preaching to her, too, instead of just to me."

"Lady Diana is not my niece," the reverend said absently, returning his attention to the newspaper. "You, however, are, unfortunately, my nephew, and for my sister's sake, my responsibility."

Dolefully, Edward looked up from his bread. "I think she's seeing another man."

"Lady Diana?" His uncle smiled at so preposterous a suggestion. "Her governess keeps much too close a watch over her charge for that. An admirable little woman, Miss Wood, and devoted—*devoted!*—to that noble family."

Edward sighed again. A large fly had flown in through the open window beside their table, and was sauntering along the rim of his plate. "A girl that's as handsome as Lady Diana is bound to have a pack of men sniffing after her."

"All the more reason for you to show a bit more alacrity in your wooing," his uncle continued, as if everything in life could be fixed if only a bit more effort was demonstrated. "We've spoken of touring the catacombs with the ladies. What better place to make yourself agreeable, eh? There's nothing like the dark to make a lady start seeing bugbears in the dust, shrieking and clutching at you for comfort."

Edward watched the fly reconnoitering the jam and rubbing its front feet together with dainty precision.

As if he cared a whit about the damned catacombs. Maybe his uncle and that plain little governess had been fooled last night, but he hadn't. The girl hadn't been ill, not by half. When she'd come back to their box, she'd had the same tousled, used look of the shopgirls and scullery maids who stumble giggling from the bushes at Vauxhall Gardens, clutching the hands of their guilty lovers. No wonder she'd been so deuced quiet on the way back in the carriage; she hadn't been feverish, only sleepy after whatever mischief she'd been pursuing.

But he wasn't fooled. He wasn't fooled at all.

"It's not so easy as that, uncle," he said, pushing the jam towards the fly. "If I'm going to ask the lady to marry me, I want to be sure she's not already got another man's brat swelling in her belly."

"Edward!" His uncle snapped the newspaper down with indignant distaste. "I'll hear no more of that vile sort of talk about the lady."

"I don't want her fobbing her bastard off on me, that's all," Edward grumbled. "That's only fair, isn't it?"

"With £20,000," his uncle said, "she'll be the one who'll decide what's fair. Beggars can't be choosers, Edward, and at present you're firmly among the beggars."

Edward grunted, unwilling to admit to such a bleak future. What kind of world was it when a gentleman with as much wit and promise as he could boast was made to grovel for his very existence around the petticoats of a woman like Diana Farren?

The fly had stepped onto the crust of his toast, and was already nibbling at the jam. Edward scooped a large blob of the glistening jam onto his knife and dropped it directly onto the fly. Trapped, the fly's legs tried to flail through the heavy, sugary red mass that smothered it. Edward leaned closer, watching as the fly's movements became more and more feeble, and finally stilled.

"Edward." His uncle had finished and was prepared to return to their rooms, his chair tucked beneath the table and his newspaper folded under his arm. "Are you quite done with your breakfast, Edward?"

"Done enough." He gave a final shove to the plate with the dead fly, and thought of how much his own life felt much the same. "It was cold, anyway."

"You do look better this morning, my lady," Miss Wood said, her expression still full of worry as she searched Diana's face. "But I wish to be certain you're out of danger."

"I never was in any danger at all, Miss Wood." Restlessly Diana pushed herself upright in her bed, eager to be permitted to rise and dress. From what she could see from the window, it was a beautiful day, cooler again as it had been last night, and she didn't want to squander it by lying in bed with Miss Wood hovering over her. "I'm perfectly fine."

"So you keep insisting." Miss Wood sighed, and folded her hands at her waist. "But his grace your father has entrusted me with your care, and I must be certain you are as well as you say before I risk your health."

"My health is *fine.*" She thumped her pillow for emphasis, the same pillow in which she'd hidden the note the boy had given her at the door last night. She still hadn't been able to read it. Miss Wood's vigilance had kept her by Diana's bedside throughout the night, never once leaving her alone, and making Diana wonder with frustration if her governess ever intended to sleep again. "Most excellent and *fine.*"

"You needn't be rude, my lady." Miss Wood sniffed, wounded. "Perhaps we might consider a short drive along the Corso in the carriage."

"Oh, a drive, please, Miss Wood!" Diana exclaimed, throwing back the bedsheets. A drive along the Corso wasn't ideal, true, but it was much better than remaining here. She could always catch a glimpse of Antonio out riding among the other fashionable folk, or perhaps he'd be waiting by the carriage in the piazza, as if by accident. She didn't doubt he'd find her again. He always had before, somehow knowing exactly where she'd be even before she knew herself. It was part of his magic. "I should like a drive above all things!"

"I will do my best, my lady," Miss Wood said. "I cancelled the hired carriage earlier this morning, but perhaps Signor Silvani can arrange for another."

"Go, go, ask him now," Diana said, sliding from the bed and dancing around it. "Please, ask if it is possible!"

Yet still Miss Wood hung back. "We won't be able to rely upon the company of Lord Edward and Reverend Lord Patterson. When I told them earlier that you were unavailable, I believe they made other plans for the rest of the day."

"Then we'll go by ourselves, Miss Wood, the way we always did before!" Diana exclaimed, not entirely disappointed to be without Edward at her side. "You see I'm entirely recovered. I'll dress, and be ready in an instant."

"Very well, my lady." Miss Wood was watching her closely, intent on spotting any signs of the fever recurring. "I'll send Deborah to you."

She curtseyed, and closed the bedchamber door after her. At once Diana dived back onto the bed and pulled the crumpled letter from its hiding place inside the pillow. Her fingers shaking with anticipation, she cracked the seal, and unfolded the single sheet. This would be the first letter she'd had from Anthony, the first time she'd been able to read his endearments in his own hand.

But to her dismay, the letter wasn't from Anthony at all, and there wasn't a single endearment anywhere in it.

My Lady,
You may think you were Rid of Me, but I have found you
At Last. Well now it is time to make things Even between
us. One hundred guineas would be Fair. Bring them to
me tomorrow (that is, Wednesday) at two o'clock to the
Fontana di Trevi.
Come alone My Lady do not Fail me or I vow I will tell
the Gentleman you now Love how you are a Cheating
Lying Whore to those men who Dare Trust you.
Will Carney

She made herself read the letter again, praying that she'd somehow gotten it wrong. *Will Carney*. Oh, dear Lord, what could have possibly brought Will Carney back into her life?

She gulped, fighting back tears of shame and fear. She crumpled the letter in her fist, then thought better of it, and smoothed it out over her knee.

Will Carney was the reason for her being sent abroad with her sister Mary earlier this summer. He'd been a new groom in her father's stables, tall and handsome with piercing blue eyes and a thick shock of pale-yellow hair that had reminded her of the manes of the horses he'd tended. He had been on the staff at Aston Hall for only a few weeks before he'd begun flirting with her—a teasing whispered word here or there as he'd helped her mount her horse, a wink when only she could see—and she'd been fascinated by his daring. Most men were far too intimidated by her father to take such a risk, especially the men in his employ. The Duke of Aston was the most exalted authority in their county, and on the few times when he'd been crossed, his vengeance had been thorough and swift. In any other circumstances, Diana would have gone no further with Will. She was not a fool, even if the groom was.

But on the night of her sister's farewell party, before she left for Dover and Calais, a young gentleman whom Diana had much admired had chosen to announce his betrothal to another young lady, and Diana had drowned her disappointment and humiliation in an unladylike consumption of her father's punch. Thus fortified, she'd decided to show the young gentleman exactly how little he meant to her, and she'd gone to the grooms' quarters behind the stables to find Will. Will had misinterpreted her interest as true ardor, and it had been a good thing—a very good thing—that her sister Mary and Miss Wood had come to rescue her from Will's embrace when they had.

But it had likewise been a very, very bad thing that Father had followed them and witnessed the whole sordid scene. In short order, Diana's London season was cancelled and replaced by this dismal educational tour of France and Italy, and Will had been taken in chains to the coast, and given over to the press gang in Portsmouth to serve on one of His Majesty's navy ships.

But how had Will escaped to find her here? How had he jumped his ship and deserted his duty and tracked her clear to Rome? Who had written this letter for him, and therefore knew her secret as well? She'd remembered him as good-natured if not terribly clever; she'd never have believed him capable of blackmail like this.

She studied the note again, her heart pounding as she tried to think, *think*. She should show it at once to Miss Wood. This was exactly the kind of problem Miss Wood was supposed to be protecting her from, wasn't it? She'd contact the proper magistrates or constables here in Rome and have Will arrested and punished, and that would be that.

At least that was what would happen in England. The Romans were charming, delightful people, but their authority struck her as appallingly careless and corrupt. She'd seen that from the first, when it had taken three days and countless bribes for them simply to clear Roman customs. The few disputes she'd witnessed in the street—an accident between two wagons, a thief running from the market with a stolen length of sausages trailing beneath his coat—had turned into violent and uncontrolled brawls, with no authorities appearing at all. She hadn't any confidence that her dreadful secret would remain private, or that Will would be arrested in time, or that he'd even be caught at all.

Her father had sent her on this journey in the first place not only as a punishment, but also to let any hint of the scandal drift away from her name before she was presented at Court and began the serious task of finding a husband. But if the same scandal surfaced luridly here in Rome—Lady Diana Farren conducted an intrigue with her father's groom, in the very stables!—she could be sure it would reach London in next to no time, and her reputation would be in irredeemable tatters before she ever returned to Dover.

Here in Rome, a continent removed from the domain of the almighty Duke of Aston in Kent, Father's word would be powerless to protect her again. Painfully proper Edward would likely have no further interest in her, especially not once the Reverend Lord Patterson expressed his views.

Yet the real question for Diana was this: Will vowed to tell "the Gentleman you now love" if she failed to comply with his demands. But did he mean Edward, or Antonio? Or was he simply fishing, guessing that she'd have at least one gentleman paying her attentions? If she went to Miss Wood, then she'd have to explain about Antonio, and that—oh, that she could not do.

But where would she find the money that Will demanded? Miss Wood handled all their funds. Diana had almost no coins in her own possession. She had brought no jewelry of any value with her—Father had forbidden it, saying jewels would only tempt thieves—and she'd nothing else that she could sell for that much money.

She'd seen the Fontana di Trevi on one of their drives, and it wasn't far away. At two o'clock in the afternoon, the time Will had chosen, most of the city was napping through the warmest part of the day, including Miss Wood, Edward and his uncle. She could likely slip away, use the hired carriage and driver that Signor Silvani kept waiting for them each day, go to Will, and return to the Piazza di Spagna without any of them knowing.

She refolded the letter, her mind racing. If she could only explain to Will that it was Father who'd sent him away, not her, then perhaps he'd forget this blackmailing foolishness. Even if he didn't, then she could try to convince him to keep his secret to himself until she returned to England and could arrange things for him then.

And if he wanted more than her assurances, if he still threatened her for money, why, then—then she'd have to think of something else.

"My lady?" Her maid Deborah curtseyed expectantly in the doorway. "Miss Wood said you wished to dress for driving. Shall I fetch the blue day gown, my lady, or the yellow with the matching parasol?"

"The blue gown, Deborah, thank you." Hurriedly Diana refolded the note, and as soon as the maid had turned away, she bent down and tucked it under the bed, between the mattress and the rope springs. That same hiding place had served her sister well while they'd traveled through France, when Mary had been keeping a valuable painting away from thieves, and Diana didn't doubt it would work now for her, too.

"Are you coming, my lady?" Deborah asked, holding the blue gown out in her hands. "Miss Wood said if you wish to go driving, you must be ready at once. But if you've had a change of mind—"

"I'll be ready, Deborah." Diana slipped from the bed, full of new resolve. She wasn't going to weep and wail. She'd be strong, the way her sister was, and solve this problem one way or another. "You needn't worry. I'll be ready."

"You are thinking of the English girl, Antonio, aren't you?" Lucia's smile was smug as the waiter set the dish of ice cream before her. "You prattle on and on about your new horse, yet you're thinking of her instead. Don't try to lie to me. I can see the truth in your eyes."

It was just as Lucia said, so Anthony didn't bother to lie. "I was thinking of her, yes," he said, as carelessly as he could. "Though I cannot see why you believe it your duty to monitor my thoughts."

"Why shouldn't it be?" she asked, languidly dipping her long-handled spoon into the swirled mound of pale-pink ice cream. "Considering our little wager, I'd be terribly remiss if I didn't take an interest."

Anthony leaned back in the rickety wooden chair, impatiently tapping his fingers on his knee. He should be at his stable with that new horse, and he would be, too, if Lucia hadn't waylaid him in the street on his way back from the Piazza di Spagna. He certainly didn't want to be here in this café, sitting at one of these wretched little tables that was practically in the street itself, protected from passing carriages only by a slender railing and a striped awning that was no protection at all. He hated the display that went along with sitting here almost as much as Lucia relished it, as if they were a pair of porcelain monkeys for sale in a shop window.

But for Lucia, that was the point of so public a meeting. She wanted to prove to Rome that while she remained in the keeping of her amiable Signor Taribarelli, she was still willing to entertain the attention of other gentlemen, and perhaps open to another, more generous offer if one should happen her way.

Anthony watched her toy with the strawberry ice cream from the bowl of her spoon, her little tongue lapping at it like a cat's. She was smiling, yet her dark eyes looked past him, always aware of who might be noticing, who might approach. Once he'd been amused by how blatantly she played her games. Now all he saw was her desperation, brought on by the unhappy realization that with each day, her beauty was fading. He guessed she was at most twenty-four or -five; she'd never told him, nor would she. But with Diana Farren's fair country face fresh in his mind, Lucia's suffered sadly by comparison.

"You're thinking of her again," Lucia said, and winked coyly. "That's good for my wager, Antonio. I know you met her at the Teatro delle Dame. Dandolo told me."

Anthony sighed. "Dandolo couldn't keep a secret if his life depended upon it."

"I didn't realize it was a secret to be kept." She winked broadly. "A place made for wickedness, that theater."

He narrowed his eyes, the only change in his expression. "How do you know I met the lady at the theater?"

"Because I was there, too." She turned the spoon in her mouth and licked it. "I saw you in your box, and she with her dull English party in theirs. Then while Dandolo sang, you both disappeared. Where else could you have been but together?"

Once again his thoughts raced back to Diana in his arms, how she'd come to him so willingly, how she'd given herself to the pleasure he'd offered her with a fierce, startled innocence that promised so much more. Since then her memory had haunted him, her cries echoing in his ears, her scent seeming to linger on his very skin, no matter how he tried to wash it away. "Perhaps we were discussing Dandolo's aria."

"And perhaps you were not," she said, pointing her spoon at him for emphasis. "Consider how many scores of maidenheads have been give up in those very boxes while mamas and governesses were distracted by the singers! Why should your little English virgin be any different?"

"Because she is, Lucia," he said, stating what he thought was ridiculously obvious. Why else, really, would he have spent most of this day loitering outside Diana's lodgings like some miserable puppy, hoping for even a glimpse of her? At her lodgings, they'd said the English lady was indisposed, and had kept to her bed. Only he knew that as she'd lain there, she would have thought of last night, of him and nothing else. "One doesn't deflower a lady in an opera box."

"No?" There was an edge to her voice, and to her smile, too. "What a novel idea, Antonio, especially from you. Unless *one* has lost his usual nerve and cunning. Unless *one* has shifted from seduction to making love. Unless *one* has been felled by this milk-faced chit, just as I wagered *one* would be."

Purposefully he kept his voice mild, unwilling to rise to her challenge. "Seduction should not be so very far removed from making love, darling."

"What a curious sentiment to hear from your lips, Antonio!" she said, twisting the spoon back into the mounded ice cream. "Not like you in the least."

He watched the next pink spoonful slide slowly between her full lips. "I'll interpret your comment as concern for your wager."

"Oh, that infernal wager!" she exclaimed. "What did she do to bewitch you so? Did she use her lips upon you? Did she use her tongue, her—"

"Don't ask me, Lucia," he warned, "because I'm not telling you."

She tossed back her head, making the tiny false birds that nested on the crown of her hat tremble and bounce.

"Dandolo saw you leave the theater," she said, her voice rising. "Alone, he told me, all alone. He said you had the look of a hungry man denied the meal he craved. Did she refuse you outright, Antonio? Is that it? Is her little Eden hung with forbidden fruit?"

Antonio smiled. What would Lucia say if she knew the

truth, that he'd been the one who'd resisted, not Diana? A month ago, he himself wouldn't have believed it. To have a beautiful young woman panting in his arms and to resist her—why, it was unnatural, preposterous, a rejection of his constant philosophy to seize whatever pleasure life offered him every day!

Yet somehow, with this girl, he didn't care about world-weary philosophies. Instead he cared about her. Although she was as young and beautiful and fresh as a golden new morning, it was her spirit that fascinated him most, a spirit that matched his own. She was different from every other woman he'd ever desired, a tantalizing mixture of innocence and English propriety that hid a very real passion. He'd had a glimpse—only a glimpse—of it last night, and he'd been unable to put her from his mind ever since. Was it any wonder that he wanted to *win* her, not just seduce her?

And was it, perhaps, time to make himself and his feelings more openly known to her?

"You foolish man," Lucia crowed scornfully. "Look at you! Why, I could claim my stake as winner now. You fancy you're in love with that chit, don't you?"

"Lucia, Lucia," he said, not bothering to deny her accusation. "You don't begin to know what love is."

"*I* do not know what love is?" Lucia smacked her open palm flat down on the table, her eyes wide with disbelief. "You would dare say that to me, Antonio? To *me?*"

He shrugged, no answer at all. For the sake of their friendship, he didn't want to explain the truth to her. It wasn't just the late nights and rich living that had drawn the fine lines around her eyes, or settled the hardness into her mouth. With surprise and sadness and eyes opened by Diana's innocence, he'd realized the fact that the lovely Lucia had never been truly loved in return—not by him, or by any of the many other men she'd been with in her life.

"I *will* win this wager, Antonio," she said furiously, striking the edge of the table again and again. A small dribble of ice cream had fallen into the ruffled white lace framing her nearly-bare breasts, a tiny pink blot of imperfection that would have mortified her if she'd known it was there.

"You can tell me whatever tales you please," she said, "but I know you too well for you to lie to me. You will lose, and I—I will win!"

"The best wager generally does, darling." He rose, and tossed a few coins on the table to settle their bill. "Pray forgive me, Lucia, but I've another engagement."

She looked up at him, and now her chin trembled as much as the cotton-wool birds on the brim above it.

"Go to her, Antonio," she whispered fiercely. "Go to your little chit, so you will lose to me!"

"Good day, dear Lucia." Ordinarily he'd bend to kiss her on the lips, or at least the cheek, but he decided not to risk it now. Instead he kissed his fingertips, turning his wrist to send his affection to her that way. "Until later, yes?"

"Until the devil takes you, you mean!" she cried, and hurled the dish of ice cream splattering at his head.

Anthony ducked; he knew how to dodge her missiles. Lucia's aim was excellent, but from hard experience, he'd learned that she always threw a little to the left.

She swore at having missed him. Other diners rose and exclaimed. Carriages slowed in the street to give their passengers a better view of the scene. Waiters rushed forward to clean up the shattered glass and ice cream, while the cafe's owner hurried to soothe Lucia himself, bowing and babbling as if everything were somehow his fault.

Now forgotten, Anthony slipped away, and left Lucia to the audience she always craved.

As their carriage turned, Diana adjusted the angle of the parasol over her shoulder to keep the sun from her face. More and more of Rome's aristocratic families were returning to the city from their summer villas, and the Corso was so crowded with carriages and riders that there was no room for pedestrians. There was much waving and kissing and excited cries of greeting, as if all these beautifully dressed people hadn't seen each other in years, instead of, in many cases, only a few days.

More English tourists had appeared, too, coming south from France or north from Naples, and Diana's British looks and fair hair drew her own share of admiring greetings. She sat back quite happily against the carriage's cushions and nodded to yet another young Englishman on horseback who was lifting his hat to her. For now she could forget Will Carney's note; she'd see him and deal with that tomorrow. Now she'd do her best to simply enjoy herself. Riding in an open carriage on a beautiful sunny afternoon on a beautiful foreign street with many beautiful gentlemen paying her court: this was a far more agreeable notion of international travel than dragging through dusty ruins that all looked alike.

"I must say, my lady, that the gentlemen here are quite forward," Miss Wood said, ever vigilant beside her. "They wouldn't dare greet you so informally if we were in London."

"But we're not, are we, Miss Wood?" Diana said, giving a lighthearted little twirl to the handle of her parasol. She was thinking of Antonio's handsome black horse from the Domus Flavia, and wondering if he ever came riding along the Corso, too. "Everyone's more friendly in Rome."

"They were friendly in France, too," Miss Wood said ominously, "and look what came of that."

"What came of it was that Mary met John and discovered the great love of her life, and there's absolutely no reason for us to fuss over what's been so happily resolved with their wedding," Diana said. "Besides, having gentlemen touch their hats hardly constitutes disgrace and ruin."

Miss Wood sniffed. "I still wish our friends Lord Edward and Reverend Lord Patterson had been able to join us, my lady."

"And I'm rather glad they didn't," Diana said. "They act as if they believe we're two helpless ladies in need of their protection, which we most certainly are not."

Miss Wood scowled at her from beneath the wide, flat brim of her plain hat. "We may not be entirely helpless, my lady, but there have been occasions when a trustworthy gentleman has been of great comfort and use to us."

Diana wrinkled her nose. Today Antonio was too much on her mind for her to give much thought to Edward and his uncle. Besides, Edward at his overbearing worst could scarcely be called a comfort, and when he was behaving like that, he certainly wasn't of much use to anyone.

"I should rather we depended on ourselves," she began, "and I do not agree that—"

"Buongiorno, mia bella donna."

She turned swiftly in her seat, her heart racing at the unmistakable timbre of Antonio's voice. He'd reined in his horse to ride alongside their carriage, the big black gelding champing impatiently to be held to such a snail's pace. He was dressed with careless elegance, a patterned silk scarf knotted around his bare throat at the open neck of his shirt and his black cocked hat tilted forward over his face, a pheasant's feather that no English gentleman would ever wear curling back from the crown.

He smiled, and she blushed. His smile widened, quirking up on one side to reveal a dimple she hadn't noticed before. The memory of all they'd done last night, the liberties she'd granted him so eagerly, came rushing back, and her face grew hotter still.

And she still hadn't managed to speak a single word.

Miss Wood, however, was more than willing to fill that gap.

"*Sono spiacente, signore, non non ci siamo presentati,*" she said slowly and firmly, as if speaking to a half-wit or a badly trained dog. Then for good measure, she repeated the message in English. "I'm sorry, sir, but we've not been introduced. Her ladyship is not interested in further contact. *Arrivederci, signore.*"

"Ah, Miss Wood, but you see I've already had the considerable honor and pleasure of meeting her ladyship," he said easily and in flawless English, now turning the full force of his charm towards the governess. "It seems as if I've known Lady Diana forever."

Diana gulped with horror. "Good day, sir," she managed to squeak out. "It is a—ah—a pleasant day, isn't it?"

Oh, what was he going to say next? To admit that they already knew one another, with that charming, charming smile upon his face! Oh, why had he chosen to just—just appear like this, taking her so completely by surprise! Surely Miss Wood must guess—surely she'd know! And what if he told her everything—everything!—and destroyed all the careful goodwill she'd restored and built with her governess in the course of this long journey?

Miss Wood held her plump chin at the precise angle to be most properly resolute in her defense. "You speak excellent English, *signore.*"

"Thank you, *signorina,*" he answered with an elegant

flourish of acknowledgement. "Yet I can see that you're surprised by my accomplishment in the language."

"Yes, sir," Miss Wood answered without a bit of apology as she continued her blatant appraisal. "It does surprise me to find such an excellent grasp of the language in a—ah— that is, in a—"

"In a lowly Roman?" he supplied helpfully. "In a swarthy, dangerous exotic?"

She knew Miss Wood, and she knew he'd guessed right: this was indeed how Miss Wood was judging him—though Miss Wood was far too polite to say what she was thinking aloud.

At least not exactly. "You are not English, sir," she said. "Rather, you are a native of this place, and therefore your accomplishment with the language is to be remarked."

"Signor Randolfo is a gentleman, Miss Wood," Diana said, unable to keep silent any longer. "It should be no surprise that he is accomplished."

"Signor Randolfo?" Miss Wood repeated, frowning a bit at Diana. "So you really have met this—this gentleman? Might I ask the circumstances?"

"I am honored to count Lord Edward Warwick among my acquaintances, Miss Wood," Antonio said. "I have many friends among the English visitors to my Rome."

"Ah." Miss Wood seemed to relax, though she continued to watch Diana closely. "That explains everything, *signore,* if you are a friend of Lord Edward's."

Diana only smiled, trying to hide her anxiety. Antonio had never said he was *friends* with Edward, only that they knew one another. Antonio didn't think much of Edward, and if in fact the two men had met, then she'd be willing to wager Edward wouldn't have a much higher opinion of Antonio, either. They were simply too different.

"Then might I beg the privilege of riding with you and Lady Diana?" he asked, his smile so winning that Diana could have sworn Miss Wood blushed. "What better way to pass a beautiful afternoon than in the company of two such lovely ladies?"

"Oh, yes, please do join us!" Diana said with impulsive haste that she immediately regretted. "That is, sir, we would be honored by your company."

"If you please, yes, *signore*," Miss Wood added, smoothing the gray bow beneath her chin. "Her ladyship and I would enjoy your company."

He nodded, and his gaze slipped back to Diana. His smile deepened and his eyes seemed to crinkle at the corners, a subtle change that escaped Miss Wood's notice, but not Diana's. To him this was clearly a great joke, a secret to be shared between them alone. But in that same glance came another, more complicated message: he found her beautiful and desirable, he remembered last night, he longed to see her again alone.

Swiftly she looked down, before her own glance would betray her longing to Miss Wood. Heaven help her, what this man could *do* to her without so much as a single kiss or touch!

"Perhaps we might beg you to advise us, *signore*," Miss Wood continued, fortunately unaware of what was swirling unsaid between Diana and Antonio. "Thus far we've let ourselves be guided by Lord Edward and his uncle Reverend Lord Patterson. But as excellent as their advice has been, their expertise is limited to the ancient side of the city. As a Roman, are you familiar with the more modern sights to be seen? We've read all the pamphlets and guidebooks, of course, but could you recommend which galleries we should visit to view the best of the great painters and sculptors of the last centuries?"

"We're a city rich in art and beauty, *signorina,* that is true," Antonio said, his gaze still lingering so pointedly on Diana that she felt herself blush again. "The Borgheses' villa, the Barberinis', and of course the Vatican itself. There's such artistic wealth here that it's difficult to know where to start. But as a fit beginning, I must humbly offer you the gallery in my family's own palazzo."

Diana looked up sharply. He'd already asked her to come to his palazzo with him, and she'd refused, knowing the only room she'd be sure to see would be his bedchamber. Was this, then, how he sought to convince her, by including her governess in the invitation? She tried to imagine how he'd separate her from Miss Wood, how he'd contrive for them to be alone. Her heart quickened, and her palms turned damp inside her gloves.

"You collect works of art, *signore?*" she asked, struggling to mask her interest. "You have pictures by the great artists?"

"Tintoretto, Reni, Titian, a Raphael or two," he said with a shrug, as if to say that surely every house hung such masters on their walls. "My grandfather had a weakness for Rubens, too, though he is obviously of the northern school."

"Two Raphaels!" Miss Wood exclaimed. "Oh, *signore,* how much I should like to see such rarities!"

"It would please me no end to show them to you," he said. "To you and her ladyship. Both of you must consider my home as yours."

"We would be delighted, *signore,* delighted!" Miss Wood cried excitedly.

But though he nodded, Antonio cared only for Diana's agreement.

"*Signora mia?*" he asked, the words rolling seductively from his tongue. "Will you consider my humble invitation as well, my lady?"

She leaned forward a fraction on the leather cushions, nearly level with his pale-blue eyes. She should refuse. She must not go. She should invent an excuse, any excuse, to stay away from the great temptation he presented. This invitation from him could only lead to her own ruin, there in his palazzo beneath the watchful eyes not of her governess, but of some Rubens goddess of pagan love.

Of *love.* How could her pitiful English conscience win against that, or him?

"Yes," she said softly, and smiled for the first time since he'd joined them. "Yes, *signore,* I should enjoy that above all things."

"Then it shall be," he said, his voice low and confidential, as if the crowded street were empty except for them. "I wish no more than to please you, Lady Diana."

"Pray send us word of a day and time that are agreeable to you, *signore,*" Miss Wood said, "and we shall be delighted to call upon you. We are staying in the same house as Lord Edward and his uncle, on the Piazza di Spagna."

Two other gentlemen cantered by and called to Antonio, obviously expecting him to join them. He waved and shouted something that made them laugh, and finally turned back to the carriage.

"Ladies, I must claim a previous engagement." He laid his hand over his heart, a gallant, sentimental gesture that Diana had come to associate entirely with him. "May we meet again soon, yes?"

"Oh, yes, *signore,*" Miss Wood said gaily, her cheeks pink with enthusiasm. "Until we meet before your lovely Raphaels! *Arrivederci!*"

"*Arrivederci, signorina.*" He swung his horse around, ready to join the other gentlemen, then paused to smile one last time at Diana. "*Ah, la mia bella! Chiunque gli ha detto quanto assolutamente squisito osservate oggi? La mia signora, sembri abbastanza buona da mangiare!"*

He laughed and tossed her a quick kiss on the tips of his fingers in parting as he rode away.

"Well now, that was a pleasant surprise, wasn't it?" Miss Wood said. "To come across Signore di Randolfo like that!"

"Yes, Miss Wood," Diana said automatically, watching Antonio as he joined the other gentlemen. He rode the black gelding with the same grace and ease that he did everything else, and she couldn't make herself look away. "A surprise."

"Imagine how fine his family's collection must be, with two Raphaels!" Miss Wood marveled. "Now *that* will amaze your sister!"

"Yes, Miss Wood," Diana murmured. She didn't know a Raphael from a rock, nor did she really care. Mary was the one with the gift for history and art. But when Diana could finally tell her sister of this intrigue with Antonio, of how he'd been so bold and daring that he'd settled their next assignation with Miss Wood in the carriage beside her—why, even blissfully-wed Mary would be amazed!

"The *signore* is dreadfully forward, of course," Miss Wood was saying—babbling, really, "but then all the Italian gentlemen seem to be that way. Doubtless he believes that with you, he's already made another conquest. Can you just imagine, my lady, what his grace your father would say to a rascal like that?"

She'd lost sight of Antonio now in the crush of carriages and riders, and so, with a sigh, she turned back to face Miss Wood. "You wondered the same thing about Lord John because he was Irish, and yet now that he's wed to Mary, you love him beyond reason."

"But being Irish is not the same as being Italian, my lady,"

Miss Wood said, as if this were the most obvious explanation in the world. "Except for him having been raised in a papist country, Lord John's really no different from us English. But this Signor di Randolfo—why, he's an entirely different kettle of fish, isn't he?"

"Yes, Miss Wood," Diana said, able to agree in far more ways than her governess would ever imagine. "He seemed quite different."

"Different from a fine English gentleman like Lord Edward, that's for certain." Miss Wood chuckled to herself. "Heaven only knows what kind of ridiculous, unseemly gibberish the signore was saying to you when we parted. I couldn't begin to understand it."

Diana nodded, grateful for Miss Wood's ignorance. As they'd traveled through Italy, Diana had begun to pick up more and more Italian words and phrases. She loved the sound of the language, even when she didn't always comprehend it, the rolling rhythm that made even a laundry order sound like music; it was much more pleasing to her ear than French could ever be. While she hadn't understood everything of what Anthony had said, she knew that he'd called her his beauty, and that he'd said something more about how he found her especially delicious, even delicious enough to eat—a compliment no English gentleman would ever dare make to an English lady.

But then, Antonio wasn't an English gentleman, and the more time that Diana spent in his company, the more she wondered whether she was a model English lady.

"Oh, well, my lady, it doesn't really matter what the signore said," Miss Wood announced, taking out their guidebook to identify the buildings they were passing. "If he's like all the other Italian men, he didn't mean a word of it, anyway."

But Diana wasn't so sure.

Chapter Eight

"A reception at your palazzo, my lord?" Sir Thomas Howe, the English consul to Rome, could scarcely contain his excitement as he flipped up his coattails and sat in the armchair across from Anthony's. "Your family's home is considered one of the most magnificent jewels of Rome, and for you to open your doors to your fellow Englishmen is most generous indeed."

"To be hosted by yourself, of course." Anthony wasn't surprised that Howe had jumped at his offer. The two-hundred-year-old palazzo he'd inherited as part of his mother's original dower was indeed a marvel, holding generations of paintings, sculptures and other treasures, arranged and displayed with his mother's exquisite taste. This sorry old house that acted as the English consulate managed to be both shabby and gaudy at the same time, and, in Anthony's opinion, was a general embarrassment to his father's homeland.

Sir Thomas's reception room was a perfect example: the patterned silk wall cloth was a garish bright pink, the paintings were decidedly third-rate and the bronzes on the mantelpiece were blatant copies. Even the wine that he was manfully attempting to drink for Sir Thomas's sake was some dreadful sweet Spanish brew, a most ignorant choice with so many excellent vineyards nearby. No wonder that, for the most part, he kept his distance from the consulate and its entertainments, preferring his Roman friends to the stuffy earnestness of the English visitors.

But such minor indignities were nothing if it meant he'd see Diana again. This idea of a party had come to him as soon as he'd left her on the Corso, and he'd come here to the English consulate as soon as he'd been able. Of course, he'd be taking a risk, letting her learn exactly who he was in such a manner, but the timing of it appealed to him. It would be an unexpected twist on the invitation he'd already extended to her. Now he'd not only be welcoming her into his palazzo as an honored guest, but he'd also likely upset every notion that she'd already conceived of him. To learn that he was by birth an English aristocrat, just like her—hah, what would she make of *that?* he wondered with pleasurable anticipation. He'd liked surprising her, and this might be his biggest surprise yet.

"I thought it might be an agreeable way to welcome all the English gentlemen and ladies returning to Rome." Anthony smiled warmly. "You can conjure up some sort of official occasion, I'm sure. His Majesty's birthday, or the anniversary of some battle or another."

"Oh, indeed, my lord, indeed!" Sir Thomas refilled Anthony's glass himself, clicking the heavy crystal decanter against the rim in his eagerness. "Or perhaps we could link it to one of the Roman festivals or celebrations. Our visitors do like to see the local amusements here in Rome. With a few weeks of planning between your staff and mine, we could—"

"I was thinking of something a bit sooner, Sir Thomas." Anthony forced himself to feign an appreciative sip of the bad canary. "This Friday, in fact."

"Friday! My lord, that's hardly time to make the proper arrangements for—"

"Oh, I think it's sufficient." Anthony cocked his head to one side, pleased, as if the thought had just occurred to him. "My servants are quite accustomed to obliging my impulses in such matters."

"But to assemble a proper list of guests and deliver the invitations, my lord!"

"The work of an afternoon, Sir Thomas," Anthony said with a careless wave of his hand. "I'm sure you already know the names of every last English person of quality in the city at present. I must have met the majority of them in this very room."

His brow furrowed, Sir Thomas nodded as his visions of a lavish, costly ball or masquerade began to fade.

"I can name them, yes," he admitted reluctantly. "It's my responsibility to be so informed. Upon their arrival to the city, they generally present their letters, and ask for my assistance with introductions and admission to the private collections."

Anthony smiled. "A sizable group, I should guess."

"It's increasing as the heat subsides, yes," Sir Thomas said. He spoke slowly, choosing his words with care, a most useful attribute for a consul. "And then we must include those English citizens who have chosen to dwell here in Rome throughout the year. We don't want to slight anyone, my lord."

"Not at all," Anthony said expansively. The more guests, the more easily he could separate Diana from her governess. "I'll leave it to your discretion entirely."

"But you can be sure that the guests will all be of sufficient rank and position to honor your most gracious invitation, my lord. Why, at present I can count a bishop, an earl and a dowager marchioness, all residing within the city, and most recently we've been joined by the younger daughter of a duke."

"How splendid." The daughter of a duke: simple enough words, yes, but because they referred to one particular and special daughter of a duke, Anthony had to work to keep his face fittingly impassive and his manner slightly bored.

Sir Thomas nodded vigorously. "There's also a noted classical scholar, Reverend Lord Patterson, and his nephew Lord Edward Warwick, and—"

"Oh, Lord Edward." Anthony suppressed a yawn. "Don't you find Lord Edward somewhat...*ottuso?*"

"Ottuso?" Sir Thomas's brow wrinkled with anxiety.

"Dull," Anthony explained, though he was sure Sir Thomas had comprehended the Italian word and all its more subtle meaning. "Tedious. But if you wish—"

"I understand entirely, my lord," Sir Thomas said quickly. "He'll not be invited."

Anthony smiled. He didn't fear Warwick as a rival, but he could have been an annoying inconvenience to his plans for the evening. "You needn't mention my name at all in the invitations. Let it come from the consulate. My address will be sufficient."

"Thank you, my lord, thank you!" Sir Thomas said, almost gushing with gratitude. He should be grateful, thought Anthony wryly, damned grateful. A party at the Palazzo di Prosperi would send his constituents happily back home to sing his praises, and set an almost unattainable standard for his successors. "I'm sure every one of the guests will recognize your house."

"Just as they will recognize your hospitality, Sir Thomas." Anthony set his glass down on the table and rose. Even if Diana and her governess had heard of the Palazzo di Prosperi—named for his mother's family—he doubted that they would connect it with the charming Signor di Randolfo. "Until Friday, then."

Sir Thomas hurried to stand, too. "Until Friday, my lord. I promise you a most splendid evening!"

And Anthony could scarcely wait.

"Another glass of sherry, Miss Wood?" Diana reached for the bottle, eager to oblige. In a moment or two, the servants would come to clear away the remnants of their lunch from the table before them, and the chance to refill Miss Wood's glass—and to assure the governess of a deeper nap—would be lost. "Signor Silvani's choice for us today was a fine one."

"As was the roasted squab," said Miss Wood with a small sigh of satisfaction. With dainty fingers, she held out her empty glass to Diana. "I fear the signore's cook is spoiling us dreadfully, my lady. I don't wish to think of how sadly our shipboard fare will compare on our voyage home."

"Then best to enjoy it while we're here." Diana tried not to look again at the clock as Miss Wood sipped at the wine. It was nearly half-past twelve now. She needed her governess to be soundly asleep as soon as possible, so she could steal away to meet Will Carney. She didn't know how long Will would wait if she were late, nor did she want to find out what he'd do if she weren't able to come at all.

She raised her hands over her head and yawned dramatically, trying to put the idea of sleep into Miss Wood's head. "I'm feeling quite weary this afternoon, aren't you?"

Miss Wood frowned. "I pray you're not coming down with some illness," she said with concern. "You shouldn't be weary. We've done little this morning except read and write letters."

"But letter-writing and reading can be just as wearying as riding about," Diana said. "Perhaps even more so. Page after page after page, word after word after word after word after—"

"I understand, my lady," Miss Wood said, suppressing a small yawn herself. "And I agree that a brief rest might not be amiss. It is the Roman way, you know, and while we are here in Rome—oh, that must be the servant to clear the table. *Entrare!*"

But instead of a footman or maidservant, Signor Silvani himself came through the door, carrying a thick white letter on a pewter charger. With a bow, he presented the letter to Diana, and smiled warmly.

"For the fair lady," he said. "From the English consulate this very moment. I did not trust its delivery to any other than myself."

"Grazie," Diana said as she took the letter. Their round-faced landlord was notoriously curious, and most likely he'd brought it himself not to be trustworthy, but hoping to glean something useful. Not that she blamed him; she was curious, too. She slipped her finger beneath the seal, and opened the heavy, cream-colored sheet.

"What is it, my lady?" Miss Wood asked, sipping her wine. "Not ill news, I trust?"

"Oh, no," Diana said, passing the sheet to her. "We've been invited to a party by Sir Thomas. But instead of the consulate, it's to be held at some English gentleman's private palazzo."

"Well, that's very nice of the English gentleman." Miss Wood read the letter for herself. "Though I must say Friday is rather short notice."

The small porcelain clock on the mantle chimed the half-hour, and anxiously Diana realized how fast her time was slipping away. She yawned again. "Can't we discuss this later, Miss Wood, after we've rested?"

"There's not much to discuss now or later, my lady, for of course we'll attend," Miss Wood said, refolding the invitation. "It would be ill-mannered to refuse such a kind invitation from the consul. Signore, do you know this place? The Palazzo di Prosperi?"

Silvani swept his hands out before him. "Who does not know the Palazzo di Prosperi? It is only one of the grandest and finest and most beautiful mansions in Rome!"

"Well, then, all the more reason for us to attend, my lady," Miss Wood said. "I'm sure that Lord Edward and Reverend Lord Patterson will join us in the same carriage, so that we—"

"Forgive me my grievous intrusion, *signorina*," Silvani interrupted gently, as if it truly did pain him to speak up, "but the footman from the consulate did not bring such invitations for their lordships."

"Oh, dear." Miss Wood's eyes widened with chagrined surprise. "Well, then. That seems rather like a slight, doesn't it?"

"It doesn't matter, Miss Wood," Diana said quickly, wishing that none of this needed deciding *now*. "No doubt they do things without us as well."

"That's true, my lady," Miss Wood said thoughtfully. "Very true. We shall still attend the consul's party, but we simply must take care not to mention it to their lordships, to preserve their feelings."

Diana shoved back her chair and stood, stretching and yawning and making her eyes as heavy-lidded as possible. "Later, Miss Wood, later, if you please."

"Yes, yes, my poor weary lady!" At last Miss Wood emptied the last of her sherry and rose, too, shaking the lunch crumbs from her skirts. "Here I am nattering on, and you're half asleep on your feet! That will be all, Signor Silvani. I must see her ladyship to her rest."

With guilt gnawing at her, Diana let Miss Wood help her settle onto the daybed in her bedchamber, taking off her slippers herself and covering her with a light coverlet. Ever since her sister had married and they'd left her with her new husband in Paris, Miss Wood had been especially kind to Diana, and Diana hated herself for repaying that kindness with dishonesty. If only there were some way to tell her governess the truth about Will Carney and his hateful letter and her jumbled feelings for Antonio and Edward and—well, if she could tell her *everything*.

Which, of course, she couldn't.

"You always look after us, Miss Wood," she said softly as her governess tucked the coverlet around her. "You'll rest now yourself, too, won't you?"

Miss Wood smiled, her own eyes already heavy with sleep. "I don't believe you could stop me, my lady. Sleep now, and we'll decide what we'll do next when we both wake."

Obediently Diana closed her eyes until she heard Miss Wood close the door between their rooms. Then her eyes flew open and she stared up at the painted ceiling high over her bed, angels and cherubs peering cheerfully down through the painted plaster clouds. She listened for the last squeak of the floorboards as Miss Wood reached her narrow bed, for the shuffle of her kicking off and dropping her shoes, for the creak of the rope springs beneath her mattress as she lay down, for the happy little sigh she always made when she settled with her head on the pillow. Diana listened so hard she was holding her breath, and at last she heard what she'd been waiting for: the gentle, wheezing snore of Miss Wood's sleep.

Carefully, to make as little noise as possible herself, Diana slipped from her daybed. She gathered up her hat, her parasol and gloves, tucked a few coins into her pocket, and with her shoes in her hand, tiptoed from her room to finish dressing in the hall.

"My lady!" Silvani popped from his rooms at the bottom of the stairs at the sound of Diana's careful footsteps. "What might I offer you, my lady? There is no trouble, is there?"

"No trouble at all, signore," she said. "I should like the use of our carriage, if you please."

"The carriage, my lady?" He made a great show of looking past her, up the stairs for Miss Wood. "Will the *signorina* be joining you?"

"She will not." Diana raised her chin, striving to look imperious, and pulled the veiling from the front of her hat down over her face. "Tell the driver I am ready."

"Yes, my lady." Still he hesitated. "Might I also tell the man of her ladyship's destination?"

"I shall tell him myself." She stopped before the door, waiting for him to open it. He shook his head, all the comment he'd dare make, and held the door for her before he escorted her to the hired carriage that she and Miss Wood kept ready every day.

"*L'uomo che state andando venire a contatto di e un bastardo fortunato,*" he said with a smile as he helped her into the carriage. "Good day, my lady."

"Good day." She didn't return his smile, but looked straight ahead and ignored his disrespectful comment. He'd counted on her not understanding the Italian words, but she had: The man you're going to meet is a lucky bastard.

How woefully wrong Silvani's guess was!

She waited until the carriage had moved away from the house and out of his hearing before she addressed the driver. "The Fontana di Trevi," she said. "You know the way?"

The man nodded, the only answer he ever gave to their questions, leaving Diana to her own troubled thoughts as they drove through the city.

* * *

"Damnation, uncle, she's going out!" Edward called back from the window. "She's going out alone!"

His uncle didn't look up from the fragment of pottery that he was considering with his glass. "Who's going out?"

"Lady Diana, of course." Edward leaned out the open window, sure now that she wouldn't see him as her carriage headed slowly through the crowded piazza. "Where the devil's that Miss Wood? How can she let Diana go out unaccompanied like that? When I tried to call on them this morning, she said they were spending the morning writing letters! Letters, hell!"

"Your language, Edward," his uncle said irritably. "You must learn to moderate yourself if you wish ever to have a place in polite company."

"She must be going to meet some other man," Edward said furiously. "I knew it. Why the devil else would she be hiding her face behind a veil? I've suspected her from the start, and here's the proof."

Uncle Henry scowled at him. "You've not a scrap of proof. You're slandering the poor young lady without any evidence."

"How much more evidence do I need?" Edward demanded, turning from the window. He folded his arms over his chest, barely able to contain his anger. Lady Diana was a prize, a beauty with a fortune, and he'd done his best—his very best!—to be agreeable enough to win her. He'd thought he was coming close, too, until the other night at the opera when she'd practically shoved him away. The only reason he could see for her turning so blasted cold was that she'd found another man who'd turned her head.

"Why else would she be slipping out from under her governess's thumb like this," he continued, "if it weren't to see some damned lover? She's like every other pretty woman on this earth, without a conscience or regard for anyone but herself!"

Uncle Henry laid down the pottery shard and set the glass beside it, the better to look at Edward. "Don't be ridiculous, Edward," he said. "Unless there is more to this tale than you've told me, you have neither cause nor justification for this raving at Lady Diana's expense."

Edward shook his head, gnawing at a ragged spot on his thumbnail. He wasn't about to tell his uncle about how Diana had rebuffed him. A man was entitled to his pride, wasn't he?

"Wooing a lady isn't easy, Edward," his uncle said sternly. "She's not going to drop into your lap like an overripe plum. She's the daughter of a peer. She knows her value. You cannot expect her to be as forthcoming as some dairymaid or milliner's girl. If you truly expect to ask for Lady Diana's hand, then you must be constant, and persevere until the proper opportunity presents itself."

"Oh, aye, perseverance," Edward muttered, grabbing his hat and jamming it onto his head. "That's the way to win a lying, cheating chit."

"What did you say, Edward?" his uncle demanded. "What was that?"

"I said I'm going out for a walk," Edward growled, already halfway out the door. He'd trap her at her own game, confront her with the evidence, and show her she couldn't get away with it with him. *That's* how he'd win her, not by groveling at the hem of her petticoats. "Don't look for me to return until I'm done."

In a city dominated by fountains, the Fontana di Trevi was the most famous, and the most extravagant, that Diana had seen. First imagined by Bernini, then constructed over the span of the next hundred years, the fountain was as wide as the piazza that housed it, with huge statues filling the niches on the palazzo behind it, and water spilling from an elaborate composition of stone scallop shelves, seahorses, tritons and nymphs to the large pond before it.

As the carriage drew closer, Diana tried to calm herself by remembering what Miss Wood had read to her about the fountain from her favorite guidebook. The old bearded fellow in the central arch was Ocean, and the two figures in swirling stone drapery represented Abundance and Health, though Diana couldn't tell which was which. It was all very classical and pagan, which made Miss Wood's explanation that the fountain had been conceived as a lasting monument to one pope or another seem strange indeed.

Foreign visitors clustered around the rim of the fountain, and over the sound of the falling water Diana could hear voices speaking in English, German and French. For every gawking visitor there seemed to be a guide, a beggar, a vendor, ready to offer advice, services, or dubious souvenirs, a busy pack of charming, brightly dressed greed. She'd grant Will Carney uncharacteristic cleverness for choosing such a spot for their meeting; here they'd be only another pair of unremarkable foreigners, and the babble around them would mask their unsavory conversation.

The driver stopped the carriage to one side of the piazza, and pointed toward the fountain with his whip. *"Fontana di Trevi, mia donna."*

"Thank you," Diana said, her heart thumping as she scanned the crowd for Will. *"Grazie."*

Without Silvani's meddlesome curiosity, the driver merely nodded and settled more comfortably on his bench. From the basket beneath his seat, he drew out the bundled red cloth that contained his midday meal, and prepared to wait patiently however long it took Diana to view the fountain.

"Do you know the time?" Diana asked. *"Quale ora?"*

"Due, mia donna," the driver said, then held up his first two fingers to explain more graphically.

Two o'clock: she was exactly on time. She was hesitant to leave the relative safety of the carriage and walk to stand un-escorted beside the fountain, but Will's note had specified that she come alone.

"You will wait here for me, yes?" she asked the driver. *"Qui, sì?"*

He nodded, and patted the bench with his open palm to demonstrate that he'd every intention of remaining in this place until she returned. Brandishing her parasol before her like a bludgeon, Diana climbed down the carriage's little metal step, and into the street.

She'd not taken three brisk steps before a barefoot boy with a yellow scarf tied about his head bounced up beside her.

"Lady, lady!" he said, tugging at her sleeve as he danced beside her. "English lady, yes? I talk English to pretty English lady!"

Diana pulled her arm free of his grubby fingers and fell back on her well-used retort. *"Sono spiacente, signore, noi non sono stato introdotto."*

"I am Benedetto, English lady, servant of you!" the boy exclaimed with an extravagant flourish that reminded Diana of Antonio. "I tell you the fountain. Most beautiful, yes? The fountain has magic for English ladies. You toss your coin over your shoulder, and *presto, presto!* You will come back to Rome forever! Good magic, eh, English lady? You trust Benedetto to—"

"Shove off, you little monkey!" A large figure thrust

between her and the boy, knocking him sideways across the pavement. "The lady's with me!"

"Will!" Diana stared at him, aghast. "Will, I—I didn't know you at first."

"I'd scarce know myself, sweetheart," he said, so close she could smell the stale liquor on his breath, "thanks t' what your old man did to me."

If she hadn't been expecting to see him here, she doubted she would have recognized him, he was that much changed. Instead of the bluff, sturdy young groom she remembered from last summer at Aston Hall, he now seemed shrunken and his shoulders were bent. His hair was dull and dirty and falling over his face, his clothes worn and tattered, his shoes fastened with scraps of string instead of proper buckles. He'd lost all of the rooster's strut that had caught her eye last spring, and in its place he was now furtive and wary, his red-rimmed gaze constantly shifting around the piazza and the fountain.

"You can't blame my father for having become so—so incensed," she said defensively. She wanted to leave, to run away, but she feared the scene he might make if she tried. "I know that giving you to the navy was wrong, but I—"

"*Wrong?*" he demanded roughly. "Is that all it be t'you? Your da's wrong?"

He frightened her like this, even in a crowd of people and she backed away from him, only a step or two, but enough that she felt the splattering spray of the fountain. "I told him not to do it, Will. I begged for you, but he wouldn't listen. I told him you didn't deserve such a punishment, not when—"

"Aye, m'lady, you know I didn't!" he said, his voice shaking with bitterness and anger. "My life an' livelihood snatched away from me, put in chains an' tossed in a stinkin' hulk o' a ship with a madman for a cap'n, for the length o' my mortal life—aye, now *that* be wrong, m'lady!"

"But you must have been freed," she said, trying to grasp at whatever logic she could. "You're here now, so you must have got them to let you go."

He laughed, hollowly and without any mirth. "I freed myself, m'lady. I jumped ship in Naples an' ran, here t'find you."

Before she could react, he grabbed her by the arm and drew her to the far side of the fountain, away from most of the others. He thrust the pad of his right thumb before her face, forcing her to look. The skin was distorted and tight, scarred by the letter *T* that had been burned into the flesh.

"*That* be your father's wrong," he said in a ragged whisper, "branding me for being a thief, for trying t' steal his precious lady-daughter's precious maidenhead!"

Diana stared, horrified. Even as sheltered as she'd been, she knew that any Englishman who was branded like this for theft was marked and shunned for the rest of his days, and any sailor who deserted a navy ship would be hung if he were caught.

And all of this—all—had happened to him because she'd impulsively let him kiss her on a warm summer's night.

"I'm sorry, Will," she said miserably. As appalling as his claims about his punishment were, she sadly didn't doubt them, not where Father's vengeful anger was concerned. "I'm sorry."

"To hell wit' your apology," he said. "Give me th' money."

She gulped. "I don't have it," she confessed hurriedly. "That is, not now, not that much. We—I don't travel with such sums in my possession, not when there are so many dangers to—"

He loomed over her, his fingers tightening into her arm. "Didn't you read th' letter? Didn't it make it plain what I'd do if you didn't bring th' money, who I'd tell? Only you an'

I know that I be branded for naught, but others believe my thumb. What a pretty tale it will make, eh? How you spread your legs for a groom, eager-like, and gave me—"

"Please, Will, don't!" she begged. "I'll get it soon enough, I swear! If you can only wait a little longer, until I return to England—if you could meet me there, in England, that is, why, then I'll have—"

"England? So you can see me clapped in irons for desertin', an' swayin' from a gibbet?" He swore with disgust. "No, m'lady, it's now you owe me, an' now you must pay."

"Another week then," she pleaded, fear twisting through her. "I'll find the money, I promise you, if only you won't tell anyone else! Please, Will, please!"

He stared down at her, breathing hard, his hatred washing over her. "You're no better'n a whore, *m'lady*. No, you're worse'n a whore. At least a true whore gives what she be paid t'give."

With a wordless sob, Diana tried to pull free, but he held her firm.

"You give me th' money you owe me, m'lady," he warned. "Two more days, m'lady, an' I'm generous at that. You be here again in two more days wit' what you owe me, or I tell 'em all."

He shoved her clear, and she stumbled backward, into an old woman with a basket of fruit who scolded her in a torment of oaths.

"Scusa, scusa," Diana stammered as she worked to steady both herself and the woman. By the time she looked back for Will, he was gone, and with relief she hurried alone to the carriage.

Two days, two days: that wasn't long enough to do what he'd demanded. But what choice did she have? Now she knew she'd never be able to persuade Will to give her more time, any more than she doubted he'd betray her. He'd toss her to the wolves exactly as he believed she'd done to him, and he'd spread his venomous tale to sully her father's reputation as well. An English peer was granted much goodwill and power, but not the right to take the law into his own hands as her father had by "punishing" Will Carney. The London press would cry out for retribution, her father could face prosecution and a trial, her reputation would be hauled into public display and irreparably destroyed and her entire family would become unacceptable to polite society.

All this she'd accomplished with one misjudged rendez-vous with a servant, and, her head bent in despair, Diana returned to the carriage and their lodgings.

Edward stood across the street from the tavern, keeping to the shadows beneath a tattered striped awning. The street was a low, common place, not far from the church of San Marcello, where huge pans of tripe for the poor were cooked on open fires each day. The air stank of the simmering offal, blotting out even the pervasive smells of too many unwashed Romans living in too-close quarters, the stench so foul that Edward was forced to hold his scented handkerchief close to his face to be able to breathe.

But his reason for loitering here was worth this discomfort and more. It was almost too good to be true, the kind of fortuitous accident that only happened in plays, and enough to let Edward dare believe his luck could in fact be changing for the better.

When he'd left his uncle and stormed outside, he was surprised to discover that he could still make out Lady Diana's carriage in the distance, slowed by the perpetual street traffic of Rome. On an impulse, he decided to follow her, determined to learn who the rival for his hand might be.

But he'd hardly been prepared for the little drama he'd witnessed beside the Fontana di Trevi. In the crush of visitors, he'd been able to sidle so close to Diana that he'd heard nearly every word the beggar had said to her. Or rather, as Edward had soon learned to his astonishment, not a beggar, but some rascal from her past who now wished to blackmail her over the sins they'd shared together. Edward hadn't quite caught the more sordid details—two chattering passersby had briefly obliterated the conversation—but he'd heard enough to be sure that Lady Diana was terrified of this man and the scandal he'd vowed to reveal, so terrified that she'd promised to pay him the money he demanded.

It would have been the perfect time for Edward to play the hero. He considered it, too: appearing from nowhere to rescue the lady from the filthy villain who threatened her. Such action would surprise Diana, impress her with his decisive courage, and show him to best advantage as a man of brave action— the kind of man that every woman claimed to love best.

But there'd be danger, too. The man was desperate, and desperation gave even the shabbiest of men more strength and unpredictable cunning. What if he drew a knife or pistol from beneath his threadbare coat, or knocked Edward to the pavement? Was Edward willing to risk his own life to make a show before Lady Diana? What if he were injured, or even killed, and Diana still didn't give him the kindness he deserved? She'd already shown herself to be damned perverse in her affections. Why should she behave any differently if he offered his life to defend her?

No, it wasn't a chance Edward was willing to take. What sane gentleman would? But perhaps there was another, more certain way to win the lady's thanks, if not her love, and at no personal risk to himself, either.

The blackmailer had revealed himself to be a sailor from His Majesty's Navy, wanted now for deserting his ship. The navy didn't look kindly on deserters, and punished them with rare vengeance; Edward knew this from having to sit in the tedious company of one of his uncle's cronies, a retired admiral here in Rome who vented such sentiments with patriotic fervor.

It had been simple enough for Edward now to call himself a patriot, too, and send a boy to the admiral's house with a message of righteous outrage, proclaiming he'd spotted a traitorous deserter himself. Simpler still to follow the man at a distance to the tavern, and send another boy to the admiral to say he'd trapped the cowardly weasel in his den. And far, far more simple and safe to let the admiral's men capture the blackmailer with their cudgels and pistols, and make him vanish forever into the brig of the nearest English navy vessel, followed by his inevitable hanging at some yardarm or another.

But while the blackmailer would conveniently disappear, never to trouble Diana or her father again, Diana herself wouldn't hear of it. Such sordid transactions weren't discussed before ladies. Instead, she'd continue to suffer alone, consumed by guilt and dread. Only Edward would continue to know her fearful secret, and what he'd do with it—ah, that would be his own secret.

Now Edward stepped from the awning, drawn by a noisy excitement coming towards him. Four English marines, their red uniforms bright and their muskets glinting in the afternoon sun, trotted down the street with their officer, followed by a small escort of boys and stray dogs. Two of the marines remained outside the tavern to guard the door, while the other three went inside. At once a small crowd began to gather, attracted as always in Rome by the possibility of free entertainment.

They hadn't long to wait. The marines soon reappeared, dragging the blackmailer with them, his hands ringed with iron manacles. Clearly the man hadn't come without a fight: blood dripped from his forehead and hair, and his footsteps were unsteady. The small crowd jeered the prisoner, and someone threw a clot of dirt that struck the front of his dark coat. The marines hurried him along; the show was soon done, and for all purposes, so was the life of the unfortunate blackmailer.

But for Edward, whistling happily as he sauntered back towards the Piazza di Spagna, life seemed endlessly full both of possibility and of hope.

Chapter Nine

❦

The footmen were lighting the last of the candles as Anthony walked through the Sala Grande, the most celebrated room in his entire palazzo. The spreading candelabra of silver branches and pink and green Venetian glass drops had been lowered from the ceiling for the purpose, and was being steadied by two more footmen while the last wicks were lit. Anthony paused as another man carefully pulled the velvet-covered cord that lifted the candelabra back into its rightful place overhead, the flames flickering and the blown-glass drops clinking gently against one another.

Anthony applauded with appreciation as the old-fashioned candelabra rose like some slow-moving skyrocket, gradually lighting the painted Tiepolo gods and goddesses on the ceiling far above. He'd always loved to watch the candles being lit like this when he'd been a child, part of the ceremony that marked the beginning of his parents' lavish entertainments.

He'd made a point of continuing such rituals himself, not just to honor the memory of his mother's hospitality, but also because he delighted in the blatant splendor of the candlelight and polished silver and paintings, the gilded furnishings and white marble statues, the zigzag pattern of the polished marble floors, all reflected over and over in the tall-looking glasses on either end of the reception chamber. It was one more reason among thousands that separated him from his more practical brothers, and another way that he'd always considered himself infinitely more Italian than English. His appearance, his tastes and interests, his sensuality, even what made him laugh—all were due more to his mother's flamboyant family than his father's.

Yet now an English girl—a girl completely at ease in his father's aristocratic world of London and country counties—had bewitched him with a thoroughness that no Roman lady had yet managed to do. It was as preposterous as Lucia claimed, and yet he couldn't deny it. He'd only to think of Diana Farren and he smiled. He'd realize he was doing it, and smiled all the more. He'd stopped caring entirely about the wager, and he didn't care that he didn't care. In fact, the only thing he seemed to care about these days was Diana, and even that sorry, sentimental realization merely made him smile more.

"My lord, everything is prepared for your guests." His solemn-faced butler Carlo, the real master of Anthony's palazzo, bowed low, the powder from his tied wig drifting over his blue velvet livery coat. "Exactly as you ordered, my lord."

"Excellent." Anthony trusted his staff implicitly, and he knew that the butler's assurance covered everything from the flowers in the porcelain vases on the marble-topped sideboards to the supper that would be served later in the evening. "You've opened the gates to the courtyard?"

"Yes, my lord," answered Carlo again. "An hour before, as you ordered."

Anthony smiled, hearing the question behind that polite statement. "These are the English consul's guests, Carlo, not my usual friends. These guests will come at the exact time they're bidden, from curiosity more than punctuality."

Though Anthony had his share of curiosity about tonight, too. What would Diana's temperament be towards him? The last time he'd seen her, in her carriage on the Corso, she'd been proper, even demure. Before that, in the box at the opera, she'd been overcome by passion, but he doubted she'd let herself be so fiery before her peers, let alone her governess. The real question in his mind was how she'd be towards him once they were finally alone.

"The small chamber upstairs," he began. "Is it prepared?"

"Everything is as you wished, my lord," Carlo said. "The candles are lit, and the wine and supper have been set."

The little chamber was far from the public rooms: a gem of a room, with walls hung with red velvet and furniture rich with gold leaf and an exquisitely fanciful bed supported by carved, kneeling stags. What better place to end his hunt for his own goddess Diana, later this very night?

From the entry downstairs, he heard a woman's laughter and a man's lower reply. English voices: his guests were arriving.

"There now, Carlo, what did I tell you?" He smoothed the soft lace ruffles on his cuffs one last time. Strange how he was almost nervous from anticipation tonight; he couldn't recall the last time he'd felt this way for the sake of a woman. He hoped at least she'd the decency to feel the same butterflies when she was finally, properly introduced to him.

Pausing just outside the doorway to the palazzo's grand salon, Diana took a deep breath to collect herself while Miss Wood told the footman her name. If there was one thing she knew how to do splendidly well, it was make an entrance. For these next few moments, when every head would be turned towards her, she must put aside the sick dread that Will Carney had left her with, and concentrate instead on being merely the beautiful daughter of the Duke of Aston.

At least she was confident she looked the part. She'd decided not to powder her hair tonight, instead having Deborah brush it until it gleamed like silver-gold, and arrange it simply with a single lovelock over one shoulder. She wore a new *robe à la française* that she'd had made while they'd been visiting France. The pink-and-white striped silk *cannele* rustled softly even when she stood still, and the bobbin-lace trim that edged the sleeves and the front of her skirts was so fashionable, she'd never seen it anywhere but in Paris.

"Lady Diana Farren," the footman announced with the same droning solemnity that footmen always seemed to use, whether English, French or Italian. Diana straightened her back and relaxed her shoulders, arranged her hands gracefully with her wrists turned out, and with quick, measured steps that made her skirts ripple gently across the pointed toes of her slippers, she sailed into the candlelit room.

She smiled serenely, pleased and charming but never ingratiating, and let her gaze wander slowly across the admiring faces turned towards her. She understood exactly how long to look, how much to smile, from the careful practice she'd made when she'd expected to be presented to the queen in London. It remained a useful skill, of course, but now there was a bittersweet futility to so much graceful, purposeless smiling with no possible suitors in sight, or in her future, either, with Will Carney's threat hanging over her.

But such grim thoughts would show on her face, and that would never do for a young lady of her breeding. Instead, she forced herself to concentrate on Sir Thomas Howe, their host and consul, bowing low as she approached.

"My lady," he said as he rose, his hand gallantly outstretched. "I'm honored that you could join us this evening. Even a city as beautiful as Rome is immeasurably improved with you here visiting."

"You're most kind, Sir Thomas," she murmured, lowering her eyes modestly and making the slightest dip of a curtsey in acknowledgement—more than a knight deserved from a peer's daughter, but she knew how such little niceties pleased older gentlemen, and besides, Sir Thomas had been very useful to them here in Rome. "I'm equally honored to be your guest."

She offered Sir Thomas her fingertips to raise her up, continuing the genteel charade that she was far too delicate to do so unassisted.

"Not at all, my lady," Sir Thomas said. "But I should like to present our host, and the master of this splendid palace. My lady, Lord Anthony Randolph."

Lord Anthony? She looked up sharply, her much-practiced serenity abandoning her, and clutched at Sir Thomas's hand in shock. Antonio—or now Anthony—was standing beside the consul, his smile every bit as blandly pleasant as her own. He was elegantly, elaborately dressed in dark blue, a ribbed silk that shaded subtly dark to light in the candlelight. The front and cuffs of the coat were heavily embroidered with silk and silver threads and glossy chenille that made the twisting vines and flowers come to life. Even the buttons of his coat and waistcoat were embroidered with wreaths of tiny blue flowers, forget-me-nots, as if Diana needed any more reminding. But though he might be dressed like a lord, he still had a rascal's glint to his eye, yet another shared joke between them that she didn't necessarily want to share.

Why hadn't he told her he was *English?* Why had he

masqueraded as some wonderfully disreputable Roman rogue, instead of telling her outright that he owned this—this palace, with a title to match? What sort of foolishness was he trying to trick her with? Heaven deliver her, she couldn't even conduct a proper Roman flirtation without it going so dismally wrong! A pox on him—no, a pox on all men, if this is what her sorry luck in love came to. Better to have no luck if the best she could do was a grinning, lying rogue like this!

"My lady?" Sir Thomas asked anxiously. "My lady, are you unwell?"

Swiftly she gathered herself. "Forgive me, Sir Thomas," she said, smiling warmly at the consul and not at all at Anthony. "It's only that Lord Anthony surprised me. At first glance he reminded me very much of another gentleman I once knew, but I see now that there's little real resemblance."

Beside Sir Thomas, Anthony laughed. "And how happy I am to meet you, too, my lady."

"Indeed, my lord," she said, purposefully cool. "Your palazzo is so grand, I wonder that you keep it such a secret."

"Oh, it's no secret," Sir Thomas said. "Not to anyone who's familiar with Rome. Most would say it's every bit the equal in splendor to the palaces of the Farnese and Barbarini families."

"The Prosperi have always had excellent taste, Sir Thomas," Anthony said, his gaze still intent on Diana. "As a whole, we've proven to be a discerning bunch, whether we're acquiring architecture, paintings or women."

Sir Thomas cleared his throat delicately, the only way he dared show his disapproval to his host. "To be sure, your family has made many fortunate marriages over the centuries."

Anthony nodded with acknowledgement of the comment, not the implied criticism. "My ancestors chose their women the same way they chose everything else, Sir Thomas: from appreciation and desire, not need."

He smiled at Diana, making it clear that he considered this a compliment to her.

But Diana didn't miss how he'd carefully said *women,* not *wives,* nor was she in any humor to be complimented by him.

"I suppose it must be the Roman fashion to equate women with paintings that are for sale in a common gallery," she said, "but I can assure you, my lord, that English gentlemen regard their ladies with more respect and regard."

"But his lordship *is* English, my lady," Sir Thomas protested. "Though his father lived most of his life here in Rome, he was the Earl of Markham, a most worthy gentleman, may he rest in peace. It is through his mother's blood, a noble lady of one of this city's most ancient families, that his lordship can claim to being Roman as well."

"Which is why, my lady, I can, in perfect honesty, be Anthony Randolph one day, and Antonio the next," Anthony explained with maddening ease. "It makes my life much more interesting."

"Or simply more duplicitous," Diana said tartly. "I'm afraid I remain unconvinced, my lord."

And yet it made dreadful sense. So much was now explained—his ease with English, his ability to anticipate her whereabouts, his familiarity with English manners and habits, even the blue of his eyes—that she'd wondered about before.

"But it's the truth, my lady," Sir Thomas said, now clearly aware of the tension between them, yet without a clue as to its cause. "Lord Anthony brings together the best of both London and Rome, and we are fortunate to be able to enjoy his hospitality tonight."

"And fortunate in other ways as well, my lady." Gently

Anthony took her hand from Sir Thomas. "You see, because I am English, I can respect a lady like yourself, and hold her in the highest regard. But because I am Roman, too, I can appreciate your beauty as the greatest and highest work of God's art."

Before she could answer, he raised her hand to his lips and kissed it, his lips brushing so lightly over her skin that she shivered, her thoughts flying back to the first kiss they'd shared that night in the Coliseum.

Blast him! What was it about him, English or Roman, that reduced her to this worthless state?

"Eloquently phrased, my lord, most eloquently phrased!" Sir Thomas beamed at the two of them as if they were model students in the schoolroom. "There you are, my lady! You can scarcely object to logic like that!"

Diana pulled her hand free of Anthony's, wishing she could banish the other memory as easily. "Logic was never my objection, Sir Thomas."

"Why, then you've no objection at all, my lady," he said, glancing past her to the other guests patiently clustered in the doorway waiting for her to enter first. Because Diana was the person of highest rank in the room, they had no choice, even if she dawdled all night, but it was still rude of her, and she knew it. "Perhaps if you've an interest in art, you and your governess might enjoy viewing the paintings in the palace's collection. She is with you tonight, isn't she, Miss—ah—Miss—"

"Her name's Miss Wood, Sir Thomas," Diana looked over her shoulder, searching the crowded room for her governess. Miss Wood was usually very accomplished at hovering on the edges of a party until her presence was needed, but tonight she must have been tempted by so much splendor to wander off. "She must be somewhere here, I'm sure, but I don't—"

"I'll show you the pictures, my lady," said Anthony, holding his hand out to take hers once again. "After all, they belong to my family, both English and Roman."

She hesitated, looking down at his offered hand, then back to his face, his blue eyes watching her intently. She'd seen that expression before, daring her to join him. She knew what had come from her accepting his dare, too.

Hadn't she learned anything from her disastrous rendezvous with Will Carney? Wasn't she sadder, but wiser with that sorry proof of what could come of giving in to desire and impulse? How could she possibly believe this man—any man—would be different?

"Yes, yes, my lady, no one else would know these magnificent collections quite so well." Once again Sir Thomas looked pointedly past her, to the other waiting guests. "You couldn't ask for a better guide than Lord Anthony, my lady."

"True enough," Anthony said, his smile so invitingly wicked that Diana couldn't believe the consul didn't see it, too. "And I'll give you my word, my lady, that in my company you'll never be bored."

Oh, she knew that, too, and this time she couldn't keep the guilty flush from her cheeks as she remembered exactly how he'd amused her before. Already her heart was quickening, her blood racing with the excitement she always felt when she was with him.

"Lady Diana, please," Sir Thomas said, his urgency as clear as his unhappiness at being so ill-mannered. "I can send one of the footmen to search for your governess, my lady, or—"

"Or you can be brave," said Anthony, his head cocked to one side, "and come with me. But if you wish to be a coward, my lady, why, then—"

"I am no coward, my lord." Diana didn't take his hand

so much as seize it. "Show me your wretched pictures at once. At *once*."

Sir Thomas drew back, his eyes wide with surprise, but Anthony only chuckled, and tucked her hand into the crook of his arm.

"As you wish, my lady," he said as he led her through the crowd. "My family really does have excellent taste, you know. The pictures in this house are among the most splendid in Rome. I've heard that even His Holiness envies a certain St. John by Raphael that hangs in my library."

"The Pope envies you a picture?" She narrowed her eyes suspiciously as they walked through the doorway and into a long, high-ceilinged gallery, still safely within sight and hearing of the rest of the gathering. "I find that impossible to believe, my lord. But then I suppose I should find it impossible to believe anything you tell me."

"Anthony," he corrected, "or Antonio. You may choose whichever version pleases you, of course, and I promise to answer promptly to either."

"Why didn't you tell me your father was English?" she demanded.

He shrugged, unconcerned. "It seemed of no consequence."

"But you deceived me into believing you were something you were not!"

"I did no such thing, sweet," he said easily. "Rather you chose to believe what you thought you understood. I go by both names in Rome, and no one else judges it as peculiar. But no ceremony between us, I beg you, not after—"

She flushed, keeping her gaze so directly ahead that she scarcely noticed the gallery around them. "I know perfectly well what—what occurred the last time we were together, and I've no intention of letting it ever occur again."

"I am shocked." He stopped, holding his hand outstretched in amazed supplication. "Didn't I give you great pleasure, *cara?* Didn't I—"

"It's not a question of pleasure," she said quickly, glancing over her shoulder back at the others to make sure no one had overheard. "I'm not even certain that was what you—you did to me."

She saw the skepticism on his face, enough to make her stammer on defensively, and try to explain. "I thought we'd kiss, that was all. I'd never—never—"

"No man has ever loved you?"

Expected tears welled up to blur his face before her, and swiftly she turned away before he could see them. She didn't want to cry, and she didn't know why those tears had been so quick to appear.

No man has ever loved you...

She was beautiful, titled and rich, admired and envied wherever she went. She could scarcely recall all the boys and men that had already come and gone through her short life, or all the stolen kisses and fumbled caresses that had come with them. She'd been eager for their love and approval, just as she'd yearned to feel a share of the same passionate excitement they'd all claimed to feel with her.

Yet, Anthony had been the only one who'd thought to put her desires before his own, who'd wanted to give, not simply take whatever he could. As a high-born lady and a virgin at that, she realized that the liberties she'd permitted him to take had been too many and far too free, but as a woman—ahh, she hadn't the right words to describe how he'd made her feel.

No wonder from that first night in the Coliseum, Anthony had seemed so different. No wonder that she'd simultaneously longed and dreaded seeing him again. No wonder, really, that she wished to be nowhere else in Rome than here with him.

No wonder that she couldn't think of a way to answer his question.

No man has ever loved you...

"Ah, well, no matter," he said at last, as if her silence was of no real importance. "No matter at all."

Unsure of what he meant, she glanced uneasily back at him. He was watching her just as closely as he had before, but now his earlier skepticism had been replaced by something else—something perilously like gentle understanding, even tenderness, something she'd never seen in a man's face before.

No man has ever loved you...

Swiftly she looked away again, forcing herself to concentrate on the huge, gold-framed painting that hung before her, and not on the man at her side. Cleopatra, she decided, the famous Egyptian queen: a foreign-looking but beautiful woman with a great many jewels and little clothing. Beneath waving palm trees, the queen sat sprawled with regal insolence across a golden throne, surrounded by her attendants and her wild leopards and crocodiles on silver leashes. The painting's colors were brilliant, the brushwork so vivid that Diana could almost imagine herself standing in awe in the great queen's presence.

That was better. Think of Cleopatra and her crocodiles, of anything other than what Anthony had said. If she let herself begin to cry, she feared she'd never be able to stop.

"That—that painting is as large as a small house, my lord," she said, working hard to keep the tremor of emotion from her voice. "If my sister Mary were here, she—she could tell me in an instant who had painted it."

"Tintoretto," he said. "That's the painter. I won't make you wait until your sister can tell you. And yes, *cara,* it is indeed as large as a small house, for the simple reason that it was commissioned to fill this very large wall."

"I see." She did, too, the tears gradually retreating from her eyes to wherever it was that unshed tears went. "Mr. Tintoretto must have been very happy to have so large a commission."

Anthony laughed. "I imagine he was, if he charged by the size of the canvas. His real name was Jacopo Robusti, you know, but he was called *il tintoretto*—the little dyer—because his father was a master cloth-dyer by trade in Venice, and the name stuck."

She nodded eagerly, wishing now she'd bothered to pay more attention when Mary and John had discussed pictures in the French galleries. "This painting reminds me of another artist. The same colors, the same dramatic lighting, too, as though we're watching a scene on a stage. Oh, I can't quite recall the painter's name, but it's something like Tintoretto. Another *T*-name."

"Titian?" he asked, his interest clear. "Was that the name?"

"Yes, yes!" she said, delighting herself as much as him. "It was another great big painting like this, but it showed a scene from the Bible—the breakfast at Cana, I think—but this reminds me of it very much."

"Titian was the grander master," Anthony said. "He, too, was from Venice, though he was a guest of the Pope here in Rome for several years. He painted several of my Prosperi ancestors at that time."

"Titian? Truly?" Even she'd heard of Titian. Her uncle had a tiny Titian sketch hanging over the fireplace in his library, given so much pomp and respect in its heavy gold frame that the rough-drawn painting was almost overwhelmed. Gentlemen like her uncle fought over paintings by Titian, bringing them home from their grand tours like trophies, but no English noblemen had any family portraits by Titian.

None, that is, except for Anthony.

"Truly, yes," he said, clearly unimpressed by the great prizes in his home. "We Prosperi never give up anything without a fight."

"'We'?" she repeated curiously. "Your father *was* English, wasn't he?" Anthony was so very different from any other English gentleman she'd met that she wasn't entirely certain that Sir Thomas had been telling her the truth.

"Oh, my father was as English as can be, and so are my brothers," he assured her, "but the Prosperi blood definitely courses more strongly through my veins. You'd see it for yourself in those Titian portraits. Stand beneath their blue-eyed gaze, and all you can think is what a pack of wicked old rascals my ancestors must have been!"

"Eyes like yours?" she asked, though she already knew the answer.

He widened his eyes to round blue circles, making her laugh. "So they tell me. Though more benign, I trust."

"Perhaps," she said lightly, turning back to the painting to hide her smile behind her fan. "Perhaps."

Talking about the picture this way made her feel clever and more confident and not simply pretty, more like her scholarly sister. But it wasn't just the paintings. *He* made her feel clever, too. He didn't lecture her like Edward or Miss Wood, assuming her head was empty. He asked her opinion as if her opinion actually mattered, and then listened when she gave it. She couldn't recall any other man ever doing that, and she liked it. From him, she liked it even more than all the empty praise and poetry offered up to her beauty.

"So this is by Tintoretto," she repeated, letting the rolling syllables fill her mouth. "I must remember that name, because I'll always remember the picture."

"Then you must remember me with it." He winked at her, and then quickly looked back at the painting again so she couldn't rebuff him. "I've always liked this picture, too, even as a child. It's a dreadful thing to confess, I know, but Cleopatra reminded me of my own mother."

"Your *mother?*" she repeated, shocked. In her family, her mother's memory was kept with saintly reverence. Diana knew nothing of his mother, of course, but for him to liken the pagan woman in the painting—her breasts brazenly bared and her eyes rimmed with kohl—to the deceased Lady Markham was, well, surprising. "She reminded you of your—your lady mother?"

"It was Cleopatra's demeanor that resembled Mama more than any true likeness," he admitted. "Mama had sufficient presence to turn even a kitchen stool into a throne, and make every man her subject. I doubt even Cleopatra could have held a candle to her in that regard, but then, how could a mere Queen of the Nile dare compete with a daughter of the Prosperi?"

His explanation was so disarmingly honest that she couldn't help but smile, more than enough to make him grin in return.

"There now, I told you my pictures would entertain you, didn't I?" He winked boldly, coaxing her smile to remain. "No dreary, dusty ruins with me. I'll leave those to Warwick."

She tipped her head to one side. "It was you who refused to invite Lord Edward and his uncle here tonight, wasn't it? It wasn't Sir Thomas. It was you."

"I didn't refuse anything," he said with a careless shrug. "I simply didn't do it. I like to be amused at home, and Warwick must be the least amusing man in Rome at present."

She clicked open her fan, watching him over the curved

edge. She felt more sure of herself now, once again back on the familiar territory of teasing flirtation. "That's not very hospitable of you, my lord, inviting every other Englishman in Rome save those two."

"Anthony, sweetheart." He replaced her hand in the crook of his arm, leaning closer to whisper his request as if she'd forgotten, and he wished to be discreet. "You really must remember to call me Anthony."

"Anthony." How could she not, after he'd made her forget her tears with tales of Cleopatra and Tintoretto? She knew why he'd done it, and the fact that he'd understood made him all the more rare among the men she'd known. She slid her hand along his arm fondly, unable to keep from touching him even this little bit. "Lord Edward was wounded at being left out, you know, and I cannot say I fault him for it, either."

"This palazzo is my home, and I invite whom I please," he said, his face still close to hers. "And you, my dear Diana, please me very much."

Purposefully she didn't return the compliment, or even reply to it. They'd been out here alone, away from the others, for far too long. They'd have to return soon, or surely be missed. She knew all that, every bit of it, yet she lingered still.

He was frowning slightly, perplexed. "Tell me, *cara*," he said. "Would you rather I'd invited Warwick? Have I crossed you without realizing it?"

"Not at all," she said softly, dazzling him with the truth. How could a man like Anthony ever be jealous of Edward Warwick? "You've other pictures to show me, yes?"

"Oh, yes." He brushed his fingers lightly across her cheek. "But the best ones are upstairs, for me and my closest friends alone to appreciate. You would, I think, enjoy them even more than Cleopatra."

She understood. Oh, she understood, and slowly she furled her fan, one blade at a time, to take away that slender barrier between them. He wasn't Lord Edward, and he certainly wasn't Will Carney, but Anthony was still a man—a wickedly seductive man who had already tempted her more than he'd any right to.

"Upstairs," she repeated slowly. "Upstairs, you say?"

"Upstairs." He glanced past her, back at the others through the doorway. "Where is your governess?"

"I don't know. I haven't seen her since I was announced when we arrived."

He touched her cheek again, just his fingertips, and she shivered. "I don't want her to make a scene if you're not…not to be found."

"She won't." At least Miss Wood never had before, and heaven knows Diana had given her plenty of opportunities. Her governess might come hunting for her, but Miss Wood was always discreet, the way Father expected. "And if we were only gone long enough for you to show me the other pictures, then—"

"Come." He didn't wait for her agreement, seizing her hand and drawing her along with him down the length of the patterned marble floor to the staircase at the end. He slipped his other arm around her back, guiding her, sheltering her, making sure she didn't falter or stumble. The steps were curved, a sweeping flow of pale marble beneath their feet.

With him beside her she walked faster, faster, her heart racing and her breath quick. The candles in gilded sconces made their shadows dance, and the laughter and chatter from the reception room grew more faint with every step. There were paintings hung along the wall here, too, more enormous paintings like the one of Cleopatra, with swirling gold frames that made them part of the wall. But they were moving so fast that the painted images blurred into nothing more than colors, cerulean blue and carmine red, gold and silver and creamy white, the rich intense colors of Rome, of passion.

Of Anthony.

From the stairs he led her down another passage—more marble, more gilt and silver, more paintings, as if not an inch of the palace dare be left unadorned—and at last threw open a door and stepped aside for her to enter first.

She gasped with wonder. She'd never seen such a room before, not in England nor in France nor any of the other Italian cities she'd visited so far.

While the rest of the palazzo had been conceived on a grand scale, this chamber was small and intimate and intended for the most private use. The walls and windows were hung with red cut velvet, and all the candelabras and chandeliers glittered with hanging crystal drops that magnified the candlelight like a thousand stars. A low table had been set for supper, with wine waiting to be poured into crystal goblets.

But what had made Diana gasp was the oversized bedstead, the centerpiece of the entire little room. It sat on a raised dais, two steps up from the rest of the floor. Four carved, gilded stags, nearly life-sized, knelt with their heads bent in vanquished submission at each corner of the bed's frame to support it on their backs and antlers. The bed had no curtains, only ethereal hangings of silver cloth that swept down from a ring overhead to tangle in the stags' antlers. The coverlet was red velvet, elaborately embroidered with swirls of precious threads, and the sheets and pillows were fine-bleached linen, with heavy silk fringe along the edge of the pillows.

Almost as part of the bed, a large painting hung on the wall at the head. In exquisite detail, it showed a lovely young woman clad only in a short, gauzy tunic and silver sandals, a bow in one hand and an arrow in the other, and a silver circlet crowned with a brilliant-studded crescent in her pale-gold hair.

"I told you I'd a special painting by Titian to show you, *cara mia*," Anthony said. "Not an ancestor of mine. Perhaps one of yours. But then surely you recognize the huntress goddess Diana?"

"Even I can recognize Diana," she said in awe. The painting was beautifully done, all cool silver and pale blues like the moonbeams that lit it, with the goddess so vivid that she seemed poised to speak as she looked back over her shoulder, her rosy lips parted. "Goddess of the hunt, goddess of the moon. She's beautiful, Anthony."

"So are you," he said, coming to stand behind her. He circled his arms lightly around her waist, and bent just enough to kiss the side of her throat. "When I first saw you on the balcony with the soft gray rain clouds behind you, I thought of this picture. Even before I knew your name, I saw you as Titian's goddess."

"You did?" She turned in the loop of his arms so she was facing him, her skirts brushing against his legs. She glanced up at him, at the strong line of his jaw, faintly shadowed with his shaven beard. "How could you know, Anthony? How could you *know?*"

"I cannot explain it, Diana, but I did." He lowered his face as she arched up towards him, and their lips met—lightly, tenderly, more of a pledge of devotion than a promise of passion. "I saw you, and you've been always in my thoughts ever since. Why else would I have done this now?"

"You did this for me?" she asked, shaking her head in disbelief. "This room, this painting, this—this bed?—you did that for me?"

"I cannot claim the bed," he admitted, his hands settling around her waist. "Everything else, but not the bed. Prosperi legend claims that it once belonged to Catherine de Medici. I'd rather believe it's been waiting all this time for my own goddess."

"Ohh." She bowed her head, feeling the sting of tears again as she rested her palms on his chest. No other gentleman had ever thought so much about her to make such a grand effort to please her, not like this.

Were these the signs that Anthony was falling in love with her?

And was she already in love with him herself? Was that why she'd come here with him, stayed here when there could be no doubt of his intent, wished to be nowhere else on earth than here with him?

"Look at me, Diana." With one finger beneath her chin, he tipped her face back up towards him. "Don't hide. I want you to remember me just as I remember you, and to remember this night. I want you to remember everything, *mia dea di innocenza.*"

She gazed up at him, her smile trembling. "That's not fair, for you to speak words I do not understand."

He chuckled, leaning close to kiss her. "What else would I say, but words of love?" he whispered, his mouth close over hers. "I called you my Diana, my own goddess of innocence."

Of love, of innocence: the words were meant as endearments, but came instead like a bucket of the coldest wellwater. Though she may not be well and truly ruined, she was far from the paragon he thought her to be. He believed her to be innocent, unaware of any man's touch but his own. He believed her to be what she seemed, the innocent daughter of an English lord, instead of what she was, a wanton who'd let herself be ruled again and again by passion and the temptations of men, and now faced, either blackmail or ruinous scandal.

Anthony offered her love, and all she had to offer in return was falsehood and deception.

"Is that so troubling, *cara?*" he asked, half teasing, half with concern. "Is my love so unsettling to you?"

She pulled free and turned away from him, unable to let her face betray her any further. No matter what it cost her, she owed him the truth. If he'd only been the idle Roman rogue she'd first thought, then it wouldn't have mattered, but he was an English gentleman, a lord of noble blood like her own—a gentleman of honor. There was no other way, not if she ever wanted to deserve the love and trust he was offering her now.

And yet how to find the words to tell him about Will Carney? If Will did as he'd threatened, then the scandal would spill over onto Anthony as well. How to explain to him in any way that would make him not scorn her as the shameful creature she was?

"What is it, Diana?" He slipped his hands back around her waist. "Tell me, please. Is it the prospect of love that makes you so—"

"Do not speak of love, I beg you!" she cried in an anguished wail, pulling free again. "Oh, Antonio—Anthony— you wouldn't say any of it if you knew more of me!"

"What do I care for the words of others?" he said, reaching for her again. "Come, *cara,* don't let—"

"It's a man," she interrupted. "A—another man."

His hand froze in midair, his confusion clear. "Warwick?"

She shook her head. He'd told her she must remember this night, and at least this way she'd always have the beautiful, untainted memory of how once he'd loved her, and she'd loved him.

"No," she said miserably. "It's no one you'd ever know, or meet, but he—he has a power over me that I can't explain."

"Try," he said. "Please, *cara*. Give me that chance."

But she could only shake her head again and back away, hugging her arms around her chest.

"I can't," she whispered. "I'm too much the coward to see your face if you heard the truth. I don't deserve your love, Antonio, and I don't deserve you."

And before he could stop her, before she lost her resolve and changed her mind, she turned, and fled away from him and back to Miss Wood.

Chapter Ten

Anthony sat in the shadows of the café's awning, the coffee before him untouched, the paper unread, and gazed across the Piazza di Spagna to Diana's lodgings. He knew which windows were to rooms she shared with her governess, and which window belonged to her bedchamber.

Even if he hadn't first spotted her on that little iron balcony, the house's cheerful chambermaid had been delighted to offer that information, and more: how the English young lady liked cocoa with cream, but never tea; how her lady's maid insisted on ironing her ladyship's linens herself, as if she feared Roman hands were too rough for her lady's tender skin; how the English lady and the English gentleman seemed to be forming an attachment, encouraged by the governess and the uncle, and how in her opinion the lady would be tossing herself away if she accepted the hand of that pudgy, unpleasant English gentleman.

Anthony smiled wryly, remembering the girl's indignation on behalf of the English young lady. He could hardly scorn Warwick now, considering how he'd made no more progress with Diana himself. He couldn't begin to fathom why, either.

He knew she liked him, and most likely loved him. He knew she'd been so eager for seduction, she'd practically tossed herself on the bed with the golden stags. He was experienced with women, a man of the world, and he knew the signs of a willing lady as surely as a sailor might scan the sky and seas for signs of a coming storm.

But this time, with Diana, he'd been doubly sure, because he himself had wanted so badly to be so. The wager had ceased to count. The lady herself was all that mattered. He couldn't remember enjoying anyone's company as much as he did hers, whether it was discussing that grand old painting of Cleopatra, or sensing her trust in him as he held her in his arms. Her laughter, her kiss, her quick wit, even the way she'd gasped when she'd first seen the little bedchamber he'd had prepared for them—no, there was no other woman like her, and none that he'd cared more for.

For the truth was he'd fallen in love. Deeply, passionately, inexplicably. This was entirely new to him; he'd never felt this way before, and it was…unsettling. Pleasurable, blissful, delightful, yes, but he'd been completely unprepared for the depth of the feelings he had for her. All the other times he'd fancied himself in love were nothing compared to this.

He'd laughed when Mama had predicted that one day he'd feel like this, lost beyond reason over a woman. He'd laughed and scoffed, too, when she'd warned him that love was no sport or game, but a most serious business, perhaps the most serious of all. Now, with Diana, he finally understood, and while he knew that Mama would be delighted to say she'd told him so, he sadly wished she still lived so she might explain why, with so much love between them, Diana was insisting that there was none.

He continued gazing up at her window, wryly considering

how foolish he must appear as he prayed for even a glimpse of her. Why did she think he'd care if there'd been another man before him in her life? Considering how ravishing she was, he'd have been more surprised if there'd been none. He cared only that he was the one in her heart now, and there he was determined to remain—if only she'd give him the opportunity to tell her.

Surely by now she must have received the flowers he'd sent. Damnation, he'd been sitting here for at least a quarter of an hour. By this time, even the most desultory of Roman servants would have carried them up the stairs to her rooms.

Had she taken the bouquet in her hands, cradling it beneath her face so she could breathe the flowers' fragrance? Had she closed her eyes to concentrate on the scent? The flowers he'd chosen had once again come from Mama's garden, the last of the summer's roses combined with laurel, her favorites and his, as well. He prayed they'd find the same favor now with Diana.

Had she found the card he'd tucked into the ribbon? Had she read the message—Forgive me whatever sin I have committed against you, the one I hold most dear—considered it, accepted his apology? If he went to the door and asked for her, would she come to his arms? Better yet, would that simple message from his heart be enough to make her forget whatever had stopped her last night, and instead bring her to search for him?

It was laughable, even shameful, for a Randolph to be waiting like this, on the whim of a lady. But once again his Prosperi blood overruled his English, for a Prosperi knew that true passion, true love, was worth the world. One true love will give joy for life, Mama had promised, and he'd seen it so with her. Now, with Diana, he hoped to claim his own share.

And so he would wait.

* * *

"What lovely flowers!" Miss Wood exclaimed as the maid handed the bouquet to Diana. "Did you happen to remark whose servant brought them, Anna?"

"The man wore the livery of Lord Anthony Randolph, signorina," the girl said with a dipping curtsey. "Green with silver lace. Everyone in Rome knows it."

"Lord Anthony sent these flowers?" Diana froze, holding the flowers out in her arms as if they'd just turned into a bouquet of writhing serpents. Of course he'd sent them: who else would, really?

"Surely there's a card or note, my lady," Miss Wood said, coming to peek among the red roses and laurel leaves in the bouquet. She smiled brightly at Edward and his uncle, still sitting at the table where they'd all shared their midday meal. "Lord Anthony was quite taken with her ladyship last night at his palazzo, personally showing her the finest paintings in his galleries. I'm not surprised he's sent this token to her today."

Reverend Lord Patterson snorted with disgust, refolding his napkin. "That man's a rascal and a rogue, Miss Wood, and not a fellow to be encouraged where a lady is concerned. How he can claim to be an English gentleman is beyond cognition. One look at him, and you know he's not one of us. I'm surprised you even accepted his invitation."

"We wouldn't have," Edward said, pushing his chair back from the table. "Even if we'd been invited. Randolph keeps the lowest company in Rome, disreputable women and mountebanks. Hardly suitable for ladies."

"I'm surprised, my lords," Miss Wood said defensively. "Our company last night was the most agreeable I could imagine to be gathered together in Rome, with Sir Thomas as our shared host. And the Palazzo di Prosperi is the most magnificent private palace I've ever seen."

"Gaudy, overwrought excess in the Vatican style." Reverend Lord Patterson sniffed with disdain. "I'll take the honest, honorable ancient manner over that gilded rubbish any day."

"Is Lord Anthony's servant below?" asked Diana, the flowers still in her outstretched hands. How could they babble on and on about architecture when her heart was breaking here in the same room?

"Yes, my lady," said the maid. "He said he was told to wait for a reply."

"Then return these to him, and to his master." She shoved the bouquet back into the maid's hands so forcefully that stray petals scattered to the carpet. "Pray tell him that I've no further use for either his lordship, or his flowers."

"My lady!" exclaimed Miss Wood, shocked. "Those are harsh words from you, very harsh indeed!"

"Considering that I've no wish to see Lord Anthony ever again, I feel my original words were sufficient." Overwhelmed with frustration, Diana rose, swiftly shaking the stray petals from her skirts. "Return the flowers to his lordship's servant directly, Anna."

"*Brava,* my lady, well spoken!" Edward applauded with approval. "Serve the foreign rascal as he deserves!"

Diana wheeled around to face him. "Lord Anthony is neither foreign nor a rascal, Lord Edward, and I'll thank you not to display your shameful ignorance of his character in my hearing."

Edward flushed. "I ask your pardon, my lady, but I only desired to compliment your great judgment, your wisdom, your—"

"Excuse me, Lord Edward, Reverend Lord Patterson, but

I am weary, and wish to retire to rest," she said tartly. "Good day to you both."

"An afternoon rest is an excellent idea in this climate, my lady," Edward said with hollow heartiness. "I'm sure you'll feel much restored afterwards."

His uncle nodded. "That's true, my lady. You'll wish to be rested for our tour of the Catacombs tomorrow."

But Diana was already through the passage to her bed-chamber, and in another few steps she'd slammed the door between them and thrown herself face-first across her bed.

Why had Anthony sent her flowers? He'd no reason to make peace with her, or to woo her afresh. Why didn't he *understand* what she'd tried so hard to explain last night, that there was no place for him in her life?

"My lady?" Miss Wood called softly, coming to stand beside her bed. "My lady, has something affected you? Did something happen last night that you'd like to—"

"Nothing's wrong," Diana said into her pillow, without turning her face. "Everything is perfectly fine."

"If I spoke too freely about Lord Anthony's attentions to you, my lady, then I—"

"Don't apologize," Diana said, her words muffled. "There's no reason."

Diana felt the mattress sink as Miss Wood sat on the edge, and leaned closer to lay a comforting hand on Diana's shoulder. "I suspect there is, my lady," she said, "though I've no right to ask you to confess it."

Diana didn't answer, not knowing where to begin or end. And how could she explain to Miss Wood what she hadn't been able to explain to Anthony?

"You shouldn't take offense at poor Lord Edward," Miss Wood said. "I'm sure he looks at Lord Anthony and that lovely palazzo of his and worries that you'll favor this newcomer over him, and the only way he can address his fear is to ridicule Lord Anthony. You know how gentlemen can be with one another. Like little boys, they are."

Edward *was* like a little boy, a mean-spirited, disagreeable little boy, while Anthony—Anthony was a man, and a gentleman, too.

And now he was also the man that she loved, but who could never love her in return.

"If you wish to tell me anything, my lady," the governess continued gently, "then I'm here to listen. I know that your sister Lady Mary felt she couldn't confide in me about Lord John, but I wish she had. I do. So I pray you'll tell me if there's anything amiss that I might help with between you and Lord Anthony, or Lord Edward or—or whatever it may be."

Whatever it might be: did that include Will Carney? For one tempting moment, Diana considered telling Miss Wood about Will's threats. She could be like a small girl again, running to her governess with a scraped knee that needed bandaging and easing with a kiss or a sweet biscuit. But Will Carney was no childhood mishap. Miss Wood would insist on taking his threats to the local magistrate or whatever the authorities were called here. There were no secrets in Rome—she'd already learned that—and before long Anthony would know all the sordid details of her shame, and that—that she could not bear.

"A trouble shared is a trouble halved, my lady," Miss Wood continued. "Know that when you're ready, I am here."

She gave Diana's shoulder a final pat and rose. "I'll be resting now, too, my lady, but please come wake me if you wish to talk."

Again Diana didn't answer. She listened to the governess's

footsteps leave the room, the door closing after her. Edward and his uncle must have already returned to their quarters, for all she could hear from their parlor was the clinking of plates and empty glasses as Anna cleared away the last pieces from the table. Then she, too, left, and their rooms were quiet.

Diana waited another few moments to be sure she'd not be seen, then wearily pushed herself from the bed. She gathered her gloves, her hat and her parasol. From beneath her bed she retrieved the small bundle of jewelry, tied together in a handkerchief. There was nothing of much value—the settings were mostly pinchbeck, the stones garnets instead of rubies, or merely paste—but she prayed Will wouldn't realize the difference. He'd have to accept what she brought; she'd nothing more to offer until she returned to England, and her more valuable jewels.

A half an hour later, she was standing beside the Fontana di Trevi. She kept the wide brim of her hat pulled low against the sun, but she'd cleared her veil free from her face as she anxiously scanned the crowd around the fountain for Will. She knew her blond hair and fair skin made her stand out among the other women, though she paid no heed to the admiring comments that she garnered from passing men.

Where was Will? She'd come exactly at the time and place he'd chosen. Surely he must realize how difficult it was to get away, how she couldn't linger here all day.

Spray from the fountains blew around her, dappling her skirts. The sad bundled weight of her pinchbeck jewels sat in her pocket as heavily as her conscience. The clock in a nearby church chimed the quarter-hour, then the half, and still Will hadn't come. She took the tiny watch from her pocket to be certain: one-forty, creeping towards two. She couldn't linger much longer, not at the risk of having Miss Wood wake and discover she was gone.

What if Will had somehow found out she hadn't the money he'd asked? What if he'd decided not to trust her further, and spread his ugly stories anyway? What if he'd gone to the news sheets, or to Sir Thomas, or worst of all, to Anthony?

At one forty-five, she began to walk back towards the hired carriage. Slowly she climbed into the carriage, and sat in the seat for another quarter hour, her back aching from tension. If Will were here, he'd have found her by now.

At last the driver turned on his seat and touched the brim of his hat. "Signorina?"

It was nearly two. She had no choice but to leave.

"Go," she said softly. "Just…just go."

Edward leaned closer to the cab's window, watching. This was better than any play, better, really, than anything.

Lady Diana Farren was so deucedly headstrong that he'd half expected her not to come to the fountain today, no matter how frightened she'd been two days ago when Carney had threatened her. But fear had overruled her shrewishness, and here she was. Served her right, too. He'd never seen her look so uneasy, her mouth tight, her shoulders hunched, her hands restlessly twisting some small bundle back and forth in her fingers.

Was that the blackmailer's reward, he wondered. Had she somehow managed to gather the gold that Carney had demanded? For all her fussing yesterday, the sum was likely pin money to her, less than she spent on stockings and ribbons. Rich girls were like that. Such a fortune was wasted on her, of course. No woman could ever make proper use of money. But as soon as Edward could make her his wife, then all that lovely fortune would be his to control.

He frowned a bit, remembering how quickly she'd jumped to Randolph's defense earlier. He hadn't expected that, nor had he thought of Randolph as his rival for Diana. But then all women, whether lady or whore, seemed to flock to that kind of glib, oily charm that Randolph offered, and the man's wealth was reputed to be so vast that even the Duke of Aston might be willing to overlook his foreignness if he asked for Diana first. Edward himself had had a good English mother, true, but he'd never be able to offer anything like that blasted palazzo. Of course, Edward had never been invited to it, but he'd heard enough—more than enough.

But there were other ways to compete. Edward was sure he'd stumbled across the best, and he smiled with anticipation as his gaze followed Diana pacing along the side of the fountain. It was good for him that she was so obviously frightened, her anxiety growing visibly the longer she waited for the man who'd never come. She needed a savior more than she needed a rich foreign bastard.

She needed to be rescued, and tomorrow, when their little party visited the Catacombs, Edward meant to do exactly that. He would make her see him as her salvation, her hero and then, finally, inevitably, her husband.

And when he was done, Randolph wouldn't have a chance.

"Of all the great monuments we have viewed here in Rome, I must say I anticipated this one the most." Miss Wood nodded, as if to reaffirm her enthusiasm. Miss Wood had been talking about the Catacombs ever since they'd left France, and for her they seemed to be the one thing in Rome she most wished to see. "The legendary Catacombs of San Sebastiano! Surely, Reverend Lord Patterson, there must be no more sacred place for Christians in all of Italy."

"Oh, I agree, Miss Wood," said Edward's uncle, his voice as solemn as his own pulpit. "To me, the Catacombs are the purest example of faith maintained under duress and persecution. To be sure, there is nothing to compare to St. Peter's basilica for sheer magnificence and the glorification of Heaven, but there is a sense of true humility of Christianity to be found in the Catacombs that makes the more modern Papal extravagance literally pale in comparison."

Diana listened, saying nothing, as she stared without seeing from the carriage window. She had scarcely slept these last two nights. Her heart was sick over Anthony, and her nerves were on edge from worrying about when and how Will Carney might reappear. What if they'd misunderstood one another about the date? What if he went to the Fontana di Trevi today, instead of yesterday? She'd have no opportunity to slip away this afternoon, not with this wretched tour of the Catacombs consuming their entire day.

"Are you afraid of ghosts, my lady?" Sitting across from her, Edward grinned ghoulishly at her. "They say the Catacombs are full of them, with both Christian and pagan spirits all crowded cheek to jowl."

"Nonsense, Edward," scolded his uncle. "Don't try to frighten the ladies. Viewing the Catacombs is not an easy tour, I'll grant you, but if you jump and balk at every stray shadow as a phantasm, then the edification of the experience will be lost."

"That is quite true," Miss Wood agreed vigorously. "Good Christians have no need to fear the dead."

But Diana was not so sure. Even she knew that the Catacombs were an ancient, sacred burial ground—or rather, underground—with untold numbers of bodies buried in a network of deep, winding tunnels. Diana didn't care if the graves belonged to Christians or pagans; she still wasn't sure whether she wished to go traipsing about among them.

Her misgivings increased as their carriage drew up before the church of San Sebastiano that served as the entrance to the Catacombs. The church was small, plain and tired, more like the classical ruins of the ancient empire than the newer, more exuberant churches in the center of the city.

"We sent ahead for a guide to meet us," Reverend Lord Patterson said as he helped Diana and Miss Wood climb down. "Don't know where the fellow is, though. Hold now, this must be him. *Buongiorno, guida, eh?*"

The old man put aside the broom with which he'd been sweeping the steps and came shuffling towards them. He was as sorry as the church he served: his back was bent, his long coat dusty and tattered, his breeches sagging around his spindly legs. He didn't try to answer Reverend Lord Patterson's attempts at Italian, but simply touched his forehead in respect, and motioned for them to follow him through the church and down a single flight of stairs to a low-ceilinged crypt, lined with stone sarcophagi and faded murals.

"This is not our destination, is it?" asked Miss Wood, clearly disappointed.

"Hardly, hardly," Reverend Lord Patterson said, pointing up at one of the sarcophagi with his walking stick. "These once held the bodies of the first popes, but they've been long removed and taken elsewhere. This space is only the entry to what lies below."

The guide stood at the top of another staircase, carefully lighting small wax candles in tin holders.

"*Bougie,*" he explained as he handed one to each of them. "Against the dark."

To Diana the wobbling little flames offered precious small comfort against the dark as they followed the guide down the steps.

"We'll watch for the ghosts together," whispered Edward as he took her arm without asking. "I'll protect you, my lady, whether they're imagined or real."

"I trust I won't need protecting, my lord," Diana said, pointedly slipping her arm free of his hand. But her uneasiness kept her close to him; though Edward hadn't Anthony's sheer physical confidence, she guessed he was sizeable enough to scare away any stray ghosts.

This staircase was much narrower than the previous one, winding down deeper and deeper into the earth. Over the centuries, the feet of countless pilgrims had worn a dipping hollow into each of the steps, and to Diana the hollows felt as if the steps were sucking at her shoes, drawing her down whether she wished to go or not. To distract herself, she tried counting each step as they descended, but by the time she reached two hundred, she stopped, not wanting to know exactly how far they'd come from the ground's warm sunshine and fresh air.

At last they reached the bottom of the stairs, with only packed earth beneath their feet. The guide paused, his withered face lit strangely by the flickering bougie in his hand.

"Mansions of the dead, signore e signori," he intoned in obviously rehearsed English. "Each grave in these walls holds one, two, three dead. Noble, poor, babies and warriors and martyrs, Christian and not. Many, many, many dead, *sì?*"

He held his candle up so they could see the first carved markers set into the wall like headstones in a churchyard. He shifted the candle before him, the faint light illuminating the next bit of the way to lead them. The floor slanted downward, a decline that gradually led them further into the earth, and the first passageway divided into several more, like branches on a tree. The guide confidently chose the farthest way, to the left, and they all followed dutifully, unwilling to risk remaining behind.

"Mark the flames," Edward said with surprise. "They're burning blue!"

"The damp, signore," explained the guide. "The water in the earth—it turns the fire blue, *sì?*"

"Of course," murmured Miss Wood, her round face ghoulish by the blue-tinged flame as she turned the guide's words into an impromptu schoolroom lesson. "The moisture in the damp soil would change the quality of the air, and therefore the color of the flame. Fascinating!"

But Diana wasn't so much fascinated as oppressed. So far underground, the air was fetid and heavy. As they walked, the passages narrowed further, until they were only wide enough for a single person. She and Miss Wood had been warned about the cramped tunnels, and had covered their hair with loose scarves today instead of their usual broad-brimmed hats, but Diana was still surprised by the ceiling overhead, so low that the two men had to bend so as not to strike their heads.

Cobwebs plucked and snagged at Diana's skirts, and she could hear the faint scurrying and scrabbling of tiny creatures and insects that must live here underground. Adding to that was the grim awareness that they were surrounded by hundreds—thousands!—of long-dead Romans, stacked away in these flattened niches on either side of her like so many turnips in a root cellar. Little wonder, then, that she felt so closed in and anxious, clutching her candle so tightly that her fingers hurt.

But Miss Wood seemed to have no such uneasiness, pausing to run her gloved fingertips over the nearest inscription.

"See this, my lady," she said eagerly, making Diana stop, too, as she traced the outlines of the letters with the cross beneath. "*'Iulia Filia Pacis.'* Now I know we've never studied Latin together, but that means Julia, daughter of peace. Think of that, my lady! Julia lies directly behind this stone."

But Diana didn't want to think of the dead Julia lying inches away from her face. She didn't want to keep standing here, either, and she began to hurry away.

"Stop, *signorina,* please, please!" The guide caught her arm, tugging her back. "You will be lost! All must stay together or perish!"

"That's true, my lady," Reverend Lord Patterson cautioned. "These passages are like the worst kind of country roads, wandering every which way for miles. Anyone who sets off without experienced knowledge of the way is likely never to be found again. Is it true, *guida,* that there are no other exits to the ground than the one by which we entered?"

"There are others, *sì,*" the guide admitted darkly. "But with much hazard. Only for those who know the way. Not for you, *signore.*"

"I wouldn't dream of it, *guida!*" Reverend Lord Patterson laughed heartily, and patted Diana on the shoulder. "But you see how careful we must be, my lady. I'd hate to have to tell his grace your father that we mislaid you beneath the city of Rome."

"I'll watch over her, Uncle," Edward said gallantly. "We can't afford to lose the lady, can we?"

"Thank you," she said stiffly, but this time when Edward took her hand, she let him keep it. She didn't particularly want to be lost, either, and she could think of few worse ways to perish than dying alone, in one of these dark, dank, frightening passages.

Not that Miss Wood seemed to worry. "Could you please take us to the section dedicated to the Christian martyrs, *guida?*" she asked the old man. "That's the part of the Catacombs I wish most particularly to see."

"As you wish, *signorina*." The guide touched his forehead again, and began to lead them deeper into the passages, following so many twists and turns through the murky shadows that Diana could not have found her way back even if she'd dared to.

At last they stopped before an iron gate, flaked with rust, that protected a kind of antechamber off the main passages. The guide pushed the gate open, holding his candle high.

"There are the first graves of the martyrs you seek, *signorina*," he said. "They are marked MR."

"Gracious!" Miss Wood studied the inscriptions with the same fervor that Diana herself used before the windows of a milliner's shop. "Why, there must be at least twenty martyrs in this room alone!"

"There are many more," said the guide. "Many, many, many more, *signorina*."

"Some guess as many as fifty thousand, Miss Wood," Reverend Lord Patterson said, his interest equal to Miss Wood's. "Early Christians were forced to pay dearly for their faith."

Miss Wood's eyes glowed in the blue flame. "We are fortunate to live in the age in which we do, when martyrdom is not a risk for true believers."

Although the guide was clearly bored, he dutifully held his candle close to another grave, decorated with elaborate illustrations.

"Here are the celebrated signs, signore, signorina," he said. "The lamb and the cross. The Christian at prayer. Another cross and a crucified martyr."

"Oh, these are very fine!" exclaimed Miss Wood with delight. "How vastly moving! Are these the best, then, *guida?* Are there any more to view?"

Diana fervently hoped there'd be no more, but the sad-eyed guide nodded, and held his candle towards yet another long hall. "This way, signorina. Many, many more. Most remarkable."

"You go with Miss Wood, Uncle," Edward said. "I believe Lady Diana and I have seen enough. We shall wait here for your return."

His uncle frowned. "I must trust you not to venture from this spot, Edward."

"We won't," Diana said swiftly. She'd no real wish to join them, but she was reluctant to lose their company just the same, and the light from their three little candles, too. "I give you my word. Just—just do not delay."

"We'll not be long, my lady," Miss Wood assured her, and then with an almost cheerful air she and Edward's uncle followed the *guida* down another passage. Diana looked after them, shocked by how swiftly the dark and damp walls swallowed up not only their candles' lights, but their voices as well. Everything had the same silence as the graves around them.

"I'm glad you chose to stay with me, Diana," Edward said, raising his candle to light her face. "I'd almost come to think you no longer cared for me."

"What I didn't care for was going any deeper into the ground," she admitted. "Even if it's only a hundred more paces, this is far enough."

She knew she hadn't answered his real question, and he knew it, too, his smile freezing oddly on his face.

"Well, yes," he said, and turned away from her to stare at the drawings on the wall behind them. "They should be back with us soon enough."

"I should guess so." She could think of nothing more to say, and so concentrated on jabbing her thumbnail into the soft half-melted wax on the side of the candle, making a pattern of interlocking half-moons. At least it was better than figuring out the names of people who'd been martyred in some horrifying way a thousand years before.

She sighed, still looking down at the wax. "I wonder why Miss Wood finds all these dead bodies so fascinating. Maybe she amuses herself by imagining how she'd martyr *me* for vexing her, if she had the chance. Hah, maybe your uncle's thinking the same thing about you, Edward!"

But to her surprise, Edward didn't say anything in return, which wasn't like him at all.

Swiftly she looked up, and, to her horror, realized she was alone in the antechamber.

"Edward?" she called, hurrying from the antechamber to the passage. "Edward, please don't jest with me, not now. Edward? *Edward!*"

But the same blackness that had enveloped the other three now appeared to have claimed Edward, too. As hard as she stared into the dark, she saw no light, no movement, her very shouts muted and dulled.

"Edward!" she cried again, her heart pounding wildly as she gripped her candle. She knew she must not panic, or run about, or worst of all, risk dousing her candle's tiny flame. She must stay here, the place where the others had left her, or risk being lost forever in the labyrinth of underground passages.

But where could Edward have gone? How could he have abandoned her like this, when he knew how much she hated the dark, hated the—

The man grabbed her from behind, pinning her arms beneath his own and knocking the candle from her hand. She shrieked, fighting to free herself as the candle rolled across the floor, the flame sparking, fluttering, and finally guttering out, leaving her to struggle in the blackest dark she'd ever known.

"Let—let me go!" she cried with terror, twisting about in the man's grasp "Let me go at—at once!"

"Why should I, you damned whore?" The man was breathing hard and his voice was muffled, as if he'd tied a scarf over his mouth, but she recognized the accent and the ugly words.

"Will!" she gasped. "Will Carney, for all heaven, let—let me *go!*"

But instead he jerked her arms behind her back and shoved her hard against the wall. She cried out again, shaking with fear and pain and hatred, too, of the man who'd dare treat her like this. With all her strength, she tried to break free, but he only pushed her more closely to the wall, his breath hot upon the bare nape of her neck.

Then as suddenly as he'd trapped her, Will was gone, torn away by another man—Edward? His uncle?—in the dark. Off balance, she stumbled backwards and fell to her hands and knees. Gasping for breath, she heard the men fighting behind her, the sounds of grunting and fists striking flesh and then a muted thud and a groan, with only one man's ragged breathing left.

But which man was it? Was it Will, or her unknown rescuer? If it were Edward, why didn't he speak to her, say something, anything to reassure her? Instinct told her to keep silent, and she scuttled across the damp stone floor until she reached a wall. She pressed herself into as tight and inconspicuous a ball as she could, and held her breath, and prayed the beating of her own heart wouldn't betray her.

Darkness sharpened her hearing. She heard a metallic scrape and a muted fumbling, the *click-click* of a flint and striker. A brief flash of spark to tinder, a lighted wick that glowed brighter for being the sole beacon in so much black. The candle's circle of light dipped lower, the glow finding the man sprawled on the ground: Edward, poor, foolish Edward, his fair hair tangled over his forehead and a rivulet of blood trickling from his nose to his jaw.

Horrified, she gasped, then quickly tried to cover her own traitorous mouth. But too late: the other man had heard her, and he raised the candle towards her, making her unaccustomed eyes blink and turn away from the brightness.

"*Cara,*" Anthony said softly. "Oh, my own love, what has he done to you?"

Chapter Eleven

Diana was huddled beside the wall, her skirts dirty and torn, her hair tangled and dusted with cobwebs and her eyes wide with terror. Anthony had never seen her like this, and if he'd anything to do with it, he never would again.

"Diana," he said, coaxing, not wanting to frighten her any further. "You're safe now, sweetheart. He can't hurt you any more."

She shook her head, quick little jerks. "It—it wasn't Edward," she whispered, her voice breaking. "It—it was Will, Will Carney."

"Will Carney?" Who the devil was Will Carney? Had she been so traumatized that she was imagining things? Or was there some other man lurking out there in the darkness? He'd thought there'd been only two of them in the Catacombs just now, and one of them was definitely Warwick. "Diana, *cara,* I don't—"

"He *was* here!" she cried frantically. "It was Will Carney who grabbed me and pushed me against the wall and told me—he told me—"

Her eyes filled with tears, shining in the candlelight. She

bowed her head and she covered her mouth with her hands, unable to go on.

That was enough for Anthony, too. Quickly he wedged the candle into a crack in the marble slab, and gathered her up into his arms, holding her as tightly as he could. It didn't matter who this Will Carney might be, or why she'd believe he was the one who'd attacked her, not Edward. They'd sort that out later. All he cared for now was that she was safe, and with him.

"*Carissima,*" he said in a rough whisper, holding her tightly. If only he'd followed them a little more closely, and spared her this suffering! "He can't hurt you any longer. You're here with me now."

She pushed back against his chest so she could see his face. "But why are *you* here, Anthony?" she asked, her cheeks smudged with dirt and tears. "How did you come to be here in this awful place?"

"I'd a sense you'd need me," he said truthfully. He couldn't explain it any more clearly than that. He'd long ago learned to trust his intuition; his old nursemaid had told him he'd a gift for it, but he wasn't superstitious enough to go that far. "When the servant from your lodgings returned the flowers to me, she told me you were visiting the Catacombs today. That was enough to make me decide to follow you from afar."

"But how did you find us? The *guida* said—"

"Every Roman boy is warned not to play in the Catacombs," Anthony said, "just as every Roman boy worth his salt will do exactly that. There're many ways to come and go through the hillside, if only you know them."

For the first time she smiled through her tears, a tremulous, uncertain smile, yet the loveliest he'd ever seen. "Only you did."

"Only so," he agreed. "I thought you might need me."

"I did," she said, a fresh shiver of fear running through her. "I can't begin to thank you enough."

"I did it for you, not for thanks." At their feet, Warwick groaned and began to stir. "Come, we must leave before he wakes."

"We can't," she protested. "We shouldn't, not after he was hurt trying to save me!"

"Maybe he was, and maybe he wasn't," Anthony said cynically, lighting a second candle from the one in the wall. "The truth is that you're not safe here, and I'm taking you someplace where I know you'll be out of harm's way."

"But what will Miss Wood think if I'm gone?"

"We'll leave that to Warwick to explain." He took her by the hand to lead her away. "I'll send word that you're safe through Sir Thomas as soon as we're above ground."

She glanced down at Warwick for only a moment, her eyes now more full of resolution than fear.

"I'll trust you, Anthony, because I love you," she said, the simple words taking away all the sting of the flowers she'd sent back and the evening she'd cut short. "Because I love you, I'll come."

"And I love you, too." He smiled crookedly, thinking of what a damned unlovely place it was to say such a thing. "Now hurry. I don't want to stay here a moment longer than we must."

Edward had never been more contented in his life. It was a warm and sunny day, an English spring if ever there was one, and all the sweeter still because he was lying with his head in the lap of his beautiful wife Diana, Lady Edward. She was running her fingers through his hair in that dear way that ladies had, and smiling with agreement to every question he asked her.

"Your father's put all your money in my name?" he murmured. "You're sure of that, my dear?"

"Oh, yes, Edward darling," she said, leaning forward so he had an excellent view of her bosom. "He trusts you above all others with money."

"He should." Edward sighed with contentment. "I always try to do my best for my dearest Diana."

"Look, reverend my lord, he's waking at last!" the woman exclaimed. "Oh, thank the heavens, he's going to live!"

"Ehh?" Edward forced his eyes open, squinting at the faces leaning over him. It wasn't his beautiful Diana, but her annoying little governess, and beside her round moon of a face was his uncle's, both peering down at him as though he were some odious insect on the pavement. "Where's Diana?"

The two exchanged concerned glances, while the tattered *guida* listened with open interest, and lit a fresh candle.

"Oh, dear," Miss Wood said finally. "My poor, dear Lord Edward, we were rather hoping you could tell us that."

"The lady's gone, Edward," his uncle said bluntly. "We trusted her to your care while we stepped down the way, and when we came back, you were here flat on your back and Lady Diana's nowhere to be found. Even a mongrel dog knows enough to heed an order to stay."

"Hush, hush, reverend my lord, not so sharply." The little governess slipped her hand beneath his head, and he realized sadly she must have been the one toying with his hair before, and not the Diana in his pleasant dream. "Can you recall anything, my lord? Were you and her ladyship attacked?"

His uncle snorted. "More likely she cuffed him for being too forward."

"Hush, I beg you!" scolded the governess, turning back to

Edward. "Think hard now, my lord. Her ladyship's very life may depend upon your answer."

Oh, he was thinking hard, all right, as hard and as fast as his pitiful thumped head could. He remembered planning to pretend to be Will Carney so he could then "rescue" Diana. He remembered that the plan had worked, too, with her weeping and begging for mercy from old Will. He'd been almost ready to step in and save her from himself—or rather, from the pretend Will—when his memory became a mite hazy. There wasn't supposed to be anyone else in the dark with them, but there had been, some enormous beast of a fellow, with flailing fists and a wicked temper.

But what *had* become of Diana? Had the flailing beast carried her away, or had she gone with him willingly? Didn't the bitch realize she was supposed to stay here with him, the man she was going to marry?

Oh, how his head ached!

"Damn it, Edward, think, *think!*" his uncle said crossly. "What happened here? What has become of her ladyship?"

Slowly Edward sat upright. He sneezed once, spraying blood down the front of his shirt, and fumbled for his handkerchief.

"It's not easy to tell, Uncle," he began, blotting at his nose and hoping his efforts to concoct a self-serving story would appear as mere confusion from the blow he'd taken. At least he had Will Carney's name to haul out again; that would make the whole tale credible to Miss Wood. "We were waiting here for you, just as we were supposed to, when a great savage ruffian appeared from the shadows. I tried to stop him, but he struck me down."

Miss Wood gasped with horror and clasped her hands together, but his uncle was less impressed.

"So where did this great slobbering fellow come from,

Edward?" he demanded impatiently. "You heard the *guida* himself say there's only one way in and one way out of these tunnels for most visitors, and we saw no sign of anyone else. And where in blazes is Lady Diana?"

"Most likely she went with him, Uncle," Will said. "To my amazement, she seemed to know the man, calling him by name. Carney, it was. Will Carney. Does that name mean anything to you, Miss Wood?"

From the shock on the governess's face, Edward was certain that name meant even more than he'd realized. "Will Carney here? In Rome? Oh, I can't fathom it! A large young man with fair hair?"

Will nodded, wincing at the very real pain. "I didn't get much of a look at him, Miss Wood, on account of the dark, but that would seem to be the same man."

"Will Carney here!" Distraught, Miss Wood sat back on her heels. "And with my lady! They must have been in correspondence all this time, yet I never learned of it!"

His uncle frowned. "Is there a—ah—history between her ladyship and this man?"

"A sad, sorry history, yes," Miss Wood said wearily. "I thought her ladyship had left that man behind in her past. I truly thought she had. Oh, Lord Edward, I'm so very sorry that you risked your life in the name of her foolishness!"

"I did it for her, Miss Wood," Edward said gallantly, but hung his head with what he hoped would appear properly dashed dreams. "For the dear lady."

"Buck up, the battle's not lost yet." His uncle gave him his hand to pull him to his feet. "We'll take you home and clean you up, and decide how best to retrieve your lost lady love."

"Yes, we shall." Wearily Miss Wood rose, too. "And pray that we find her ladyship before I must write such grievous news to his grace her father."

Diana had no idea of where they were headed, nor did she care. It was as if once she'd decided to trust Anthony to take her from the Catacombs, she was free to trust him in everything else as well, living minute by minute with no thought for the future beyond that, and if this was love, why, then it was the most glorious thing she'd ever experienced.

Instead of the closed carriage with liveried footmen and driver that she'd expected a nobleman like him to keep, he'd surprised—and delighted—her with a small, smart curricle painted a bright yellow. Red ribbons and tiny silver bells were woven into the matched blacks' manes, and the two large wheels were picked out in red as well. With his hat shoved down on his head to keep it from blowing off, Anthony took the whip and the reins himself, and drove them racing through the city streets. The fleet curricle was as recognizable as its driver, and it seemed to Diana that on every street corner, others shouted and waved to him, while he saluted them in return with the ribbon-trimmed whip.

She clung to his arm to steady herself, and because she didn't want to let him go. He didn't say much, and neither did she. After she'd been attacked amidst the death and smothering darkness of the Catacombs, the sun was almost blindingly bright, the sky overhead the most brilliant of blues and the summer breeze that drifted over the hills the sweetest air imaginable. The sun sparkled on the river and on the water that splashed from every fountain they passed, and white gulls danced and dived overhead.

Beside Anthony, Diana tipped back her head to watch and

laughed with pure joy, letting the sound stream behind her. Because of him, she was still alive, and each of these small pleasures had become a thousand times richer.

"Aren't you curious about our destination, *cara?*" he asked as they slowed to cross the crowded bridge over the river.

"Not really," she admitted, shoving a loose strand of her hair back from her face. Miss Wood would have seventeen fits about her not wearing a hat and letting the sun find her face, but the exhilaration she felt was well worth the unladylike pink cheeks. "All I know is that I'm above ground, and I'm with you."

He laughed. "How very flattering to be equated with the Catacombs."

"You know perfectly well that's not what I meant!" She swatted his arm, and he laughed again. "It's just that when I think of what might have—what almost—"

"Don't think of it at all," he said gently. "Better to look ahead than behind."

She sighed, her shoulders hunched. "Then perhaps you should tell me where we're going. We've gone the opposite way from your palazzo, haven't we?"

"We have," he said. "Because we're not going there. We're going to my villa. You'll be safer there than anywhere else."

"We haven't visited any villas yet," she said, seizing on the distraction. He was right, it was better to think of good things than bad. "I know we've letters of introduction to some of the families who own them, but the only things we've seen in Rome have been tumbledown ruins, because that's what Miss Wood likes best."

"Villa Prosperi is many things, but it's not tumbledown, and it's not ancient, either," he said. "The main house was begun only two hundred years ago or so, though each generation has added their mark to the house or the gardens, particularly with the *casini.*"

"Casini?"

"Little rooms," he translated. "All of ours are made to look like small, open-sided temples, and used in every way imaginable. My brothers and I turned the *casini* into forts to be captured, while my mother liked them for suppers in the summer when the main house was too hot, and Father always took his friends to his favorite to smoke their pipes in peace. You can't walk through any villa's gardens without practically tripping over *casini.* I know you English aren't given to such pleasurable informality, but I suppose the closest things you have to *casini* are your follies."

"'You English,'" she repeated, teasing him. "You're English, too."

He winked at her. "Not the best part of me."

"All of me is English," she said, "whether you like it or not."

"I like it, Diana," he said, his voice dropping lower, "all of it, because I love you."

She flushed, and shyly bowed her head. When she'd told him that she loved him earlier, in the Catacombs, she'd meant it with all her heart, but she hadn't been sure if he'd felt the same. Men were different that way. She'd learned to her sorrow that men too often said what women wished to hear, not what they actually believed. They didn't speak from their hearts, the way women did; they spoke from a far less discerning part of their anatomy.

But though Anthony had not been always truthful with her before, in this she believed him. He had cared enough for her to heed his intuition and follow her into the Catacombs, and a good thing he had, too. Men who only wished to steal a kiss didn't generally risk their lives for the chance.

Besides, Anthony was different. She couldn't really explain it better than that. It was a feeling she had that went beyond words, as foolish as that sounded. She'd never felt this way about any other man, and she sensed that Anthony felt the same about her. He might tell her a thousand other glib bits of nonsense, but he wouldn't have said he loved her unless he did.

"I didn't mean to upset you," he said, misreading her silence. "Forgive me, I shouldn't have spoken so plainly after this morning."

"Oh, no," she said quickly, blushing again. "I was only thinking of how much—how much I liked hearing those words from you."

"Ah." His face relaxed visibly. How could he possibly have guessed so wrongly? "Then I suppose I must say them as often as I can, so long as you promise to say them back to me."

She leaned up and kissed his jaw. "I love you," she whispered. "I love you, Antonio!"

"And I love you, Diana." He grinned. "Though it's hardly fair of you to kiss me like that when both my hands are occupied. I thought you English were monstrously proud of your fair play."

"'All's fair in love and war,'" she answered promptly. "That's writ by one of our most famous Englishmen, named Shakespeare, which, being English yourself, you should know."

He frowned down at her, one dark brow arched. "That's a wickedly un-English sentiment," he said skeptically. "What play, my lady? What scene?"

She raised her chin, ready to bluff, for in truth she couldn't answer. "I didn't realize you wished me to be such a scholar, my lord."

"I don't," he said. "But I'll ask any question I can imagine to keep you speaking to me a little longer. Here we are."

He slowed the curricle, turning from the road into a drive. The tall stone wall on either side was nearly covered with lush green vines. Ornate iron gates already stood open for them, though the gatekeeper hurried from the tiny stucco gatehouse to bow as they passed through.

Diana looked back, surprised that the man didn't close the gates afterwards. Her father always worried about poachers and other intruders, and took great care to protect his lands. "Do you always leave your gates open like that?"

"Why shouldn't we?" he asked, in turn surprised that she'd ask. "I don't know of a villa whose grounds are closed. The Villa Borghese, the Villa Albani, the Villa Giulia—any Roman can walk through the gardens here if they please, just as they can at St. Peter's or the Coliseum. That's how we think. The city belongs as much to the tattered old fellow who roasts the coffee beans beside the column of Marcus Aurelius in the Piazza Colonna as it does to me."

"But it's your house, your property—"

"It's Rome, not London." He smiled indulgently, then stopped, his smile now one of concern. "*Chi si contenta gode.* That's as good as the Roman motto, you know: the contented man enjoys himself."

She shook her head, unable to imagine her father or any other English lord feeling quite that content.

But Anthony misread her doubt. "Unless you feel unsafe here, Diana? Is that it? I did offer you my villa as a haven. After what happened this morning, I will have the gates barred, the footmen armed and the dogs unleashed to roam the grounds tonight if that will make you feel more at ease. Whatever you wish, *cara,* you've only to ask it."

"I'll be well enough." Yet still she edged closer to him on the curricle's seat, wanting the comfort that came from his nearness, not from any dogs or guards. "So long as I'm here with you."

"That you are, *cara,*" he said, his voice warm and low. He

looped one arm around her shoulders, pulling her so close she was practically in his lap, sitting within the loose circle of the reins. "And here you'll stay, as long as you please."

She liked that. She leaned against his chest, listening to the steady rhythm of the horses' hoofbeats and the chatter of the birds in the gardens. Already Diana could see that the grounds of Villa Prosperi were far different from Aston Hall and the other country houses in England that she'd known.

Ancient elm trees lined the drive, arching to meet overhead like a green canopy, and through them she could glimpse geometrically formal gardens, divided into long allées, green parterres and parquet circles, outlined by paths so white they looked like snow. Even this late in the season, there were bright patches of flowers amidst the green, and the southern trees—top-heavy Lombardy pines and bristling palms—added an exotic note that could never be found in England. Fountains and ponds and man-made streams shone silver-bright in the sun, while marble statues—dolphins, lions, gods and goddesses—stood like ghostly sentinels in the gardens.

And then, at last, came the villa itself: a golden yellow like the sunshine itself, iced with white marble, a perfectly proportioned exercise in curving windows, columns and arched galleries. A double staircase swept from the drive to the doorway, with red flowers spilling from the urns along the steps. Two cream-colored cats lolled sleepily in the sun on the lowest step, and with all the windows thrown open to catch the breezes here on the hill, the voice of a servant could be heard singing from somewhere inside. The entire villa seemed warm and welcoming in a way that such a grand English house never could.

"Oh, Anthony, what a beautiful place!" cried Diana, dazzled, as he drew the curricle before the front doorway. Two footman hurried to open the door, and unfold the steps. "No wonder you wish to come here as often as you can."

He grinned and pulled off his hat, and hopped to the paving stones first. She held her hand out to him to help her climb down, but instead of taking her hand, he grasped her firmly around the waist and sailed her through the air to the ground, her skirts fluttering around her legs.

She gasped with surprise, but with delight as well, leaving her hands on his shoulders for a moment longer than was necessary.

"Thank you," she said, and inexplicably her eyes filled with fresh tears when she gazed up at him. She was safe, she was in one of the most beautiful places she'd ever seen, and she was with him: what could possibly be the reason for crying in that? "Thank you for—for everything, Anthony."

"For nothing, you mean," he said softly. "For you, I could have done no less, and so much more. Now come, let me take you inside."

He led her up the curving staircase, sending the two lazy cats scurrying from the steps. Two footmen were waiting to hold the twin doors open wide for them, and as soon as they entered, the gray-haired housekeeper came hurrying into the hall, her open hands outstretched in welcome.

"Buon pomeriggio, il mio signore, buon pomeriggio!" she said in a breathless rush of Italian, her smile as sunny as the day outside, and her cheeks so plump that her dark eyes nearly disappeared in the wide arc. *"Ma perché non avete trasmesso la parola che stesse venendo? Perché mi non avete avvertito, in modo da io potrebbe fare aspettare tutto appena mantre gradite?"*

At Anthony's side, Diana's limited grasp of the language failed her before such a complicated torrent of foreign words. But that wasn't all. Most servants had keen eyes for the subtle details that separated one rank from another, and though she told herself she shouldn't care, for Anthony's sake, she did. Standing here beside him in his lovely home, how could she not feel painfully aware of how tattered and dirty and very unlike a lady she must look?

But Anthony understood far more than that.

"In English, Teresa, in English," he said gently to the housekeeper, slipping his arm protectively around Diana's waist. "My guest today is an English lady—the daughter of a duke, Theresa!—and I don't want her discomfited by having to listen to us chatter in Italian."

Tears of gratitude welled in Diana's eyes, tears she struggled to keep back as she felt his arm curl more tightly around her. She'd already wept too much today; it was better to be strong, be brave, but oh, how hard Anthony's kindness made that!

"Forgive me, my lady," Teresa said in excellent English, her smile warming even more as she curtseyed towards Diana. "With most of his lordship's guests, we speak Italian. I wished his lordship a happy afternoon, no more, then asked why he hadn't warned me that he was coming, so I might have made proper preparations."

"You know my ways well enough, Teresa," Anthony said easily. "You never need warning."

"Oh, don't I know your ways, my lord!" The woman tossed her head and rolled her eyes towards the heavens, leaving Diana to guess whether her manner was indignantly maternal, or habitually flirtatious. "You come and you go, my lord, with a score of friends, or only one, and expect me to guess the difference."

"Exactly as my parents did before me, Teresa," Anthony said, unperturbed, "nor would you wish it any other way. Now, please show Lady Diana to a room where she can wash and rest, and find her suitable clean clothes. I was fortunate enough to rescue her ladyship this morning when she was attacked while visiting the Catacombs."

"Attacked in the Catacombs!" Theresa gasped with sympathy, and touched her fingers to the silver crucifix she wore around her neck. "How terrible for you, my poor lady! That is an evil place, halfway to the devil himself. Surely the very saints must have sent his lordship there to protect you. But come, my lady, come, we'll see you put to rights."

Her face full of sympathy, Theresa stepped to one side and held her hand out towards the stairs, expecting Diana to follow her.

But Diana hung back. She wasn't ordinarily shy—far from it—but after this morning, she still felt much too vulnerable, and not even the enticement of clean clothes was enough to make her wish to leave Anthony's side just yet.

"Thank you, I believe I'm fine as I am," she said, then glanced anxiously up at Anthony. "That is, my lord, if it won't offend you if I stay with you as I am?"

"You'd never offend me, *cara*," he said, and she knew at once from the concerned look on his face that he knew how uncertain she felt. "Theresa, we'll be in the back parlor."

"I'm sorry," Diana whispered miserably as she followed him through the villa, her fingers clinging tightly to his. "I should have gone, I know, but I didn't wish to leave you."

He paused in the long hallway, and kissed her lightly on the forehead. "While you're in my house as my guest, sweet, you may do whatever pleases you. Nothing you'll do will offend me. You can shed your clothes and dance in the fountain, and all I'll do is shed my own and join you. Purely as your genial host, mind you."

She smiled, and blushed, which she suspected was exactly what he'd hoped she'd do. She turned her mouth up towards his and kissed him, a quick, shy kiss that somehow meant more than all the bolder, more brazen kisses she'd given and received from others.

And he felt it, too.

"My, my," he said softly, touching a finger to her still-moist lips. "That wasn't an ordinary kiss of gratitude."

She pressed her lips to his finger. "You're not an ordinary man."

"True enough," he murmured, and bent to kiss her again, and this time there was nothing shy or quick about it. She slipped her hands inside his coat and around his waist and pulled him closer, her breasts crushing against his chest.

No, she thought, this wasn't a kiss of gratitude at all. More like a kiss of life, of warmth, of longing and passion and most of all love, and every other thing that she feared she'd lost below in the Catacombs, and she opened her mouth further to take him deeper against her tongue.

She might be a virgin still, but she wasn't a complete innocent. She understood that she'd let him bring her here to his villa as a refuge, but if she stayed—and she'd no wish to leave, either the villa or him—then she might as well become his lover, because that was what the world would believe. No, it was what she *wanted,* to love him with her body as well as her heart, to love him completely, and to be completed by him.

And though her heart raced with anticipation and uncertainty of the unknown before her, she would not be a coward with Anthony, or her heart.

He pressed closer to her, so she felt not only the cool marble wall behind her, but also the hard length of his desire against her belly. Yet she didn't shy away from him, instead shifting her body to better fit against his, and to let him know she would never be afraid of him, not like this or in any other way.

He grunted, a sound of pure male longing, even as he then drew his body away from hers. Instead he braced his arms against the wall, over her head, making an arch over her that covered her without actually touching.

"Don't tempt me, Diana," he said, dark and low, with the rasping edge of barely-checked desire. "You don't owe that to me in return for this morning. I told you, you owe me nothing."

Without raising her chin, she looked up at him through her lashes. His protest was empty; they both knew that. Her lips felt hot and swollen, almost bruised, and fashioned more for his kisses than for idle speech. And what, really, needed saying between them, anyway?

"*Dannazione,*" he muttered, the oath he always used for frustration, and shook his head like a man determined to keep off sleep. He straightened with visible effort, grabbing her by the hand and half dragging her down the hall after him. "Another moment of that, *carissima,* and I would have taken you right there, against that wall."

"You should have," she said, her voice sounding odd to her own ears as she tried to keep pace with him. "I could have died today, and never have—have known you."

"Don't say that!"

"Why not, when it is true? If I'd been murdered, that would have been my only regret."

"*Dannazione,*" he said again, his hand tightening around hers. "You're too much alive for regrets."

"Then what of you, Antonio?" she asked breathlessly. "You want me. You *wanted* to take me there against the wall, and I wanted you to."

"But not like that," he said sharply. "Not here, Diana, and not like that."

At that moment, they'd passed beneath a crescent-shaped window high on the wall. Sunlight spilled bright and warm through the glass, and sliced across Anthony's face. Everything he thought and felt seemed laid bare before that searching sunbeam, clear enough to make Diana shiver with the intensity of what she saw.

If not now, then later, this afternoon, this evening, this night.

If not here in this hall, then in this villa, in his bedchamber, in his bed.

However would she—or he—survive until then?

"Show me your house," she said swiftly, desperate for diversion. She pulled her hand free of his and folded her arms beneath her breasts, her head high and full of daring. "Show me your villa, Antonio, and your paintings, and your bronzes, and—and whatever else you have that I should like to see."

He stared at her, almost as if seeing her for the first time.

"Paintings," he said slowly. "You wish to see my pictures?"

She nodded, quick little jerks of her chin. Her heart was beating so fast she marveled that he couldn't see it through her gown.

"Yes, I do," she said, and swallowed. "The collections of the Prosperi are famous. Everyone says so. That is my reason for coming to Rome. To see the rare things I could not see in England."

"Then come." He seized her hand and they were off again, racing back down the hall. She grabbed her skirts and bunched them in her free hand to keep from tripping, and felt the last of her hairpins fly loose and her heavy blond hair come cascading down over her shoulders. Yet still he pulled her along, up the curving white marble staircase, past impassive, bowing footmen and wide-eyed maidservants. She did slip once on the polished floor, and he caught her around the waist, his embrace so firm and sure that she didn't doubt that if she'd fallen, he'd carry her the rest of the way in his arms.

At the end of the upstairs hall, he pushed open the last set of doors, and swept her inside. The corner room was of course a bedchamber, with an enormous curtained bed standing in a small alcove to one side. Tall floor-to-ceiling windows on two sides of the room were open to the breathtaking view of Rome spread before them, the orange tile roofs scattered around St. Peter's dome like a child's toy village as the sun slipped low on the horizon. There were no curtains, there was no glass, only shutters held open to let in both the view and the sweet late-afternoon breeze.

But all that Diana noticed later. What caught her eye first was the stone floor inlaid with different colors of marble to form a giant star like a mariner's compass rose, as Anthony drew her to stand in the exact center marked by a lapis-blue circle.

"There," he whispered fiercely, close behind her with his arms clasped around her, one just below her right breast, another lower, over the front of her hip. "There are your paintings, my English Lady Diana, pictures like you'll never see in your chilly London. Prosperi pictures, *carissima,* pictures that only I can show you."

She looked, and she saw, through her eyes and his, as well.

"Is this your—your bedchamber, Anthony?" she asked, wondering how even he could sleep surrounded by such images.

He smiled, not looking away from the paintings. "No, no. This room's for guests, and always has been. The most special guests, *dolce.* Like you."

Surely none of the pictures Diana had seen on their tour had ever been like these. Surely if they had, Miss Wood would have bustled her away from pagan Rome and back to Aston Hall as fast as was possible.

The paintings were murals above a marble dado, frescoes painted into the plaster walls when they'd still been wet. The compositions were elaborate, the figures nearly life-sized, with the scenes on the two interior walls rising up seamlessly across the top of the walls into a coved ceiling, with laughing winged infants—*putti*—frolicking and peeking over billowing painted clouds and blue skies overhead.

"It's an allegory of love, *cara*," Anthony explained, his breath warm against her ear. "Venus giving her blessing to lovers everywhere."

"Carnal love, you mean," she whispered, unable to make her voice say anything more as she stared at the extravagantly painted walls.

"Passionate love, *mia amorata*," Anthony said, his hand reaching up to gently cradle her breast. "Love that lasts for eternity. Prosperi love."

In the center of the wall was Venus herself, wearing nothing save for her jewels, rising in a froth of waves from the sea. Surrounding her on the flower-strewn shore were a score of other castaways, two by two, and all as naked as the goddess they worshipped. Worship they did, too, in couplings beyond Diana's wildest imaginings, their bodies wrapped around one another and their faces contorted with ecstasy. The women were as beautiful as Venus, with full breasts and hips to please their ardent partners, who were in turn as muscular as any Roman god, and as prodigiously endowed. Nothing was hidden; everything was revealed for the admiration and titillation of whomever was granted this bedchamber.

"I knew you'd like these pictures, *cara*," he said as his hand slipped inside her bodice. He filled his hand with the tender flesh, gently teasing one crest to a stiffened peak as Diana's breathing grew more ragged. "I knew they'd please you."

"I've—I've not seen any like them before," she stammered. Her gaze kept returning to one couple in particular: a woman with long golden hair like her own, her beautiful legs spread wide as she rode a dark-haired man with a striking resemblance to Anthony. The man's fingers dug deep into the soft skin of the woman's hips, holding her tightly astride him as he plunged deeply into her, while the woman's eyes were closed and her lips parted as she felt the waves of pleasure building. She'd never thought it possible for a woman to be atop a man like that, but the longer she looked, the better she could imagine it, and want it, too.

Anthony kissed the side of her throat, his hands roaming more freely now, and she moaned in response.

"I knew you'd like them," he whispered, "just as you liked Dandolo's song. You remember what we did then, Diana? Do you remember the pleasure I gave to you that night?"

She remembered, and she wanted more, both to take and to give. She longed to be the woman in the painting, giving the pleasure to Anthony and not merely taking, and her head fair spun with new possibilities.

"I—I remember, Antonio," she gasped, unable to keep from pressing herself against his hand as she had that night at the opera. "I—I *remember*. But—but please not like that again, Antonio."

She twisted about in his embrace to face him, slipping her hands inside his coat to draw him close, and kissed him hungrily, urgently. With the image of the painted woman still fresh, she dared to tug his shirt free of his breeches, dared to slide her hands inside and felt his warm, smooth skin and the muscles beneath.

He caught his breath at her touch, a small groan of pure pleasure. "Ahh, *dolce,* how can you refuse me, yet then do that?"

"I'm not refusing you anything," she said in a husky whisper. "All I wish is to love you as you've loved me."

Chapter Twelve

⟨ornament⟩

Anthony's pale eyes were heavy-lidded with desire as he looked down at Diana.

"You wish to love me?" he asked indulgently. "Then what, pray, have you been doing before this?"

"I've been letting you seduce me," she said fiercely. "You can't deny it. Because you are so much more worldly than I, you know more of how to—to please me. But I'm learning, Anthony, and I can be a most excellent student if I set my mind to it."

"Is that true?" He looked down to where he'd pulled open her bodice, using the backs of his knuckles to graze the tips of her nipples, smiling as they tightened. "You have the most beautiful breasts, *cara*."

"Thank you," she said. "But, you see, I've no grounds to be able to return the compliment, a difference I mean to address."

Ignoring his caresses as best she could, she began to unbutton his embroidered waistcoat, and when she'd finished, she shoved it off his shoulders along with his coat.

Laughing, he shook the garments to the floor, and held out his wrists for her to unbutton the ruffled cuffs. "Here you are, *signorina cameriere*."

"What have you called me now?" Briskly she undid the row of polished bone buttons, trying not to notice the manly beauty of his wrists and hands. If she let herself be distracted here, what would happen to her when far more interesting parts of him were revealed? "Or isn't grammar to be part of my education?"

"Oh, nothing ill," he said, raising his arms over his head so the heavy, unfastened cuffs flopped down around his elbows. "I only called you lady valet, or lady gentleman's man, or whatever it is in English. Come, I'm waiting for you to remove my shirt."

"Hush." She reached down to the shirt's hem, and pulled it upwards and over his head like a billowing flag of fine white linen, letting it fall through the air to the floor. "See Antonio, this is much more fair. Now I can tell you that you, too, possess the most beautiful, beautiful chest, quite worthy of…of…"

"Of Adonis?" he suggested helpfully.

"Quite," she breathed. He *was* beautiful; after seeing so many artfully carved marble statues of gods and athletes and warriors on their tour, she'd no idea that she'd be struck so by real flesh and muscle. His shoulders were elegantly broad, his belly flat, his chest covered with whorls of dark hair that narrowed intriguingly towards the band and fall of his breeches. She reached out to touch his shoulder, her fingertips running lightly across the long puckered swash of an old scar. "How did you come by this?"

"An ancient duel," he admitted. "I was a hotheaded boy, taking offense at everything and nothing. A tendency that, fortunately, I've since outgrown."

"No more duels?"

"And no more outraged honor," he said easily. "I've found there's many more agreeable ways to spend one's time than challenging the world to foolish little battles. But where's your sense of English fair play now? You've left me to shiver here half naked. I expect the same of you, *mia dolce.*"

"You're hardly shivering," she scoffed, and he wasn't. Though the sunlight was fading into twilight, the room still held the afternoon's heat, and the breeze that wafted through the open windows was as gentle as a caress. His skin glowed beneath her fingers, so warm to her touch that if he did shiver, it wouldn't be from cold.

"You took my coat, my waistcoat and my shirt," he said. "By rights, I can now claim three articles of your dress."

"Very well," she said, willing to play along. She bent down, untied her garters, and, hopping on each foot, pulled off her stockings.

"There," she said, grinning breathlessly. "Stocking, stocking, garter, garter. That's *four* articles, so you can't call me unfair."

"Yes, I can," he said, catching her arm and spinning her around. "Extremities don't count, and you know it. Your gown, my lady, your petticoat and your stays. Those are the three articles I demand."

While she laughed, he deftly unlaced the back of her bodice and pushed it forward and off her shoulders to the floor. Next came the knot at her petticoats, sending her skirts in a puddling *shush* of muslin around her ankles. Last came her stays, and there it seemed to her he took his time, pulling the heavy cord through each eyelet with excruciating, teasing slowness, making her feel how her body relaxed as he freed it of the whalebone and buckram inch by inch.

"You're slow as a tortoise," she said, twitching to make him hurry. "You'd never keep your place as a lady's maid."

"Patience, patience," he scolded. With his palm, he swept

aside the tangled mass of her hair to brush his lips over the nape of her neck. "I thought you wished to be a proper student of love, not rushing along with breakneck haste."

"I said I wished to give *you* pleasure." Feeling the last eyelet finally give way, she shrugged her shoulders free of the straps to make her stays fall away, now dressed only in her shift. The linen was so fine that it revealed as much as it veiled, a heady realization that only made her excitement grow. She stepped clear of her discarded clothing, and turned to face him, looping her arms around the back of his neck to pull him close. With only the sheer linen between them, her breasts rubbed against his bare chest, the sensation a tantalizing surprise. "I want demonstration, my lord, not dry lecture."

He chuckled, sliding his hands from her waist over her hips, and down further to caress the full roundness of her bottom. He pulled her hips against his, and she could feel the hard proof of his desire pressing against her. She'd never been so close to naked, like this with a man before, and she thought she'd be shy, even hesitant after granting such freedom.

But because she was here, in this room so far from home with the man she loved more than any other, she felt only desire and love and, yes, wantonness, too. Her body almost vibrated with anticipation, feeling both taut and soft at the same time, with that same wondrous sensation that she'd felt that night at the opera concentrated low in her belly.

"Disrespectful students don't deserve demonstrations," he whispered, kissing her brows, her forehead, her nose, everywhere but her lips. "How can you expect to give me pleasure when you think only of yourself?"

"But I think of myself only as to the best way to please you," she said, sliding her fingers into the black silk of his hair.

She moved her hips against his, making him groan. "Where's the selfishness in that, Antonio, I ask you?"

"If you cannot see it, Diana," he said, his breath hot against her skin, "then you leave me no choice but to show you."

Before she could protest, he hooked one arm beneath her knees and lifted her from her feet to carry her the short distance to the bed. He climbed the single step to the bedstead, and settled her on the Genoese cut-velvet coverlet. Sinking deep into the featherbed beneath her, she chuckled with wry delight, and arched her back, stretching her hands over her head as she watched him drawing off his stockings.

"What kind of demonstration was that?" she asked, still laughing softly. "Was that a demonstration of your manly strength, to carry me here?"

"What an impudent student you are!" he said, his dark hair falling about his face as he unbuttoned the fall of his breeches. "I'll show you manly strength, yes, but only if you'll promise to be more obedient."

She opened her mouth to reply, and at once forgot whatever clever retort she'd intended. He'd finished unbuttoning his breeches—heavens, how had tailors ever persuaded impatient gentlemen that so many buttons were necessary to keep their privates covered?—and as he shoved them down over his hips, his erection sprang free, hard and eager for her, and far larger than she'd envisioned. If she'd never stood unclothed before a man, then in turn she'd never seen a man in a similar state, either, and the sight of Anthony there before her was at once fascinating, yet daunting, too, and she felt her teasing, playful bravado begin to wilt away.

He saw her doubt, and as he joined her on the bed he took care to lean forward and kiss her gently, with unexpected sweetness.

"*Mia colomba bella,*" he murmured. "I won't hurt you, not if you trust me."

She tried to smile up at him, pushing her hair off her face. "What is that you called me?"

"My beautiful dove," he said, trailing his hand along her cheek and down the side of her throat. "That is what you are to me, among so many other things."

"I'm sure most are not so polite as that." His hand had traveled lower, along the ridge of her collarbone, and down to caress her breast through the fine linen. Her breath was quickening again, the pleasure of it making her forget her anxiety. "I'm sure you...that is, I'm sure you have...could have called me other things, and I'd not know the difference."

"I'd never do that to you," he said, his thumb across her nipple making her twist against the coverlet. "*La mia signora appassionata.* That means you're my passionate lady. Which, my dearest, you most certainly are."

"Hah," she said, all she could manage in response. With maddening lack of haste, his caress had wandered lower again, below her navel to the same place he'd tormented so before, and she ran her tongue along her suddenly dry lips.

"*La mia sirena di desiderio,*" he murmured, pulling the sheer linen of her shift across her thighs and higher, until she was bare to his gaze. "The siren to my desire."

"Yes, yes," she said, more in response to his touch than to his words. Her legs whispered apart, wickedly offering herself to him, and as he dipped his fingers deeper, she pushed her hips up to meet him, realizing she was already shamelessly wet from wanting more, and from wanting him. The air was full of their mingled scents, the musky fragrance of desire.

"*La fiamma cara alla mia anima,*" he said, leaning down to kiss her again as he stroked her harder, his finger—no, two fingers, better, but not enough, not nearly enough!—sliding deeper, harder. "The dear flame to my soul."

She reached up and drew him down, pulling him over her, desperate for more. He shifted his body between her legs, drawing her knees around his waist. She was already so lost in the building pleasure that she scarcely realized the moment when he replaced his fingers with something hotter and far larger. She gasped and instinctively tried to draw back, but he held her hips tightly, keeping her there beneath him until he'd filled her, and their bodies were joined as closely as a man's and a woman's could be.

She whimpered, more from uncertainty than pain, and he shushed her gently. His face was strained, his breathing as ragged as her own from holding back.

"It's done, *cara*," he said hoarsely, keeping his full weight from her on his arms. "Only once, and never again. Now there's nothing but pleasure."

She stared up at his pale eyes, unconvinced. There was no pleasure now, that was certain, only the fading ripples of what she'd been feeling.

Yet before she had to answer, he startled her again, this time rolling over onto his back and taking her joined with him. He steadied her with his hands on her hips, holding her astride him with her knees bent and her hair streaming over her shoulders.

"There," he said, breathing hard. "You wished to pleasure me. All you must do is please yourself, and you'll please me, too."

She nodded, taking a deep breath. She felt less full this way, and less trapped. Tentatively, she tried moving, lifting herself up and sliding slowly down, and it was…good. She braced her hands on Anthony's chest and pushed herself up and down again, and it was even better.

"That's—that's it, Diana," Anthony said, spreading his

fingers not only to guide her movements, but to caress her full hips and bottom. His dark hair clung damply to his temples, his eyes watching her face with rare intensity. "Remember the painting you liked, *cara,* how that woman worked to please her partner by riding him, taking him deeper with each stroke, and found her own ecstasy with him."

"I remember," she whispered, and as she did, she felt the sweet tension beginning to build within her again, the heat and glow gathering low in her belly. She pulled her tangled shift over her head and tossed it aside—it seemed no more than a foolish scrap of empty modesty now—and gently she began rocking up and down, trusting her instincts and the growing pleasure her movements brought. "I *remember.*"

"Then look there, Diana," he said, his voice as dark as his eyes. "Look, and see us the same way."

She followed his glance, and caught her breath. She hadn't noticed the tall looking glass on its gilded stand, tipped to the exact angle to reflect her and Anthony on the huge bed: her pale skin against his darker body as they twined around one another, her rose-tipped breasts soft and full as she arched her back to welcome him more deeply. Behind them through the open window the last crimson of the setting sun streaked into the evening sky, their own version of Venus's blessing.

"That—that's better than any—any painting," she said, her words broken by the shuddering pace of their movements as he thrust his hips off the bed to meet her, lifting her higher. "Oh, Antonio, that's—that's better."

"*Il fuoco dolce del—del mio lombo,*" he said hoarsely, "the sweet fire of my—my body. *Dannazione,* I cannot bear much more. Here, *cara,* move against me."

He pressed his fingers to the same place where she'd found

such bliss before, and she cried out with the intensity of it. She could feel him within and without, and she couldn't have held back her pleasure now if her life had depended on it. She coiled tighter and tighter and then burst in such a rush of joy and love that she cried out with it, wild and keening, just before he, too, found his release, thrusting furiously into her.

For a long time afterwards they didn't speak, their limbs still intimately tangled as she lay atop him, her ear over his heart. She could hear its steady beat, so much slower than it had raced earlier, and she thought how Anthony himself had come to be the heart of her world, her life, her love. The sky had darkened and filled with stars, and the first nightingales had begun their song in the gardens below.

Lazily he twisted a strand of her hair, watching how the pale ringlet seemed to caress his finger. "Happy?"

Slowly she lifted her head from his chest to meet his gaze, pillowing her chin on her clasped hands. "Very," she whispered. "And you?"

"Yes." He smiled at her, his teeth pale in the half light. *"Il mio amore un allineare, il mio amore soprattutto altri*. My one true love, my love above all others."

"Oh, Antonio, I do love you," she whispered as she kissed him, her heart so full of love and joyful life that she could hardly contain it.

Her one true love, her love above all others.

Her Antonio.

Edward lay in his bed in his dressing gown, relishing that most comfortable state of a nearly done nap, still half asleep, but not yet half awake. Such were the easy pleasures of being a hero. He'd never been one before, and the novelty was still ripe and golden to him. Of course, his heroine Lady Diana was still missing somewhere about Rome, but he'd no doubt she'd pop up soon enough, and be ready to throw her arms around his neck with gratitude. He didn't really care what kind of mischief she'd been up to. Having her goods be even more soiled likely increased his chances with her, anyway. He wasn't that particular, even for a hero. She could have had a small army of lovers from Calais to Rome, yet as long as she had that dowry and her father's titled name, he'd be willing to marry her.

He sighed happily, adjusting the pillow beneath his head. The cook had concocted some foul-smelling plaster of mashed garlic for his bruised forehead, but it had seemed to work. Yes, he was feeling thoroughly fine, or he was until he heard the voices coming up the stairs towards his door.

He frowned, listening: his uncle and Miss Wood, no surprises there, but another voice, too: Sir Thomas, the consul. What the devil could he want?

Swiftly Edward pulled the second pillow from beneath his head and closed his eyes to look more wan and weak, just as his uncle opened the bedchamber door.

"Nephew?" his uncle called softly, more softly than Edward could ever recall hearing. "Sorry to disturb you, Edward, but Sir Thomas has come with wonderful news. Her ladyship is safe and unharmed!"

"She is?" Surprise made Edward sit upright, until he recalled how he was supposed to be poorly, and sagged back down against the pillows. "Ah, that is, thank God, her ladyship is delivered!"

"Well, not quite, my lord." Sir Thomas stepped into the ring of the lantern's light. "The lady is safe, yes, but not quite delivered back here."

For a man who was bearing such glad tidings, he seemed

awfully nervous, even suspicious, and Edward felt his happy glow of heroism begin to dull to his usual gray wariness.

"My lady is as good as safe," Miss Wood said promptly. "She's with Lord Randolph."

"Randolph!" This time Edward's groan was real. "How the dev—that is, how did his lordship become involved in this affair?"

"I'm not quite certain, my lord," Sir Thomas admitted. "But I received a note from Lord Randolph, assuring me that because he believed the lady still to be in great danger, he'd taken her into hiding with him, where she'd be safe under his protection."

"I must go at once to his palazzo and collect her ladyship," Miss Wood said happily. "Sir Thomas, may I beg your assistance for a bit longer so you might escort me there?"

Sir Thomas's discomfort grew. "I don't believe either Lady Diana or Lord Randolph is at the Palazzo Prosperi, Miss Wood. After receiving his note, I at once called there in hopes of finding the lady, yet his staff knew nothing of either of them."

"Then how do we know Lord Randolph himself isn't the villain?" demanded his uncle. "Certainly the man's reputation with women is not to be trusted, especially not with an English lady. When I think how my poor nephew here has risked his very life in her defense, only to have some low foreign rascal carry her off to—"

"Please, my lord, please, no idle accusations," Sir Thomas cautioned sternly. "Despite what gossip you may have overheard, please recall that Lord Randolph is not only the son and brother of a peer of the realm, but also, through his mother's ancient family, one of the best-regarded noblemen of this city. Most likely he can offer the lady far better protection than the Roman authorities."

"But who shall protect her against him, Sir Thomas?"

Edward asked gallantly, struggling to rise higher against his pillows. Now that he knew his uncle would back him, this seemed the best and more heroic course for him to take. Besides, swarthy rascals like Randolph were always beguiling women, and the last thing Edward wanted was to have a man like that as a rival. He still remembered that first night he'd met Diana and how she'd been so fascinated by her glimpse of Randolph that she'd nearly jumped from the balcony into his carriage to join the other whores. "Can you answer me that, Sir Thomas?"

Sir Thomas frowned and looked very grim. "I understand your concern, Lord Edward, but—"

"Perhaps you don't realize that I have a certain—a certain understanding with the lady," Edward said. "I have a more than passing interest in her, you see, as well as an interest in her virtue."

"Her virtue is perfectly respectable, my lord!" Miss Wood cried indignantly. "If you have an understanding, my lord, then you, of all men, should be the last to slander her!"

"I never slandered her," Edward said defensively, scrambling to retreat. "That is, I would never wish to say anything against her. It's only that Lord Randolph is the sort of man who frequents the company of prostitutes, and he—"

"Prostitutes, my lord." Miss Wood drew her small person up as straight as she could. "How dare you equate my lady with—with—"

"I don't believe my nephew is doing anything of the sort, Miss Wood," said his uncle, shooting him a glower that quite clearly ordered him to be quiet. "He's merely as concerned as the rest of us for her welfare. To that end, Sir Thomas, I trust you are making every effort to locate Lady Diana and Lord Randolph?"

"Most certainly, reverend my lord," Sir Thomas said quickly.

"Even now, I've sent messengers to every place I suspect Lord Randolph may have gone. I expect word from him, and the restoration of the lady to her friends, at any moment."

Miss Wood nodded with such agreement that Edward's hopes sank even lower. He wouldn't have a chance with Diana if the governess were against him, too.

"There's ugly gossip about nearly all unwed gentlemen," she said now. "Our brief acquaintance with Lord Randolph has shown him to be only a courtly, gracious gentleman, and certainly a fit champion for my lady."

"Indeed," Sir Thomas murmured with a vagueness that likely fooled only Miss Wood. "I fear I likewise have no word of this other man you suspect—William Carney, I believe the name was—though from his description, I expect even the Roman authorities will have little trouble finding him. A sizeable fair-haired Englishman with a branded thumb—yes, he should be easy to find, I think."

Or perhaps not, thought Edward with satisfaction. With any luck, Carney should be back in the tender care of the navy, and far, far from any possibility of revealing how impossible it would have been for him to be in that Catacomb this morning. The rewards of quick thinking, Edward decided, thoroughly pleased with himself.

Now if only Randolph could be as easily removed...

"Thank you, Sir Thomas," Miss Wood was saying, clasping her hands together to show her gratitude. "Your assurances have helped put me more at ease, and made me long only to have my poor lady restored to me."

"And to me, Sir Thomas," Edward chimed in, placing his hand over his heart with what he hoped was a convincing show of devotion. "My most fervent wish is to have the fair lady safely and happily returned."

Sir Thomas bowed solemnly. "May God see fit to grant you that wish, Lord Edward, and soon. It's all any of us will ask on this day—Lady Diana, both safe and happy."

The next morning, Anthony stood at the window in a yellow silk banyan and nothing more, sipping his coffee and skimming over the letters the footman had brought with the breakfast tray. Only one was of any real importance, and even that needed no reply. He was completely free to devote his day to the single thing that mattered most, and that was Diana.

He returned to the bed, watching her as she slept. Sweet creature, she must be exhausted; it seemed they'd made love the entire night, with each time better than the one before. He felt both sated and exhilarated after such a night, but then he hadn't been a virgin. There certainly wasn't any doubt in his mind now: just as he'd suspected, his darling Diana had proved herself made for passion, with a surprising gift for wantonness and experimentation that was, he suspected, most rare in English ladies of her rank. Strange to think how it seemed as if he'd always known her, instead of having less than a fortnight's acquaintance. Stranger still to realize that, in her, he might actually have found the one single woman he was destined to love above all others, exactly as his mother had long ago promised.

He sat on the bed beside her, unable to keep away any longer. Her cheeks were flushed with sleep, her lips rosy and swollen from his kisses. The sheets were twisted around one thigh, but beyond that she was gloriously uncovered to his eyes, like some beautiful pagan nymph created for his specific delight. Surely she put all the painted ones along the wall to shame.

His Diana, his love.

His *love:* hah, had he ever dreamed he'd come to declare

such a sentiment and mean it with all his heart? If he could, he'd keep her here with him forever, and never leave.

But she deserved more from him, and he meant to oblige. He leaned down and kissed her bare shoulder, and she stirred, waking slowly.

"Antonio, dearest," she muttered, rubbing her face into the pillow before she finally opened her eyes enough to look up at him. "Is it morning?"

"It is, *cara*," he said, kissing her lightly. "In fact, it's nearly noon."

"Noon?" She sat upright and squinted at the window, and the daylight now streaming across the inlaid floor. "How can that be?"

"Because morning follows night, and noon comes after that," he said. "Would you care for coffee or tea? I had both brought."

"Brought by servants?" Belatedly she grabbed the sheet and clutched it to her breasts. "They came in here?"

"Oh, they're very discreet," he said, gently pulling the sheet from her hands. "They'll swear they saw nothing and no one. In fact, that's what they told Sir Thomas's messenger when he called last night, asking after you. Despite my assurances, *mia amore*, it would seem that your governess is quite concerned about your welfare."

"Poor Miss Wood," she said unhappily. "She must be worried to death about me. I should go back, shouldn't I? Oh, you needn't answer that, because I know I must. Especially after what happened with Mary in Paris, I must. But, oh, Antonio, I wish I didn't have to!"

"I wish you didn't, either," he said softly, leaning forward to kiss her again. "You tempt me sorely to keep you here, Diana, sorely. But I'm afraid you're right, and we must go back to the city and face whatever we shall."

He rose, and brought back the large silver breakfast tray, setting it on the bed before her. She pointed at the teapot, and he poured it for her, the fragrant liquid filling first the cup, then spilling over into the dish.

"I must ask you now, sweet, and I've a reason for it," he said as he handed it to her. "Yesterday you said you'd been threatened by a man named Will Carney. What was he to you?"

"Will." She flushed miserably, and stared down at her tea, the fragrant steam curling up around her face. "He was a groom at Aston Hall. He flattered me, and I believed him, and met him in the stables. Father caught us, and was so angry that he sent me to the Continent instead of to London."

"Then I owe Carney my sincerest thanks," he said, striving to lighten her mood, "else by now you'd be wed to some thick-witted heir, and I'd never have met you. Was that all?"

She shook her head, curling her hair behind her ear. "Father punished Will, too, not just by dismissing him, but by giving him over to the press gang to serve in the navy. You don't wish to cross Father, you see."

"So it would seem," he said dryly, wondering what the vengeful father would say if he'd seen the various postures Anthony had shared with his daughter this past night.

"Father's a good man, truly," she insisted with the confidence of all loyal daughters, "but he's very proud of his rank and his station, and he hates for it to be compromised in any way. He has quite a temper."

"I suppose English dukes are like that," he said, his image of her father's wrath multiplying tenfold. That prideful duke would likely dismiss Anthony as some ill-bred, foreign monkey, brown and distasteful. No matter that the Prosperi had bloodlines back to the Caesars, to a time when every English duke's ancestors were still cowering in a mud-covered hut. Anthony had met his grace's kind before, and he'd just as soon not meet one again, so long as he could keep the man's daughter.

"But if Will were banished to the navy, why did you believe he was in the Catacombs?"

She looked up at him, her mouth pinched. "Because he'd found me here in Rome. He'd deserted his ship and was black-mailing me. He said if I didn't pay him, he'd tell everyone about how I'd—I'd been his lover. Which I never was."

"I know that," he said softly, and he did, too. "You didn't give him any money, did you?"

She shook her head again. "I hadn't any to give. Miss Wood keeps all our funds, and she would have suspected if I'd asked her."

"He won't trouble you again on that score, or any other," he said, reaching out to pat her cheek. "Nor was he in the Cata-combs with you, no matter what you thought. My agents have learned that Carney was taken up by a group of British marines earlier this week, and is safely imprisoned and waiting his punishment."

She shook her head, confused. "Then who was in the dark with me? Who was it that struck Edward? Oh, Antonio, he sounded so much like Will!"

"I do not know," he said evenly, though of course he'd a very good idea. He'd suspected Warwick had been the man he'd fought in the dark even before he'd learned of Carney's arrest, and now he was sure of it. Not that he'd upset Diana by telling her; she'd already suffered enough. But he'd make damned sure that that cowardly bastard Warwick knew he knew, and he'd be just as sure to keep Diana forever from his path.

"A gypsy, a beggar, some other half-mad vagrant," he said. "We may never know now exactly who he was."

"No," she said, still troubled as she stared back down at her tea. "Anthony, I'm sorry that I'm not exactly as you might have believed me to be, or that before I met you, I'd—"

"Hush," he said, and silenced her with a kiss. "Why should I care about the past? I love you, Diana. I love you, and I want to spend this day and every other after it with you. Is that enough?"

"Oh, yes," she said, her eyes brimming with tears. "It's more than enough, Antonio. More than enough for us both."

Three hours later, Diana sat as close as she could beside Anthony as they drove back to the Piazza di Spagna. They rode in the same little curricle as they'd driven yesterday, and yet in that short time, it felt as if everything in her world had changed forever. The closer they came to her lodgings, the more uncertain she felt.

It wasn't that she doubted Anthony, or the love they shared. How could she, when last night had been the most wondrous of her life? But she worried over more practical matters, and how swiftly Miss Wood's sense of honor and decorum would puncture last night's passionate magic. When her sister Mary had found love with John, he'd quelled any possible objections with a properly (if hastily) arranged marriage performed by an indisputable Anglican minister. There was no knowing yet how Father had responded to the news—correspondence was notoriously slow between England and the Continent— but not even he could object to an *affaire de coeur* that ended in a marriage.

But Father could object very much to her blissful idyll at the Villa Prosperi, conducted beneath the gaze of those scandalous paintings. He'd take one look at Anthony, and see only the part of him that was not English, and be blind to the part that was a peer's son. Father would demand to know why he insisted on living abroad, and had never set foot in London, as any proper Englishman must. He'd see popery and too many words he couldn't comprehend, red wine he couldn't digest and food not seasoned to his tastes.

Most of all, he'd see Anthony as the seducer and the ravisher of his younger daughter. And, while Anthony had spoken over and over about how much he loved her without once mentioning marriage, to her endless sorrow, Father would be right.

Yet Diana knew she'd never regret a moment spent with him.

"Here we are, *cara,*" he said, guiding the curricle to a post before their lodging house. He tossed a few coins to the boy outside to water the horses, then hopped to the pavement, and held his hand out to Diana to help her climb down.

She looked up at the windows that belonged to her rooms and wondered if Miss Wood were there, watching for her return. Would her governess be able to see the difference in her? Was her face changed by what she'd done, or did she move in a way that at once would mark her as a woman of experience, no longer an innocent girl? Could all the world see the love she felt for Anthony?

"You look beautiful," he said softly, squeezing her fingers. *"Bellissima amore."*

She smiled shyly, loving the rich sound of the Italian endearments in his mouth. When he told her she was beautiful, she believed him, and she *was,* as much from his love as from the careful attention the maidservants at the villa had taken with her dress and hair this morning. She took his hand more firmly, and stepped down, ready to face whatever lay before her.

Signor Silvani, their landlord, met them first at the door, throwing up his arms with rejoicing so loud and heartfelt that soon his whole staff came running and shouting to join him.

By the time Diana and Anthony had climbed the stairs, Miss Wood had heard the din and stood waiting on the landing, ready to throw her arms around Diana as if she'd been lost for weeks, not less than twenty-four hours. She cried, and Diana did, too, though she was sure the governess wept for reasons other than her own.

"I can't begin to tell you how glad I am to have you back, my lady," Miss Wood said, finally disentangling herself from Diana to curtsey to Anthony. "And you, my lord, how can I ever thank you for the great service you have done us? Please, my lord, please, come into our parlor with us."

"I shall be honored, *signorina.*" Anthony reclaimed Diana's hand, winking at her when the governess turned her back. She grinned and followed him into the parlor. This was the first time he'd been inside her rooms, yet because he was with her, he seemed to belong.

And then she saw both Edward and his uncle, standing awkwardly before their chairs in the room as she entered with Anthony. She'd forgotten almost entirely about Edward after they'd left him behind in the Catacombs. At least, save for some sort of bandage across his forehead, he seemed none the worse for wear, but she still felt shamefaced yet relieved to see him here now.

"Good day, reverend my lord, Warwick," Anthony was saying, but the other two men showed no such cheer towards him.

"You are unharmed, my lady?" Edward asked, pointedly ignoring Anthony. "You have not suffered in this man's company?"

Diana gasped at his rudeness. "Lord Edward, please! I must beg you to be more considerate in your comments towards—"

"No matter, *cara,* no matter," Anthony said softly. "Warwick will believe whatever ill of me he chooses. But I've one sure way to put an end to his questions, and to all others that may follow you, too."

He turned to face her, and there before the others, he dropped to one knee on the floor. His smile told her what would follow, yet she couldn't accept that it was truly happening, and she pressed her other hand to her mouth in disbelief.

"My dear, Lady Diana," he said, entirely in English so there'd be no misunderstanding. "You have already honored me with your love. Now before these witnesses, please grant me the final joy and happiness, and say you'll be my wife."

Chapter Thirteen

There, he'd done it.

He'd told Diana he loved her before a trio of English witnesses, so there'd be no changing his mind even if he wished to. After a life of making love to women, he'd sworn to love only one for the rest of his days, and asked Lady Diana Farren to marry him.

The next moment seemed to stretch nearly that long. She stood before him, her little fingers swallowed up in his hand, her blue eyes enormous and shining with unshed tears. She'd covered her mouth with her other hand, making him guess her reaction to his proposal.

His proposal. Damnation, he was offering her his entire *being*.

Why wasn't she answering? Why wasn't she accepting him, the way he'd felt sure she would? He'd thought he'd won her last night, the way she had him. Hell, for as long as he could remember he'd never been denied anything he'd ever wanted, and he wanted her more than anything else.

Please, dear love, please….

She let her hand fall from her mouth, pressing it instead over her heart. She smiled, at him, for him.

The most beautiful sight he'd ever seen.

"Yes," she said softly, just for him, then raising her voice louder so the others would hear, too. "Yes, yes, Anthony, I *will* marry you!"

She flung her arms around his shoulders, and he seized her around the waist, raising her with him as he rose to his feet. He buried his face against her hair, breathing deeply of her scent. His Diana, his love, and now to be his wife.

"Not yet you don't, my lady!" Miss Wood exclaimed. "You can't agree to this on your own!"

Anthony looked over Diana's head. The governess was so agitated she was nearly hopping up and down, her face flushed and her cheeks puffed out.

"Please put her down, my lord," she ordered when she caught his eye. "She's not your wife yet."

"But I *will* be, Miss Wood!" Diana turned around in Anthony's embrace to face her. "As soon as it can be arranged, I *will* marry him.

"Not without your father's consent, you won't, my lady." Miss Wood took her by the arm, trying forcibly to pull her from Anthony's arms. "We must discuss this—this match, my lady, and we must consult with his grace your father before any marriage is made."

"But that could take months, Miss Wood!" protested Diana with gratifying misery. "I'm of age now. I don't need to wait for Father's consent. I can accept Lord Anthony's hand myself."

"Now, now, Lady Diana, guard your temper," Reverend Lord Patterson said, stepping forward with his hands clasped sternly behind his back. "Mind the Commandment to honor thy father. You owe obedience to his grace, especially whilst contemplating the holy sacrament of marriage."

Anthony looped his hands around Diana's waist—lightly,

yet possessively, too. As far as he was concerned, she was already his. He wanted that understood. The wedding would be but a formality.

"Whether I must wait ten days or ten years, I'll still wed Lady Diana," he said. "Though his grace might find a long delay more…scandalous to the family."

The clergyman tipped his head to one side as he scowled at Anthony. "What exactly are you implying, my lord?"

"I've no implication at all, reverend my lord," Anthony said mildly. "Only the truth. That last night this lady and I did lie together as man and wife, and the sooner the rest of the world acknowledges our union, the less talk there will be. Or are noble-born brides with great bellies the fashion in London society these days?"

"How dare you speak like that of Lady Diana?" demanded Warwick, his hands knotted in ineffectual fists at his sides. "She's a lady, Randolph, not one of your common strumpets!"

"She's going to be my wife, Warwick," Anthony said, curling his hand more closely around Diana's waist, "and I'll be the one who'll happily defend her good name and honor."

"My lady, is this true?" Miss Wood asked, her earlier angry flush now reduced to unhappy pallor. "Last night, did you… did you…?"

"I did, Miss Wood," Diana said with such pride that Anthony wished to kiss her at once. "I love him, and he loves me, and that was reason enough."

Miss Wood heaved a shuddering sigh of despair. "Oh, my lady," she said. "However will I tell this to his grace your father?"

Diana slipped away from Anthony to rest her hand on the governess's shoulder. "Father will understand, Miss Wood, once he realizes that we're in love and—"

"In *love*, my lady," Miss Wood said bitterly. "How many

sorrows, how much mischief, how much ruin, has been committed in the name of love?"

Anthony took a step closer to Diana, wanting her to know he'd stand beside her through this. "I know this is something of a surprise, Miss Wood, but I have only the most honorable intentions for Lady Diana's welfare and future, and I—"

"Forgive me, my lord, but I have heard enough." Miss Wood seized Diana by the arm. "Come, my lady, we'll leave these gentlemen, so I might speak to you in private."

With a cursory curtsey to him and the other two men, Miss Wood firmly led Diana into the next chamber, and closed the door after them with a decisive thud. His last glimpse of Diana was her lovely face turned over her shoulder towards him as the door closed, her expression both anguished and beseeching, yet also full of love.

Already he missed her.

"My lord, I beg that you will likewise excuse us." Reverend Lord Patterson's bow was curtly polite, while Warwick was so obviously simmering with resentment and rage that he couldn't even manage that much, shifting furiously from one foot to another with his hands still clenched in those ridiculous fists.

"You don't deserve her, Randolph," he finally blurted out, his round face livid. "You—you're not worthy of her at all."

Anthony only smiled, refusing to take offense. "That's for the lady to decide, isn't it?" He turned to leave, then turned back as if just recalling something else.

"Oh, and Warwick," he said with careful nonchalance, "I've news this morning that might interest you. It seems that her ladyship was mistaken. That other fellow in the Catacombs couldn't possibly have been William Carney. Carney was arrested for desertion the day before, after an informant notified your British marines."

His eyes bulging with undisguised panic, Warwick chewed furiously on his lower lip before he answered. "Carney was…ah, ah…arrested? Well, then, it was some other bastard who struck me while I was trying to save her ladyship."

"Perhaps," Anthony said, and smiled. "Wouldn't want your bravery in the dark to go entirely to waste, eh? *Arrivederci, signore. Arrivederci.*"

Diana sat on the straight-backed chair in the center of her bedchamber, her hands folded in her lap, and tried very hard to look contrite. Contrition had always worked before with Miss Wood, as did apologies, and a certain amount of groveling. But she'd never erred quite this seriously before, and she'd never seen Miss Wood so—so distraught, either.

"You're ruined, my lady," she was saying now, clipping each word with brittle emphasis. "You do realize that, don't you? You're ruined, and you've only yourself to fault."

"If I were still interested in a London season, then yes, Miss Wood, I suppose I am ruined," she admitted. "But since that's no longer my wish, and—"

"*Your* wish, my lady!" Miss Wood exclaimed, pacing before Diana with such short, agitated steps that her gray petticoat jerked out over her feet. "What of the wishes of those who better know what is right and proper for you? What of the wishes of those who truly love you, and care for you, and wish you to find lasting happiness in life?"

Diana raised her chin, and watched Miss Wood as she paced back and forth. "But with Lord Anthony I will find lasting happiness."

"Bah!" Miss Wood brushed her protest aside with a sweep

of her small, plump hand. "That is what he has told you, a cunning, foreign gentleman with no respect for your position or person, and you, my lady, were foolish enough to believe his seduction."

"I believe him when he says he loves me because it's the truth," Diana said defensively. "I know it is. And he's neither cunning nor foreign. His father was as English as mine."

"Oh, what his grace your father would say to such a slander." Miss Wood shook her head. "And consider what he'll say if you present him with this man's dark bastard child."

Diana's cheeks warmed. How strange it felt to realize that Miss Wood was still (and likely always would remain) an unequivocal virgin, while she herself was not. To loll about deliciously naked in Anthony's embrace at the Villa Prosperi was one thing, but it was another entirely to hear her stern little governess speak so bluntly of the possible consequences of such lolling.

"That is why we wish to marry, Miss Wood," she said. "Because we love one another, and because we—we would welcome any children."

"Love, love," said Miss Wood. "So you're back to that sorry song again!"

"It's the most beautiful song in the world, Miss Wood!" Diana cried, unable to keep contrite any longer. She swept from her chair, her arms outstretched as she tried to think of the words to make her governess understand.

"My Anthony is kind and handsome and gentle," she began, "and amusing, too. Everything a good husband should be. His family is old and respectable, he is wealthy, and well regarded by all who know him. And he loves me. He loves me, and I love him, more than anything. Can't you understand that, Miss Wood? Can't you *understand?*"

For a long moment, Miss Wood simply stared at her. Then she sank down into Diana's empty chair and dropped her head to her hands, her eyes squeezed shut as if in great pain.

"I've lost you, my lady, haven't I?" she said sorrowfully. "Because of this *love* I cannot understand, I first lost your sister, and now I've lost you, too, and once his grace your father learns of it, I'll lose my place, and likely never find another once other families hear of this—this disgrace."

"Oh, Miss Wood!" In a wave of guilt, Diana dropped down beside her governess, resting her hands on the other woman's knees. "I'm sorry, so vastly sorry! Yet even if I hadn't met Anthony here in Rome, I would have gone back to London and married a gentleman there, wouldn't I?"

"But I've failed his grace your father, you see," she said, her voice muffled with unhappiness. "He entrusted his dearest daughters to my care, and see what a dreadful job I have made of it."

"But you haven't failed, Miss Wood, not at all," Diana said. "We've found love and happiness, and we were very near to outgrowing a governess, anyway. You'll find another place, I'm sure. How could Father fault you for that?"

Without answering, Miss Wood looked at Diana dolefully, for they both realized exactly how displeased Father would likely be with his daughters' tastes in husbands. Instead she sighed, and took Diana's hands in her own, their faces level.

"Has this—this attraction been going on since we came to Rome?" she asked. "I tried to take such care with you after Lady Mary ran off with Lord John, but it seems I've been just as blind with you and Lord Anthony."

"Not blind, Miss Wood," Diana said loyally. "It's happened very swiftly."

"Then you are certain Lord Anthony is the gentleman for

you, my lady?" she asked, searching Diana's face for any doubt. "This is not simply base desire and attraction between you two? You're sure he can make you happy?"

Diana nodded eagerly. "He can and he will, Miss Wood. And after last night, when he—"

"I needn't hear another word of last night, my lady," Miss Wood said hastily. "That must remain between you and—and your husband."

"Then you consent?" Diana asked, her hopes soaring. "You won't try to stop us?"

"I'm not sure I could," Miss Wood said with a weary smile. "I want you to be happy, my lady. And I can still go on to Venice alone."

"Oh, thank you, Miss Wood!" Diana hugged her tightly. "Thank you so much!"

"Yes," Miss Wood said, pushing her gently aside to fumble for her handkerchief in her pocket. This would be as close as Diana would ever get to seeing her governess weep, but then she supposed she'd given Miss Wood plenty of reason now for tears, both good and bad.

Miss Wood blew her nose with a small snuffle. "Though I must warn you that my consent is not the same as his grace your father's. Prepare yourself for his anger and hurt, my lady, and the likelihood that he will withhold both his blessing and your dowry from this match."

"Hah, Anthony won't care," Diana said proudly. It pleased her that he wouldn't; if she'd gone husband-hunting in London, then her worth and her title would have been the first concern of any suitor.

"I hope you're right, my lady," Miss Wood said, and sighed again. "But at least you've had the decency not to run off in the night like your sister did in Paris. We won't have the sort of wedding that could have been arranged at Aston Hall, but it can be done properly."

"I'll send word to Anthony to return, so we can tell him," Diana said eagerly, already on her feet and halfway to the door. She doubted she'd be permitted to return to the villa with him, but still she'd treasure every minute she could steal away in his company.

"No, no, stay, my lady, please," Miss Wood said, and the emotion in her voice was enough to make Diana pause. "Tomorrow will be soon enough. Give me one more night to—to keep things as they were. Can you grant me that, my lady?"

She looked back at her governess, the woman to her and her sister when their own mother had died. For Diana, this wedding would be the beginning of a splendid new life, but for Miss Wood, it could only mark an ending.

"Dear Miss Wood," she said softly, returning to put her arms around the other woman's shoulders. "Of course we can wait until tomorrow to tell Anthony, if it will please you, and then we'll make a more public announcement of our betrothal after that. One more day! What ill could possibly come between us in that tiny amount of time?"

That evening, Anthony stood in Lucia's parlor, waiting for her butler to return. There'd been a time when he'd always gone upstairs to her bedchamber unannounced, and was warmly welcomed there, too, but those days—and nights— were long past. And, after this visit, there was a good chance that he might never pass through Lucia's door again.

He glanced at his reflection in the looking glass over the fireplace, smoothing back a stray lock of his hair. He didn't look like a changed man; he wondered if Lucia would spot the difference in him. Either way, he wanted her to hear his news from him, and not from one of her gossipy friends. As an old friend, she deserved to be treated honorably, though Lucia being Lucia, he doubted she'd see it that way.

He could hear her singing as she came down the stairs to him, her trills lighthearted and merry. That was good. A merry Lucia was always preferable to the one that shrieked and smashed porcelain shepherdesses.

So far today matters had gone far better than he'd any right to expect. Praying his luck would hold a little longer, he turned expectantly towards the door.

"My dearest darling Anthony!" Lucia swept into the room, the high lacquered heels of her slippers clacking across the polished marble floor and her arms held out towards him. Her plum silk dressing gown flowed around her as she walked, the thin fabric clinging to her body to reveal the full, fluid curves of her breasts and hips. "Come, darling, where's my kiss?"

"It's wherever you left it last, Lucia," he said dryly, kissing her cheek instead of her proffered lips. How like Lucia to be draped in amethysts and diamonds, yet not bother with stays.

"That's unkind between friends, Anthony." She pouted, and hooked her arm into his so the fleshy weight of her breast pressed into his side. "*Old* friends."

"I've called on business, Lucia, not friendship." Pointedly he untangled his arm from hers, and reached into his coat pocket, drawing out a small leather pouch. "I'm here to concede. You've won."

"Won?" Her dark eyes narrowed suspiciously, staring down at the pouch in his hand. "What have I won, darling? What pretty prize have you brought me?"

He was certain she'd guessed already, but he was willing to play along.

"One hundred Venetian gold pieces," he said softly, placing

the pouch into her open palm with a muted *clink* of the coins inside. "My forfeit in our wager. I told you, Lucia, you've won. I've asked Lady Diana Farren to marry me, and she's accepted. We'll be wed as soon as it can be arranged."

She stared down at the pouch in her hand, then back up at Anthony.

"You can't marry her," she said slowly, refusing to accept his explanation. "It can't be true. You're jesting with me, aren't you? But wait, we've reached the other part of the wager now, haven't we? The part where as your old friend I persuade you from such folly?"

But Anthony only shook his head. "I won't be persuaded otherwise, Lucia. Yet, if you wish me to sing as I'd promised as loser, why, then, that I could—"

"Oh, that—that matters not at all," she said, her agitation growing. "But for you to marry that milk-faced English virgin—no, darling, it *can't* be true!"

"Not a virgin any longer," he said, folding her fingers around the pouch. "But Diana seduced me, Lucia, not the other way around. I love her, and she loves me, and now I'm going to marry her."

"*Marry* her," she said, spitting the words as she once again stared down at the pouch of gold. Her fingers tightened, like claws around the gold. She was shaking, her heavy earrings trembling against her cheeks, and when she looked back up at Anthony, tears were sliding from her eyes, cutting through the black paint that outlined them.

"I'm sorry, Lucia," he said softly, not wanting to wound her any more. He *was* sorry, too, for her sake: sorry that he'd loved her without being in love with her, sorry that fate had determined she'd always be a mistress, never a wife. "I'm sorry."

She drew back her hand and hurled the bag of coins at his

head so fast he barely had time to duck. The pouch struck the wall behind him and burst, the gold coins clattering to the floor.

"You marry her, Anthony," she said in a venomous, hissing whisper. "Marry her, and be damned together!"

She turned and fled up the stairs in a trail of purple silk, and he let her go.

A single gold coin rolled across the floor, struck his foot, and fell to its side. He settled his hat on his head, and left without waiting for the butler to show him out, closing the door gently, so gently, behind him.

Edward sat alone in the back of the taverna, glumly sipping the tumbler of red wine to make it last, and to keep the sullen serving girl from offering to fill it again. He didn't have the money to keep his glass full; hell, he didn't have the money for anything.

The taverna catered to young Englishmen on their Grand Tours, and even on a quiet night like this, the tables were filled with shiny-faced gentlemen and their tutors, drinking too much and talking too loudly. There were girls, too, pretty Roman girls who were a cut above the ones Edward had discovered would boldly ply their trade against the arches in the Forum. The taverna girls would sing like ladies, or play an instrument similar to a small lute called a mandolin, but mostly they were there to amuse the young English gentlemen. As much as Edward might long for their company, they never came to his table, for even they could sense his taints of poverty and of failure.

He'd never had the faintest chance with Diana Farren. All the times he'd thought she'd been smiling at him with favor, or laughing at his jests, or taking his arm because only he, Edward Warwick, pleased her—he'd imagined the lot. He'd even wasted his last great attempt at rescuing her in the Catacombs, as she'd spared him so little thought that she'd forgotten him completely and run off with that rascal Randolph instead.

He scowled at the wine, muttering sour, unformed oaths. She'd didn't care for him. She never had. If he'd ever gotten up the courage to ask for her hand, she likely would have laughed in his face.

That's what Uncle Henry had told him this afternoon. It hadn't been humiliating enough to see her return fresh from Randolph's bed, or have to witness his damned proposal to her. No, his dear uncle had been ready to ladle the salt onto those fresh wounds as soon as they'd returned to their rooms, reminding him exactly how great a failure and disappointment he'd been since, it seemed, the instant he'd been born.

He allowed himself another taste of the wine, letting it slide down his throat. The tumbler was almost empty now, his third, and he still could remember every hideous detail of the day. Why, he couldn't even manage to get drunk properly, and with another disgusted oath, he emptied the glass and thumped it down on the table.

But no one noticed, not even the sullen serving girl. Instead every eye was on the woman who'd just entered the taverna with a liveried footman as her escort. She stood just inside the doorway, as aware of her entrance as any grand actress on the London stage. Scanning the room, she stepped closer to the lantern that hung on the wall and slowly turned the hood of her cloak back from her face. Every man seemed to sigh in admiring unison, she was that breathtakingly, sensually beautiful.

Edward was no exception. Now *that* was a woman to make a man die happy, he thought as she slowly made her way between the tables and benches. Her clothes were costly and fashionable, her jewels dancing in the light, and yet there was something intangible that made it clear to him that she was not a lady...*and she was coming to his table.*

He rose so fast he nearly tipped over his chair. "*Buon-buona sera,*" he managed to stammer. "Ah, ahem, *signorina.* Yes."

"Don't trouble yourself, my good Lord Edward," she said with a languid sweep of her hand. "I speak English, yes? May I join you, please?"

"Yes, yes, of course," Edward said, waiting until the footman settled her in the other chair before he, too, sat. It didn't matter that his pockets were empty and he'd no more credit. He had to order this magnificent creature whatever she wished, and he raised his hand to summon the barkeep. "What can I offer you, *signorina?*"

"Thank you, no, my good lord," she said, smiling as she swayed closer. "I've come to speak to you, yes. I've come with certain information, to use as you please."

He smiled stupidly, unable to stop. He must be more drunk than he thought, grinning like this. "I am your complete servant, *signorina.*"

She nodded, baring teeth as fine as pearls. "You have been disappointed in love, yes? By the English Lady Diana Farren?"

"Yes," he croaked, stunned she knew of it. "She has chosen another, the unfaithful bitch."

She leaned across the table, laying her hand on his arm. "*He* is the unfaithful one, my good lord. Antonio Randolph. He seduced her on a wager, no more."

"A wager?" Edward exclaimed. "How do you know this?"

She winked slyly. "I know, my good lord, because Antonio made his devil's wager with me."

Now Edward knew where he'd seen her before, that first day he'd met Diana, and Randolph had passed beneath their window in a carriage full of low women. She'd been one of them, the most beautiful, and the one who'd practically been riding in Randolph's lap.

So this was Randolph's mistress, and he felt a ripple of envy that one man had had so much good fortune. Then he realized the power of what she'd just told him: Randolph had made a wager with his whore that he could steal Diana's maidenhead. All that nonsense about how much Randolph loved her had been exactly that: nonsense.

Maybe Edward hadn't lost Diana just yet. If she were to learn how false her lover had been, if he only dared enough, then maybe he could yet be her shining hero. What else did he have to risk, anyway? Diana could still choose him to marry, and that lovely fortune of hers would at last be his.

"You will make use of that knowledge, my good lord?" she asked, her gloved fingers pressing seductively into his forearm. "You will share it, yes?"

"Yes," he said, his grin even wider. "By God, yes."

"Another bite, my greedy bride?" Anthony held the silver spoon mounded with lemon ice just beyond Diana's open mouth. "Another little taste?"

"If I am greedy, Antonio, then it is because you have made me so." Laughing, Diana grabbed his wrist and brought the spoon to her mouth herself, licking the spoon clean of the sweet yellow ice. "We must have more of that at our wedding breakfast. I'll ask Sir Thomas to send us the recipe."

"I'll make certain you'll have silver buckets filled with the stuff, if it pleases you so much." He leaned down and kissed her, and she chuckled again, delighting in the combination of his warm lips against hers, chilled from the ice.

"We shouldn't," she said, pulling away from him and glancing back at the other guests who crowded the consulate's front room. Since Diana was so far from home and family, Sir Thomas had graciously, if hastily, put together this gathering for her and Anthony to announce their betrothal to the rest of well-bred Rome and the other English living and visiting there. Even with such short notice, not one person who'd been invited had sent their regrets, and she and Anthony had been surrounded by fascinated well-wishers the entire evening.

"I promised Miss Wood I'd behave until the wedding," she said. "Oh, Anthony, we shouldn't, not here."

Now Anthony dropped the spoon back into the dish, and set them both on a table nearby.

"If we shouldn't here, *cara*," he reasoned, taking her hand, "then we'll go where we should. This way, to the garden."

"We shouldn't, Antonio," she protested, but she followed him anyway, slipping through the crowd and out the back door, into the moonlit garden. "Truly."

"Truly, truly, truly," he teased. He turned her so she faced him, and gently eased her back against the wall, where they couldn't be seen through the windows by the others inside, even as the sounds of their conversation and laughter spilled into the garden around them.

"Truly, yes," she whispered, arching eagerly into his embrace. "Oh, I've missed you!"

"It's been less than a day, *mio amore*, yet it's as if I've waited my entire life for you," he said, then kissed her so hungrily that she'd no words left to whisper in return. He pressed his body against her, letting her know how much he wanted her, and urging her to forget her promises to Miss Wood.

"Here, *cara*, now," he said, his hands on her bottom lifting her against his hips. "They'll all be so close, yet no one will know except for us. But I'll have to cover your mouth so they won't hear you, won't I? We don't want them to hear my demure little bride when I make her scream with pleasure."

To be only a feet away from so many others, yet hidden here in the dark to make love—oh, the very idea was both so wicked and so very, very appealing. She felt the cooler air on her thighs above her garters as he tugged her skirts higher, and with the same eagerness she'd shown with the lemon ice, she reached for the buttons on the fall of his breeches.

"Let's drink a cheer to the happy pair!" called Sir Thomas. "Come, come, a full glass in every hand. Where are they now? Has anyone seen Lady Diana and Lord Anthony?"

"*Dannazione,*" Anthony said, swiftly dropping her skirts. "Later, *cara,* later, I swear to you."

Her blood still racing with unfulfilled desire, she quickly smoothed her skirts and followed him back into the room, praying that they'd all accept her rosy cheeks as a maidenly blush, not the feverish flush of passion. *Later,* he'd said, and knowing that he'd somehow keep that vow made her heart again quicken.

"Here now, my handsome lovebirds," Sir Thomas said, beckoning them to stand with him in the center of the room. "It's a rare treat for me to have such a merry duty as this one. But Cupid is determined to find us English even here in Rome—ha, perhaps I should say especially in Rome!—and this night we celebrate the finest love-match I've ever seen, joining together two of our nations' most noble families. To the lasting happiness and love of Lady Diana and Lord Anthony!"

"To Lady Diana and Lord Anthony!" came the echo, followed by cheers and clinking glasses.

Diana gazed up at Anthony, smiling in spite of her tears of joy. Had she ever, ever been so happy?

"To all my good friends, both English and Roman."

Anthony plucked a glass from a footman's tray, and raised it high. "I thank you for your wishes for my lovely bride and for me, and for the great love that we've found together here—"

"That's a lie!"

Like everyone else, Diana gasped and jerked her head around to see what man had dared interrupt Anthony.

But Lord Edward had made it easy to find him. He came striding into the room as others stepped aside for him, startled and wary of a man who'd behave either so rudely, or so madly. He stopped before Anthony, his fists knotted at his sides and his head high, a man determined to speak his mind.

"I know the truth of your—your attachment to this lady, Randolph," he declared. "It's time everyone else did, too."

A murmur of scandalized concern rippled through the crowd. Diana pressed her hand over her mouth, and Anthony curled his arm around her shoulder to reassure her.

"Are you drunk, Warwick?" he demanded. "Otherwise, you had better have a good reason for interrupting this gathering."

"My reason *is* the truth, Randolph!" Edward shouted, and Diana wondered if anyone else noticed how the sweat streamed down his forehead, darkening his fair hair at his collar, or how his fists were shaking with nervousness at his sides. Had he really lost his wits, to behave like this?

Appalled, Sir Thomas belatedly waved for two thick-set footmen to come remove Edward.

"The truth, sir, is that you are no longer welcomed in this house," Sir Thomas said brusquely, and was greeted with a spattering of applause. "You two, remove this man at once to the street."

"A moment, Sir Thomas," Anthony said, making the footmen pause. "Before Warwick leaves, I'd like to hear what foolishness brought him here."

"No foolishness," Edward said. "I told you, I've only come to tell Diana—Lady Diana—the truth about you."

He swallowed hard, his Adam's apple bobbing above his neckcloth as he turned to face Diana.

"My lady," he began, his gaze filing with a disturbing mix of anger and devotion. "My lady, I have learned from an impeccable source that this rascal's interest in you is entirely false, and that he made a base wager with his—his mistress that he could—could seduce you."

As another gasp ran through the guests, Diana shook her head with disbelief, unable to fathom why Edward would humiliate himself like this. "Don't say such dreadful, false things, Edward, I beg you!"

"But what if they're not false, my lady?" He looked back to Anthony with lopsided triumph. "Tell her I'm wrong, Randolph. Go on. Tell her I'm the liar, not you!"

Diana looked to Anthony, sure he'd answer as Edward demanded. But instead his mouth was pressed in a tight line, his handsome face rigid with fury.

"Lucia," he said tersely. "Lucia told you that, Warwick, didn't she?"

"Who's Lucia?" Diana asked, but neither man heard her.

"Your *mistress* Lucia, Randolph," Edward answered boldly. "You made the wager with her. You placed a stake of a hundred gold pieces with this—this *whore* that you could make this lady—"

"Enough, Warwick," said Anthony curtly. *"Enough."*

"Not quite." Edward took one step closer to Anthony. "On behalf of her ladyship and her honor, Randolph, I challenge you to a duel."

"No!" cried Diana, pushing herself between them. "Are you mad? I don't want this, I don't want you to—"

But Anthony caught her, gently steering her to one side. "I accept, Warwick. Tomorrow, at dawn; there's no need to wait. My seconds will call on you later this evening."

Sir Thomas stepped forward, his hand raised for peace. "Please, my lords, I beg you, reconsider this impulsive act that can only end in tragedy."

But Anthony shook his head. "I'm sorry, Sir Thomas, it's too late for reconciliation. Diana, come with me."

He took her hand and pulled her with him into the empty front hall. There'd be no kissing now, not that Diana wanted any at the moment.

"Tell me you won't do this, Anthony," she demanded breathlessly. "Tell me you won't let Edward goad you into risking your life over nothing!"

"You are not nothing, *cara,*" he said, though the muscles in his face still remained taut, his blue eyes full of anger. "Besides, I won't risk my life, not facing that impotent little bastard."

"He won't be impotent if he's holding a sword or a pistol." She threw her arms around his waist, trying every way she knew to implore him. She loved him for his passion, but she'd never before seen that passion turned down such a wrong path, and the furious determination he showed frightened her almost as much as the duel itself.

"You told me before you'd stopped dueling," she pleaded, her voice rising with emotion, "that it was a young man's foolishness, that you had better things to do with your life. For my sake, please, please don't do this!"

"For your sake, I have no choice." He took her by the shoulders, holding her steady so she'd have to meet his eyes. "You're going to be my wife, Diana. It's my duty not only to defend you against insults like Warwick's, but to defend both our families' names and honor as well."

"But not like—"

"Listen to me, Diana," he said. "Lucia Paolini was, in fact, once my mistress, long before I met you. She has been no more than a friend for years, and now I doubt even that. What she has done, telling this to Warwick, is vengeful and unforgivable."

"You believe that I'm jealous of a woman you knew long ago?" she cried, incredulous. "That she should matter so much that you risk your life in a *duel?*"

"That day I saw you on the balcony, beneath the rainbow," he continued, almost as if she hadn't spoken. "I did make a wager with Lucia about you. But once I'd met you, that was done. *Finito.*"

She cupped her hands around his face, holding it close to hers.

"Then let this be done, too, Antonio," she whispered urgently. "If you love me, call off this duel with Lord Edward now."

"Mia bella sposa." For the first time since that terrible moment when Edward had entered the room, Anthony smiled, so tenderly that fresh tears stung her eyes. He cradled her face as she'd held his, and kissed her. "My beautiful bride. I love you more than life itself, *cara.*"

"I love you, too, Antonio," she whispered, her hopes rising as he kissed the tears from her cheeks. "Oh, more than anything!"

"Cara, cara," he said, his voice rough with longing. "It's because of our love that I cannot do what you ask. Now let me go. I've much to do before tomorrow's dawn, and then— ah, then how happy I'll be to see you again!"

Stunned, she could only watch him leave, and take her love, her life, her joy and happiness with him.

Chapter Fourteen

"**Y**ou are certain this is what you wish, my lord?" Signor Franchetti looked over his steel-rimmed spectacles at Anthony, his pen poised in his gnarled fingers. "Considering how brief your acquaintance has been with her ladyship, you're being surprisingly generous."

"I intend to marry her at the end of the week, Franchetti," Anthony said. "I already regard her ladyship as my wife, and I intend to provide accordingly for her and any children that may bless our union."

The solicitor's wispy white brows arched towards the front of his snuff-colored wig. "You are not being premature in that hope, my lord?"

"No, Franchetti, I am not." Anthony knew that the man's long service to his family permitted him a certain frankness, but that was still no reason for Anthony to have to explain to him every detail of his circumstances with Diana. "Draw up the papers, and I'll sign them."

"Very well, my lord." With a final sniff of disapproval, the solicitor bent over the draft, copying out Anthony's will with the new revisions in place.

Anthony turned away to stand at the window, staring without seeing into the night sky over the city. Behind him Franchetti's pen continued to scratch over the page, changing his will to acknowledge Diana as his wife in every way except fact. She was already a wealthy woman thanks to her father. He doubted she'd need the provisions he was leaving her, but in case she was carrying his child, he wanted no doubts left about its paternity. For her sake, he was determined to behave as honorably as possible.

Wearily he rubbed the back of his neck beneath his collar. He'd done everything he should. God knows he'd enough experience in such affairs, though he'd thought he'd never need it again. He'd checked and cleaned the pistols himself. He'd met with his seconds, old friends, who, of course, had tried to persuade him not to fight. He'd listened to Sir Thomas again, too, pleading that for Diana's sake he must not do this. But it was for her sake that he'd accepted Warwick's challenge in the first place. He wasn't going to allow anyone to say he didn't love her, or that he was marrying her only to satisfy that idiotic wager.

While he'd always thought he favored Mama's Prosperi blood more, there were definitely other things that had come from Father alone. He had an impeccable, ingrained sense of honor and of how an honorable gentleman behaved that was purely English. That was why this duel mattered so much to him: now that he'd fallen in love with a true English lady of the highest rank, he wanted to treat her with all the regard and honor she deserved. If that meant facing death from another man's pistol at dawn among the mists of the Forum—the place they'd arranged—then so be it. His darling Diana was worth that to him, and far, far more besides.

He linked his hands behind his head and closed his eyes.

He was exhausted, but he knew better than to go to bed, where he'd only toss and turn and think of her. Better to face Warwick with that edginess to sharpen his reflexes. He should win, and have his satisfaction; he doubted Warwick had much skill with pistols, and less nerve. But duels were unpredictable. Sometimes one party turned tail, and never showed at all. Authorities could arrive at an inopportune moment, making everyone scatter. An opponent could turn skittish, and pull his trigger too soon. Too often guns misfired, or simply didn't fire at all.

No, better not to think of that. Better to think of Diana, and how delicious she'd been asleep in his bed with the sheets tangled around her and her hair spread over the pillows, the room fragrant with the scent of their lovemaking.

What would their children look like, he wondered. Gold and ivory like her, or dark like him? His brothers were both red-cheeked and fair, as had been Father, so the odds would lean towards that. Strange to think how many other women he'd had, yet this was the first time he'd ever considered a baby as a desirable result. He hoped she was with child, their child. He'd like that. A child born from so much love, much as he had been himself, would be fortunate indeed.

"We're ready, my lord." Franchetti squared the papers and slid them across the table to Anthony. He beckoned to his clerk, and to Anthony's butler and manservant, all of whom had been rousted from their sleep to serve as witnesses.

Quickly Anthony read the document, making certain that all the clauses he'd requested had been added, and then signed it.

"Thank you, Franchetti," he said, smiling as he set the pen down. He'd always made a point of revising his will before a duel or a long journey, but this time he'd felt a special urgency with his marriage pending. "At least that's done."

"I'm afraid there's one more matter, my lord." The solicitor reached into his leather portfolio, and drew out a small letter. "Considering the circumstances, it seemed proper to give this to you tonight."

He handed the letter across the table. To his shock, Anthony at once recognized his mother's seal on the back, the curling primrose pressed into the blood-red wax, and when he turned it in his fingers, he saw Mama's distinctive handwriting as well, the small, precise, upright letters that she'd learned as a girl at convent school.

"The dowager marchioness instructed me to give that to you on the day of your wedding, my lord," Franchetti explained as he gathered up the new will and his other papers. "I realize that this is a bit, ah, premature, my lord, but since you have legally recognized Lady Diana as your wife, I believe her ladyship would have wished you to have it today instead."

Anthony held the letter in his hands, feeling oddly as if his mother was once again in this room with him. They'd been close, so close that his brothers had teased him mercilessly about how much she'd always babied him, her clear favorite among her children. Mama had died over ten years ago, yet not a week passed that she didn't return to his thoughts.

"Do you know the contents of this letter, Franchetti?" he asked, turning the letter over in his hands. "What she wrote?"

"No, my lord," the solicitor said. "But I will tell you that I've held it for many, many years. Her ladyship gave it to me soon after you were born. Both she and your father regarded your arrival so late in their lives as something of a miracle, so I should dare to guess it's something of that nature."

Anthony nodded, for the notion made sense. His parents had told him much the same thing, both separately and together; Father had even credited his birth with bringing fresh vigor to their marriage, a confession that at the time had embarrassed the twelve-year-old Anthony no end.

Yet still he held Mama's letter in his hand unopened. He wasn't sure why. He'd no reason to be wary. Most likely it was only one of her characteristic letters, effusive and sentimental.

"Will there be anything else needed, my lord?" the solicitor asked pointedly, clearly yearning for his own bed.

"No, no, that is all," Anthony said. "Good night, *signore,* and many thanks for attending me at such an hour."

"Your servant, my lord, and good evening to you." He bowed, backing away. "And might I also extend my wishes for a favorable outcome in tomorrow's adventure, my lord. I should not like to see the young lady made a widow before she's a proper wife."

"Neither would I, Franchetti," Anthony said with a weary smile. "And I like to hope she would agree."

The solicitor left and the servants went with him, and at last Anthony was alone. When he'd been young and hotheaded, he'd fought—and won—perhaps a dozen duels, with pistols and with swords. Each of those times, he'd spent the night before drinking and boasting and whoring, activities designed to keep him from thinking overmuch about his own mortality. But this time he was alone in that darkest hour between midnight and dawn, and all he had for company were an unopened letter from his dead mother, and the memory of how he'd left his almost-bride weeping from fear she'd never again see him alive.

He chuckled ruefully, thankful that none of his old companions could see him now, and dropped into the chair before the last glowing embers in the grate. With fresh resolution, he cracked his thumb beneath the wax seal on his mother's letter,

and unfolded the single sheet. What could it be, really, besides
her blessings on his wedding day?

My darling Tonio,

*If you are reading these words, then I know this day
is the happiest of your life & I pray that God has granted
me the joy of sharing it with you. You of all my children
will marry for love, & for love alone, and I wish you every
blessing possible to rain upon you in this life & the next.*

*But I must tell you more, Tonio, because with your
own great love, you will at last understand. As dear as
your father is to me, he was not my only love. There was
another before him, a boy more sweet & dear for being
first, an artist of great gifts that my father judged too
poor to wed a Prosperi & sent away. Last year Fate did
cross our paths again, & for the sake of bittersweet
memory we did one night succumb. You, my darling, innocent Tonio, were born of that union, the child not of
my sin, but of my first & truest love.*

*My beloved John, the father of your heart, knows noth-
ing of my infidelity to him, for I would not have him love
you less on account of my weakness. To him, you will always be his. I tell only you, Tonio, & beg your forgive-
ness & your understanding & your love & your blessings,*

A thousand kisses, my precious angel,
Mama

Anthony frowned down at the words his mother had
written so long ago, and then read them again, praying that
this time they'd make more sense. They had to be true.
Mama would have had no reason to invent such a story. He'd
only to look in the glass to remind himself how he'd never

favored anyone else in his family except his mother. His head was spinning, his stomach lurching. Of all the things he'd thought his mother might write, he'd never—never—expected this.

The kind, gentle, honorable Englishman he'd been raised to believe was his father now wasn't.

The great romantic passion he'd always believed his mother had felt for his father—no, not his father, but the Earl of Markham—he must remember that now—was clouded, tainted and false.

The family he'd revered, the brothers he'd loved, the name and title he'd been proud to bear, the country and the values and even the language he'd spoken as his own—none of it was any longer rightfully his.

He could continue to live as he had, and no one else would be the wiser. To reveal such an ancient sin would only slander his mother's memory, and accomplish nothing. His brothers were so wrapped up in their English lives and families that he doubted such a revelation would interest them now, anyway. This house, the villa and his income had come to him through his mother and were still his.

But his whole sense of who and what he *was* had been shattered, and would never be the same again. How could it?

He was the bastard son of some nameless artist and his adulterous mother.

He was no better than a cuckoo, dropped into the nest of the poor, cuckolded Earl of Markham, where he'd crowded aside the other legitimate fledglings for more than his share of the earl's love and affection.

But most of all, he no longer had any right to the hand of Lady Diana Farren, the first daughter of his grace the proud and vengeful Duke of Aston.

* * *

Diana was still awake in her bed when she heard the caller pull the night bell to wake the porter at the front door of their lodgings. She listened to Signor Silvani finally answer, his voice grumpy with sleep. Not a visitor or doctor, or another lodger returning late, no one he needed to be agreeable to. She heard the landlord close and once again shoot the heavy bolt on the door, and finally begin his slow climb up the stairs, muttering to himself. A message: he must have a message, then, an urgent message that couldn't wait for morning, for one of them upstairs.

Diana sat up, swinging her legs over the side of the bed, as if this would make her hearing more keen, and rubbed her eyes, sore and swollen from weeping. She glanced at the tiny brass carriage clock on the table beside her bed. Nearly four, and not long until dawn.

Was Edward lying awake in his bed across the hallway as well, or had he spent this night elsewhere? She'd heard nothing from the rooms he usually shared with his uncle. Was he feeling any guilt or remorse for this unforgivable challenge that had already caused so much pain?

Across the city, Anthony must be awake, too, preparing however gentlemen prepared for duels. Perhaps this message that Silvani was carrying up the stairs came from him. Perhaps he'd called off this foolish duel after all, or—

"My lady?"

Though she'd been hoping the message was for her, she still jumped when she heard the landlord's knock. She grabbed a shawl to throw over her night shift and hurried to answer before Miss Wood woke, her bare feet padding across the floor.

"My lady." Silvani's face was puffy with sleep, his night's growth of bristling whiskers turned silver by the candlestick's light. He handed her a folded letter, sealed with a blob of wax. "For you, my lady."

"Thank you, *signore*." She didn't wait to close the door, but tore the letter open and with trembling fingers turned the sheet towards the landlord's candlestick.

My lady,
No matter what may pass this day, I release you from
your promise to wed. I am not the man you took me to
be. You owe me nothing.
Farewell, cara,
A.

She stared at the note in disbelief. What nonsense was this? If not for the small, wrenching bit of familiar fondness in the closing, she wouldn't even think this had come from Anthony, it was so coldly formal.

Swiftly she scanned the handful of words again, searching for any hints or clues. She'd no experience with how gentlemen prepared themselves to risk their lives, whether in battle or duels like this. But she did know Anthony, and this—this *disavowal* was completely beyond the character of the man she loved. She sensed there was something more here than simply the duel, something that had wounded him, that could make him write this to her.

"I trust no unhappy news, my lady?" Silvani asked.

"Not at all." She refolded the letter, creasing it between her fingers. She knew what she must do. No matter that ladies never watched duels or other affairs of honor. No matter that Miss Wood had expressly forbidden her to do so, or that Anthony himself had told her last night that he would see her again when this was done, and not before. After this formal, forlorn little note, she knew where she belonged.

"Send for a carriage for me, *signore*," she said. The night was just beginning to fade, with dawn not far ahead. "As soon as possible, if you please."

Silvani bowed. "For you and for Miss Wood, my lady?"

"For me alone," she answered firmly. "And pray show every haste, *signore*. I've not a minute to waste."

Edward sat in the closed chaise drawn up on a street near the Forum. Night had barely begun to give way to day, and the sky overhead was still dotted with stars. A little more time yet before he was tested, a little more time. He took another swig from the bottle of wine, settling it back between his knees when he was done.

"That bottle's no more than false courage, Edward," his uncle said. "Better to contemplate the state of your soul, and trust yourself to God's hands than to cheap red wine."

"How cheerful for you to say, Uncle," Edward said, disgusted. He'd gambled that Randolph would prefer pistols to swords, and when Randolph's second had chosen the guns, Edward had considered that an excellent omen. He was good with pistols, a damned fine shot, if he said so himself, which was certainly more than his uncle would say. "You're safe enough. No one ever takes a shot at a second."

"No, they don't, and a good thing for you, too, else I wouldn't have agreed," his uncle said, patting the cover of the Bible in his lap. "It's not seemly for a man of the church to participate in this sort of ritualized carnage, but who else in Rome would you have asked?"

"That's a fat lot of comfort you're offering, Uncle," Edward muttered. Ever since his uncle had found him in the taverna a little past midnight, he'd been preaching the same sermon of unworthiness, and Edward was sick of it. Why, he might throw himself in front of Randolph's gun just to be free of

Uncle Henry. "You're supposed to give guidance and peace in the face of death, not rip my head off."

"Why, when it's your head—or more specifically your mouth—that's led you into the face of death?" His uncle's disapproving frown deepened. "I've heard Randolph's never lost a duel. Not one. No one's challenged him in years for that very reason."

"Then it's past time someone did," Edward said. "I've confidence in my abilities, even if you don't."

His uncle grunted, unconvinced. "It's not only a question of abilities. How you could possibly believe that such rash action will persuade Lady Diana to choose you over him is beyond me."

"Ladies like heroes," Edward said, refusing to abandon this idea. Why should he, when it had such perfect beauty? He'd relish the chance to take a fair shot at Randolph, and show him up as a coward, making Edward the hero. He could still picture Diana as his wife, gazing up at him with the same adoration she now squandered on Randolph. Maybe he'd even claim Randolph's mistress, that divine Lucia. He could listen to her praise his courage as she rode his cock. Hah, that would show Randolph, wouldn't it, when—

"Ladies like live heroes," his uncle said bluntly. "I don't suppose you considered that, either."

Edward only smiled. He'd every intention of being a live hero. He didn't mean to die, and he'd do whatever he must to make sure of it. He reached for the bottle again, just to be sure his hands were steady when he pulled the trigger.

"Well, here's the beginning of the end," his uncle said, tapping his gloved knuckles lightly against the glass. "That's Randolph's carriage now. Prepare yourself, Nephew. Be a man for once in your life, and don't foul your breeches."

* * *

Anthony stood beside the three ghostly columns, all that remained of the ancient Temple of Castor and Pollux. This was the place agreed upon for this morning's duel, a popular place among Roman gentlemen for such actions. It was suitably melancholy and remote, important to young men risking their lives over a hand of cards or a woman, yet enough of the paving stones of what had once been streets before the temple remained to provide a long, straight, clear path that was perfect for the ritual of killing.

It was familiar to Anthony, too, an advantage he'd have over Warwick. He'd fought here at least three times before, though by now the details had become hazy in his memory. But this morning, this duel, he knew he'd never forget, because this one was about Diana.

"It's still early, Antonio," called his cousin Gianni, his second, standing by the carriage. "Come back inside, where it's warm."

"I'm well enough, Gianni," he said, waving his cousin away. As cheerful as Gianni was, Anthony didn't want company, not now. He'd tucked his mother's folded letter inside his shirt, where it would be found if he were killed. Then Diana would know, and he prayed that she would understand and forgive him.

The early-morning air was cool, and he liked how it made him feel alert, heightening his senses. He'd already shed his coat, and the finely pleated linen of his shirt caught the light breezes that always ruffled through the Forum. This was what he wanted, to feel, not think, not remember.

He turned towards the horizon, gazing upward and away from the earth. Though the sun was no more than a pale lemon band across the horizon, the kestrels that nested in the ruins had begun their day, their silhouettes sharp and dark as they wheeled in the sky.

What would it be like to fly so high over Rome? he wondered. To be weightless and unburdened and free of all earthly cares and sorrows and shames? Once he'd looked up towards a rainbow and found his golden Diana. Now he wished he could be like the kestrels and gaze down on her window, into the room where she still must be sleeping, her lips parted and her lashes feathered across her cheek, waiting for him to love her again.

"Antonio!" Gianni called again, and this time when Anthony turned, he saw Warwick and his uncle waiting for him, along with the surgeon. All were dressed in black, as was proper for so solemn an occasion.

It was time to forget Diana, and set her as free as the kestrels. It was time.

Leisurely, he joined the others. Warwick was shrugging out of his coat with an eagerness Anthony hadn't expected. The man's face was impassive—had he done this before, too?— but the damp rings of sweat beneath the sleeves of his shirt betrayed him just the same.

With the box of pistols beneath his arm, Gianni bowed to the two Englishmen. The uncle's starched clerical bands fluttered up towards his chin, and he clutched an old-fashioned Bible in his hands; Anthony had forgotten the man was an English minister. How useful, in the event that last rites might be needed.

"Good day, gentlemen," Gianni said in English, for their benefit. "Before we begin, I should like to inquire if his lordship can be persuaded to retract his unfortunate challenge?"

"Regrettably, no," said the uncle, glancing pointedly back at Warwick. "Lord Edward regrets that he is unable to oblige, and stands by his words."

"Very well," Gianni said, and bowed again, presenting the

mahogany box with the pistols, an elegant brace that Anthony had had made for himself years ago in Florence. "Then honor must be served. Pistols, my lords."

Like a child faced with a choice of chocolates, Warwick let his fingers hover greedily over first one pistol, then the second, before he finally pounced and grabbed one, pulling it away as if he feared Anthony would try to take it.

Anthony, of course, didn't. He'd tested both pistols last night, and knew they were equal. He held his lightly, warming the polished butt in his hand. Like all the most modern dueling pistols, these were fitted with hair-triggers, extra springs in the lock that would make the pistol fire at the slightest pull, and without disturbing the aim. Unlike a fight with swords, it no longer took much talent or even nerve to blast a man's fool head off.

"One last time, my lords," asked the uncle dolefully. "For the sake of your immortal souls, can you not be reconciled? Edward, I beg you to consider the love your poor mother bears you, and the pain your actions will bring her."

"A man who makes wagers with whores about a lady's virtue doesn't deserve the lady," Warwick said doggedly, jutting his chin out for belligerent emphasis. "That's *my* answer."

"No reconciliation," Anthony said curtly.

Warwick's uncle seemed to sag. He patted his hand once on Warwick's shoulder, then stepped back, his head bowed over his Bible. "Then may God have mercy on you both."

"Very well, my lords." Gianni cleared his throat, the sound echoing oddly through the ruins. "I shall ask you to take your positions."

Anthony turned so his back was against Warwick's. He held the pistol with the muzzle towards the gray morning sky, the barrel resting lightly against his collarbone.

"Five paces apart, my lords," Gianni continued, "then turn inward."

Anthony heard the chaise behind them, the wheels clattering over the broken stones of the road. He turned to look, though he already knew who it was.

"Oh, *cara,* no," he said softly. "Not here, not for this."

The chaise drew to a halt on a rise a short distance away, and Diana stood, holding to the back of the seat to keep her balance. She didn't call out, or scream at them to stop, or make any move to come closer. She simply stood there in the chaise, dressed all in white with the first light of dawn glinting on her golden hair like an angel.

"Why, that's Lady Diana!" Reverend Lord Patterson exclaimed. "She shouldn't be here, not now. It's not fit for her to watch such a scene. We must send her away."

"No, let her watch," Warwick said sharply. "She should see which of us is the braver."

Anthony turned, aghast. "For God's sake, is that all this is to you? A *contest?*"

"She came here to watch," Warwick said, his eyes too bright with excitement. "Women have a taste for bloodsport. She knows what to expect."

"The hell she does." How could his Diana know what a lead ball could do to flesh and bone at close range, or how much blood could drain from a man's body in only a minute? "She hasn't the faintest damned notion of what could happen here."

"My lords, please," Gianni said quickly. "I must remind you that your pistols are primed and loaded. If you don't wish to continue, then we—"

"Continue," Anthony barked, resuming his place, and Warwick instantly followed. Anthony stole one final glace to where Diana stood in the chaise, her hands pressed to her mouth as she watched. Was she praying for him, his angel?

"Five paces, my lords," Gianni repeated.

She was stealing his focus being here, weakening him, robbing the power from his anger. Instead she was making him think of how infinitely much more he'd prefer to be with her beneath the velvet coverlets in the enormous bed at the villa, how her skin would be warm and fragrant with her womanly scent, how she'd sink into the featherbed beneath him, how tightly she'd hold him with her thighs curled around his waist, sleek and wet and willing and *he must not think of this now.*

Or he would die.

Silently, Anthony counted his steps across the cracked paving stones and tufts of grass, then turned. Warwick was already facing him, his eyes blank. Anthony studied him critically, now less a man than a target. An inexperienced duelist always aimed for the face, the head, but it was always better to aim lower, towards the wider target of the chest or belly.

Oh, Diana, *cara mia,* are you still watching from the hill?

"I will count to five, my lords," continued Gianni. "One, two, three, four, five. Upon the final word, you may fire at will. Are you ready, my lords?"

"One, two…"

I love you, my darling dove. Even if I die, that will never change.

"Three, four…."

It shouldn't have ended like this, Diana, I swear it. I want the life, the love that you give me, not this. Damnation, I must be sure to watch Warwick's arm….

The flash came first, brilliant yellow-white, the way only gunpowder can be, a half second before Gianni called five, and well before Anthony's finger could squeeze the trigger.

Too late to think of Diana now, or of anything else but that Warwick had cheated, and now he'd be the one to suffer for it....

He felt the sharp stab in his upper arm, the pain that began small and swiftly grew, streaking down his arm and up to his shoulder with the slower spread of blood, his blood, warming his own chilly skin inside his sleeve. Around him rumbled the shock and outrage from the other men, matched by his own furious oath at being gulled by the oldest trick in the coward's book.

But his fingers still held the pistol, no bones broken or tendons severed. He'd come here expecting to die, almost seeking it as his destiny, and yet it hadn't happened. He was still alive. He'd been winged, that was all, and ten paces away was Edward's ashen face, his mouth slack, hanging open with shock and terror. The wisp of gunsmoke drifted from the muzzle of his spent pistol, and his shirt was as broad a target as any man could wish.

"Take the bastard now, Tonio!" shouted Gianni in outraged Italian. "Send the Englishman to hell, the double-damned coward!"

Everything seemed squeezed into this single moment, as if it were being compressed through the narrow neck of a bottle: Warwick's stunned face, the gaunt-cheeked surgeon kneeling to open his bag, the uncle pressing his Bible over his heart, the gray dawn sky and the red blotches on the white marble there at his feet. But what remained clearest was Warwick, dropping to his knees with a keening wail for mercy, his face turned loose with horrified anticipation, hovering there just above the sight on Anthony's pistol.

He'd expected to die, not kill. He'd wanted to free her. Didn't Warwick realize that? Didn't anyone else understand?

He thought of Diana behind him, watching this foolishness.

Was she there still, waiting, weeping for him though his wound was slight? He'd hate to see her cry, especially when it was his fault.

Was this how it was supposed to be, then, and not end with his death?

I love you, *cara,* my bride, my darling.

With Warwick kneeling before him, Anthony lowered his arm, the pain slicing down its length and back again through the torn flesh, and pointed the pistol's muzzle to one side. With a little grunt of pain, he squeezed the trigger and fired into the ground.

"There—there is my satisfaction," he said. He let the pistol slip from his fingers and turned towards the chaise, towards salvation, towards Diana.

She could not make herself look away.

Even though Diana knew Anthony could die, she remained. Even though she might see things that would haunt her as long as she lived, she watched. How could she not? This was Anthony, her love, and her fate was too entwined with his for her to do otherwise now.

The morning was chilly and damp, her white gown far too light. But she'd wanted him to see her in the early light, and know she was there. She didn't try to stop the duel, fearing that would only spur him on instead. She'd stood and watched, dreading what would happen next even as she longed for it to be over.

Then Anthony had sought her out, his gaze like a caress across the distance, linking them together. Hope, sweet and pure, rose up in her heart as she dared to believe he'd choose her and her love instead of this awful fate.

But how could love ever triumph over honor? She watched him shake his head, refuse her silent plea, turn away from her and towards the other men. He took up his pistol, marked his paces, faced Edward, listened as his second counted.

One, two...

She whispered every heartfelt prayer she knew, anguished pleas and beseechings and bargainings for Anthony's life.

Three...

Saints in heaven, but she loved him, her darling, dearest love, the one man meant to be her lover and her husband. She always *would* love him, no matter what happened next.

Four...

An eternity seemed to stretch between each number, yet time was racing past too fast.

God help her, she could not watch any longer, and she whipped around with a sob just as a shot echoed across the park. One shot, only one shot, and a disjointed garble of voices.

Not Anthony, oh, dear God, not Anthony!

"My lady, my lady!" cried the driver. "Are you all right, my lady?"

"My betrothed," she gasped. "Lord Randolph—"

"He is the victor, my lady," the driver assured her, "and he lives, though the other man played false and fired first."

She felt her knees buckle with relief beneath her, and she slipped into the seat behind her. She twisted enough to look back down the hill, to where Anthony stood, still tall and proud, clearly the victor as the driver said. She watched as he lowered his pistol, and emptied it harmlessly. At last he turned towards her, and she finally saw the bright red stain on the sleeve of his white shirt.

"Oh, Anthony, no," she cried, shoving herself from the seat. She bunched her skirts to one side and jumped down, not waiting for the driver to help her, and ran stumbling across the uneven ground, driven by her desperation to reach him. *"No!"*

The other man was supporting him now, holding him upright. As she ran, Diana could see how much Anthony was leaning on him for support, and how another man, a surgeon, was already tearing away the bloody sleeve to tend to his arm.

"Anthony!" she cried as she reached him. "Oh, my love, my love!"

"Diana." He was ashy pale, yet still he smiled at her. "I didn't die."

"Of course you didn't," she said through her tears. She longed to hug him, to touch him, to reassure herself that all this blood—so much blood!—meant nothing. "Hush, now, let them tend to you."

But he was fumbling into his shirt with his good hand, pulling out a crumpled letter that he handed to her.

"Read that, Diana," he said, his breathing harsh. "I'm—I'm not what you think."

Swiftly she opened the letter and read it, then looked back at him. "This is from your mother, Anthony?"

"Just—just last night," he said, wincing. "I'm not the—the man you believed."

"But you *are*, Anthony," she cried, now understanding his note to her earlier and the pain behind it. She'd learned both the joy and the pain that love could bring; how much his mother must have suffered beneath this awful secret, kept hidden for a lifetime! "You're still the man I love more than any other."

"My lady, we must take his lordship back to the city," the surgeon said, his long face grim with concern. "He can't be tended properly here."

Anthony shook his head. "But your father, *cara,* your father will not—"

"Hush," she said, taking his face into her hands, heedless of the blood that fell on her white gown, so much blood that it frightened her. "I'm no slave to my father's pride. I love you, Anthony, and nothing will change that."

"But your rank, your place—"

"Are nothing, my sweet Antonio, compared to the love I have for you," she said. "Now please, please let your friends take you home."

Yet still he refused to be led away. "Marry me, love."

"Antonio," she said through her tears. "There's no one else, and never has been."

"*Cara mia,*" he whispered. "My bride."

She leaned up and kissed him quickly, then let his friends half carry him to the waiting carriage as she followed.

"Diana, please!"

She turned. Edward was standing before her. His hair was flattened to his head with sweat, his shirt streaked with dirt, and the hand he held out to her now was trembling. She remembered hearing the single shot first, and how the driver had said that Edward hadn't waited for the end of the count, but had cheated and fired first.

"Diana," he said to her, and tried to smile. "I did it for you, you know. I was defending you. Your honor. I did it for you."

"Don't say that, Edward," she said sharply, remembering how close he'd come to killing Anthony, how she stood here now with Anthony's blood on her gown. "Everything you did was only for yourself. *Everything.*"

His mouth twisted, and he took another step towards her. "Diana, please. If we could only begin again—"

"No," she said. "Be grateful the second gun was in Anthony's hand and not my own, Edward, for I doubt I'd have been so merciful."

Without waiting for his answer, she turned and ran back to Anthony, and their future together.

Villa Prosperi
December, 1784

Diana lay propped against a small mountain of pillows in the middle of the bed, gazing out the windows at the gray December sky, a porcelain dish of orange slices on her lap. The tall windows were closed now, for even in Rome December was too chilly to have them open, but the view remained, the bright tile roofs of the houses and shops fanning out around the great dome of St. Peter's in the clear light of early morning. The fire in the grate popped and crackled cheerfully, while Venus and her followers continued their never-ending frolic on the walls around the room. After the wedding, Diana had chosen this room as theirs instead of the more sedately decorated master's bedchamber down the hall, giving as her reason that she preferred the wicked company of the lovers in the murals.

"At Aston Hall, we'd have had our first snow by now," she said, idly plucking another orange segment from the dish. "Always by Christmas, anyway."

"No snow in Rome, thank God." Anthony settled himself higher on the pillows beside her. "But I'd say oranges are a fair enough trade for snow, aren't they?"

"Oh, I suppose." She smiled indulgently, and slipped the orange segment into his mouth. "And I rather like the trade for a husband, too."

"That, *cara*, goes without saying, or argument." He slipped his hand behind her head and drew her face down to kiss her, his mouth tasting sweet from the orange. "You make such a splendid mistress for the villa, I should hate to have to give you up."

She swatted his arm—his good arm, not the one that had been wounded in the duel. The scar was still livid, and still ached, an ugly reminder to them both. He'd healed faster than the surgeons had predicted, being well enough within three weeks to stand beside her at their wedding. It had been a simple ceremony, especially for the daughter of an English peer, with only a handful of guests, but that was what they'd wanted. She'd come so close to losing the man she loved, that all that mattered to her was marrying him, not the spectacle surrounding it.

And it had proved wise not to wait. By Diana's reckoning, she was already two months gone with their first child, her breasts full and tender and her belly just beginning to swell— a splendid match for Anthony's pride in having sired what he was certain was a son.

Now he slipped his hand beneath the coverlet, resting his palm protectively over the gentle round of her belly, and their unborn child within. "What time is it, sweet?"

"Oh, not nearly time to rise," she said, sliding the last piece of orange into his mouth. She set the empty dish on the table beside the bed and wriggled down lower beneath the coverlet to face him. "Another hour at least, if you can bear that."

"For your sake, I'll try." He sighed so manfully that she laughed, a laugh that turned into a happy sigh as he pulled her close.

"You seem happy enough," she whispered, kissing him lightly.

"I'm lying in a warm bed with the woman I love more than any other," he said. "Why in blazes shouldn't I be happy, sweet wife?"

"No reason at all," she said softly, resting on his chest. "I do love you, Anthony."

"And I love you," he whispered, his smile crooked. *"Chi si contenta gode, eh?"*

She grinned in return, for this was one Roman proverb she knew by heart. "The contented man enjoys himself."

"Then content me again, Diana," he said, pulling her closer. "Content me again."

MILLS & BOON

Historical

On sale 5th December 2008

Regency

MISS WINBOLT AND THE FORTUNE HUNTER

by Sylvia Andrew

When respected spinster Miss Emily Winbolt jeopardises her reputation by tumbling into a stranger's arms, her rescuer is none other than distinguished Sir William Ashenden. He needs to marry – but Emily longs to believe he wants her not for her fortune but for herself…

Regency

CAPTAIN FAWLEY'S INNOCENT BRIDE

by Annie Burrows

Battle-scarred Captain Robert Fawley knew no woman would marry him – except perhaps Miss Deborah Gillies, a woman so unfortunate that a convenient marriage was ideal. Accepting his pragmatic proposal, Deborah is halfway to falling in love with him…

MILLS & BOON
Historical

On sale 5th December 2008

Regency

THE RAKE'S REBELLIOUS LADY
by Anne Herries

Tomboy Caroline Holbrook can't imagine settling into a dull, respectable marriage. Her zest for life and alluring innocence draw the attention of Sir Frederick, the most exciting man Caroline has ever met! But she really should resist this rakish bachelor…

HER WARRIOR KING
by Michelle Willingham

Blackmailed to marry, Patrick MacEgan would not be forced to bed his Norman bride. Yet Isabel de Godred wanted to ease the burdens of her proud warrior king. As queen she aided an alliance between their people. As his wife she longed to comfort him…

A WESTERN WINTER WONDERLAND
by Cheryl St John, Jenna Kernan and Pam Crooks

CHRISTMAS DAY FAMILY
FALLEN ANGEL
ONE MAGIC EVE

MILLS & BOON
Super Historical

On sale 5th December 2008

THE OUTLAW'S BRIDE
by Carolyn Davidson

When an outlaw meets an outcast!

Shunned by her tribe, Debra Nightsong simply wanted
to tend her farm alone – until a mysterious stranger arrived.
He *said* he meant no harm, yet his brooding presence
unnerved her – perhaps there was pleasure to be found in
the arms of this outlaw…

On the run and in search of a hideout, Debra's farmhouse
was just perfect for Tyler. He vowed not to take advantage
of the mesmerising beauty, but he soon regretted his words!
Could they both have finally found a place to
belong…together?

Celebrate 100 years of pure reading pleasure with Mills & Boon®

To mark our centenary, each month we're publishing a special 100th Birthday Edition. These celebratory editions are packed with extra features and include a FREE bonus story.

Plus, you have the chance to enter a fabulous monthly prize draw. See 100th Birthday Edition books for details.

Now that's worth celebrating!

September 2008

Crazy about her Spanish Boss by Rebecca Winters
Includes FREE bonus story
Rafael's Convenient Proposal

November 2008

**The Rancher's Christmas Baby
by Cathy Gillen Thacker**
Includes FREE bonus story *Baby's First Christmas*

December 2008

One Magical Christmas by Carol Marinelli
Includes FREE bonus story *Emergency at Bayside*

Look for Mills & Boon® 100th Birthday Editions at your favourite bookseller or visit
www.millsandboon.co.uk

FREE

2 BOOKS AND A SURPRISE GIFT!

We would like to take this opportunity to thank you for reading this Mills & Boon® book by offering you the chance to take TWO more specially selected titles from the Historical series absolutely FREE! We're also making this offer to introduce you to the benefits of the Mills & Boon® Book Club—

★ **FREE home delivery**
★ **FREE gifts and competitions**
★ **FREE monthly Newsletter**
★ **Books available before they're in the shops**
★ **Exclusive Mills & Boon® Book Club offers**

Accepting these FREE books and gift places you under no obligation to buy; you may cancel at any time, even after receiving your free shipment. Simply complete your details below and return the entire page to the address below. You don't even need a stamp!

YES! Please send me 2 free Historical books and a surprise gift. I understand that unless you hear from me, I will receive 4 superb new titles every month for just £3.69 each, postage and packing free. I am under no obligation to purchase any books and may cancel my subscription at any time. The free books and gift will be mine to keep in any case.

H8ZEE

Ms/Mrs/Miss/Mr...Initials ....
                                                                      BLOCK CAPITALS PLEASE

Surname ....

Address ....

....

....Postcode ....

Send this whole page to:
The Mills & Boon Book Club, FREEPOST CN81, Croydon, CR9 3WZ